# DEAD ROOM FARCE

# DEAD ROOM FARCE

## Simon Brett

Thorndike Press • Chivers Press
Thorndike, Maine USA   Bath, England

This Large Print edition is published by Thorndike Press, USA
and by Chivers Press, England.

Published in 1998 in the U.S. by arrangement with
St. Martin's Press, Inc.

Published in 1998 in the U.K. by arrangement with
Victor Gollancz Ltd.

U.S. Hardcover   0-7862-1564-X (Thorndike Mystery Series Edition)
U.K. Hardcover   0-7540-3515-8 (Chivers Large Print)
U.K. Softcover   0-7540-3516-6 (Camden Large Print)

The text of this Large Print edition is unabridged.
Other aspects of the book may vary from the original edition.

Set in 16 pt. Plantin by Rick Gundberg.

Printed in the United States on permanent paper.

**British Library Cataloguing in Publication Data available**

**Library of Congress Cataloging in Publication Data**

Brett, Simon.
    Dead room farce / Simon Brett.
       p. (large print) cm.
    ISBN 0-7862-1564-X (lg. print : hc : alk. paper)
    1. Large type books.  I. Title.
    [PR6052.R4296D42    1998b]
    823'.914—dc21                                            98-28871

*To David and Jacqui*

# Chapter One

That September morning Charles Paris had his trousers round his ankles, but it was for entirely professional reasons. He was taking part in the final London rehearsal for the forthcoming three-month tour of *Not On Your Wife!*, a new farce by the prolific British farceur, Bill Blunden. Charles was playing Aubrey, the older lover of Gilly, wife of Bob, the advertising executive who was pretending that his young mistress Nicky was in fact the property of his hapless neighbour, Ted, played in this Parrott Fashion production by the well-loved comedy actor, Bernard Walton. In the scene they were rehearsing, Charles Paris, as Aubrey, had just arrived for a bit of illicit afternoon pleasure with Gilly . . .

*The set is the sitting rooms of the two flats, divided by a common central wall. The flats are identical in dimensions, and both have French windows opening on to a balcony running along the back of the stage. Gilly and Bob's flat (Stage Left) is smart and fashionable; Louise and Ted's (Stage Right) scruffier and more lived-in. Louise sits in her flat in an armchair, reading a magazine. (The lights on this area are dim; the lights are up on Gilly and Bob's flat.) Gilly, an attractive redhead in her thirties, has just let in Aubrey, her wealthy lover, in his fifties. As soon as they enter the room, they go into a clinch.*

AUBREY: I'm sorry I couldn't come any quicker.

GILLY: I never want you to come any quicker.

AUBREY (*after a tiny pause to give the audience time to pick up on the innuendo*): I got tied up.

GILLY: You naughty boy! And I thought I was the only woman in your life.

AUBREY (*tiny pause*): No, no, one of the secretaries at the office had made a cock-up and I had to have her on the carpet.

GILLY (*tiny pause*): I don't think you're making things sound any better, Aubrey. (*starting to undo the buckle of his trouser belt and pulling him by the belt towards the bedroom door*) You're going to have to make it up to me. In bed.

*With her spare hand, she opens the bedroom door.*

AUBREY: Oh dear. I'm not sure that I'm up for this.

GILLY (*as she pulls him through into the bedroom*): You'd better be!

*They disappear into the bedroom. The door slams shut behind them. There is a moment's silence, then the doorbell is heard. It rings a second time. Gilly comes bustling out of the bedroom, followed by Aubrey. He has his trousers round his ankles, to reveal boxer shorts that are a bit too young for him.*

AUBREY: Oh Lord, who could it be?

GILLY: I don't know, do I? But, whoever it is, they can't see you here. I'm a respectable married woman.

*The doorbell rings again.*

AUBREY (*trying to run in three directions at once and finding it difficult with his trousers round his ankles*): Oh, goodness! Where can I go?

GILLY (*pointing to the French windows*): Over there.

AUBREY: Over there? But we're on the fifth floor. (*letting out a wail*) I'm too young to die!

GILLY: No, I didn't mean over the rail. (*hustling him towards the French windows*) I just meant on to the balcony. You can come back in when whoever it is has gone.

AUBREY: But suppose they don't go? Suppose it's your husband. He might never go. He lives here.

GILLY (*opening the French windows*): He also has a front door key, so he wouldn't use the bell, would he?

AUBREY: He might have lost it.

GILLY (*pushing Aubrey out on to the balcony*): Not as much as you seem to have done, Aubrey.

AUBREY (*as she closes the French windows on him*): Ooh, my good Gawd! It's cold enough out here to freeze the ba—

*The closing of the French windows cuts off the end of his line. Running her hands through her hair to tidy it, Gilly hurries towards the door to the hall. On the balcony, Aubrey, shivering and still with his trousers round his ankles, scurries off towards Stage Left. Unable to proceed further in that direction, he scurries back the other way. He has just gone out of sight behind the central division between the two flats, when Gilly returns from the hall, ushering in Willie, a flamboyant interior designer, who wears a brightly coloured silk suit with a diaphanous scarf floating around his neck.*

WILLIE: Ooh, I'd nearly given up on you. I thought you must've been having a bit of an afternoon snooze. Go on, were you having a bit?

GILLY: Very nearly.

WILLIE (*tiny pause*): I'm your interior designer. (*reaching out to take her hand and give it a flamboyant kiss*) I'm called Willie. (*coyly*) Not without reason.

GILLY (*tiny pause, gesturing to the flat*): Well, here's the flat. This is about the size of it.

WILLIE: As the bishop said to the actress. (*looking round the flat with disapproval*) Oh dear. Who on earth did this for you? These designs have got all the razzmatazz of a civil servant's Y-Fronts.

GILLY: That's why they need changing.

WILLIE: That's what the civil servant's wife said.

*Gilly watches anxiously, as Willie continues to look disparagingly round the flat. On the balcony, Aubrey's head has appeared behind the French windows, peering nervously round from the central division.*

WILLIE (*still facing out front, taking out a notebook*): Maybe we should start with those dreadful 1950s French windows. Hm, is the balcony only as wide as the windows themselves? (*He turns to face Gilly.*) Or do you have a bit on the side?

GILLY (*guiltily*): No, I certainly don't! What on earth gave you that idea?

WILLIE: Well, let's see just how bad these windows really are.

(*He swings round in a flamboyant gesture. Just*

11

*in time, Aubrey's head disappears behind the central division.*) What do you keep on the balcony?

GILLY (*very quickly*): Nothing.

WILLIE (*moving towards the balcony*): I bet you do. Everyone does. I bet you've got some revolting old crock out there . . .

GILLY: No, I haven't!

WILLIE: . . . some mouldy old creeper that took your fancy . . .

GILLY: No.

WILLIE: Well, let's have a look!

*He throws the French windows open. Gilly covers her face with her hands in horror. As Willie opens the windows, Aubrey appears suddenly on the balcony outside the French windows of Louise and Ted's flat. (The lights now go up to half-full on Louise and Ted's flat.)*

WILLIE (*picking up a flowerpot with a shrivelled plant in it*): See, I knew I'd find some wizened old weed out here.

GILLY (*her hands still covering her eyes*): It's all right, I can explain everything. He's the window cleaner!

WILLIE: What?

GILLY: Yes, and his ladder fell down!

WILLIE: His ladder?

GILLY: Yes. (*taking her hands away from her eyes and seeing what Willie is holding*) Oh, *that* kind of weed. Yes, yes, of course.

*Willie gives her a strange look. (The lights go down on Gilly and Bob's flat and up to full on Louise and Ted's.) Aubrey, afraid of being seen by Willie, opens the French windows, and steps into the other flat. He still has his trousers round his ankles. Louise looks up from her magazine in horror.*

LOUISE: Oh, my goodness! (*thinking he's the escaped prisoner, 'Ginger' little*) Are you Little?

AUBREY (*looking down at his boxer shorts*): Quite possibly. But it is very cold out there.

LOUISE: No, I mean — are you 'Ginger'?

AUBREY: Certainly not! (*He pulls his trousers up.*) Nothing funny about me. I'm as straight as the day is long.

LOUISE: But today's the shortest day.

AUBREY: You don't need to tell me. (*He turns away from her modestly to try to zip himself up. As soon as his back is turned, Louise reaches in panic to a drawer in a desk beside her chair.*) Ooh, it was so cold out there. Goodness, I thought I'd —

LOUISE (*producing a pistol from the drawer and pointing it at Aubrey's back*): Freeze!

AUBREY: Exactly. (*He turns back to face Louise. Seeing that he's looking down the barrel of a gun, he throws his hands up in the air.*) Aagh!

*His trousers once again fall down.*

13

The general feeling about the runthrough had been pretty good. At the end, Rob Parrott, of Parrott Fashion Productions, who had watched it, was cautiously complimentary. True, there was a lot still to do; and true, everything would be different when they actually got the show on to the proper set in Bath; but at least for the time being *Not On Your Wife!* seemed to be in pretty good shape.

The director certainly thought so. But then David J. Girton was not the most demanding of taskmasters. His background was in BBC Television Light Entertainment. Until recently he had been a staff producer/director with an extensive portfolio of inoffensive sofa-bound situation comedies behind him. But the changing world of the BBC in the 1990s had seen him edged out, still brought back on contract to produce the occasional series — in particular, the relentlessly long-running *Neighbourhood Watch* — but now with freedom to 'do other things'.

*Not On Your Wife!* was one of those 'other things'. David J. Girton had worked a lot in television with the show's star, Bernard Walton, and that was the reason for his appointment. Bernard Walton's contract stipulated that he had director approval and,

14

rather than going for a dynamically creative figure, the star had opted for someone who wouldn't interfere too much with the way he intended to play his part.

Because there was no question who was in charge of the production, Bernard Walton dictated the pace and emphasis of rehearsals. He selected which bits should be worked on in depth (the scenes he was in) and which should be hurried through on the nod (the scenes he wasn't in). And the whole schedule was fitted around his commitments. The reason their last London rehearsal was on a Thursday was simply that Bernard Walton had a long-standing commitment to play in a charity Pro-Am golf tournament on the Friday.

As well as having the star's approval, David J. Girton was treated with easy tolerance by the rest of the company. Many of them were comedy actors he already knew from television, though he hadn't worked before with Charles Paris, who Bernard had suggested as a possible Aubrey. Charles had appeared at the end of the first afternoon of auditions, and been extremely flattered when the director had cancelled the second day's calls and offered him the part on the spot, expressing his opinion that the actor demonstrated the requisite quality of 'seedy gentility'. At the time Charles had seen this as a reflection of his own brilliance, but closer acquaintance with David J. Girton suggested it might have more to do with the director's constitutional indolence.

Because, the longer rehearsals went on, the clearer it became that this production of *Not On Your Wife!* had been entrusted to a seriously lazy man. The business of television sitcom, in which David J. Girton had learnt his comedy skills, was, for an experienced hand, not a particularly onerous one. True, the studio days could be stressful, and there was always the risk of flouncing and door-slamming from the various service departments involved. But, for someone who'd been around such a long time and who always worked with the same tolerant studio team, a long-running sitcom did not present an over-taxing work schedule. Daily rehearsals from ten to two, and a camera script in which only the lines changed from week to week, had left David J. Girton with plenty of time to enjoy the good food and wine which had contributed to his substantial girth.

So, doing theatre rehearsal hours — usually from ten to six with the statutory Equity coffee and lunch breaks — gave him the impression he was working hard. To have actually worked hard during those hours would, to David J. Girton, have seemed like gilding the lily. He was content to block out the play's basic moves, take long lunch hours, lop a bit off the end of the working day, and basically let Bernard Walton get on with it.

This suited most of the actors very well. It certainly suited the star. Bernard Walton reckoned he 'knew about comedy', and worked tirelessly on his own part, incorporating his familiar repertoire of elaborate takes and reactions, without any reference to the other actors around him.

This behaviour, which in more serious areas of the theatre would have been regarded as appallingly unprofessional and selfish, was accepted amiably by the rest of the cast. They were all old comedy hands, who knew better than to get into competition for laughs with their star. Many of them had been in plays by Bill Blunden before, and were aware that his dramatic structures offered each cast member an unchanging ration of funny moments. So long as those moments were played right, the laughs would come. Only the star was allowed to embroider his part. And any attempts to upstage him would simply throw out the predictable but durable mechanism of Bill Blunden's plotting.

So David J. Girton, as director, was content to be a chubby, bonhomous presence around the rehearsal room, and to punctuate the days with his two catch-phrases, 'Anyone fancy a little drink?' and 'Anyone going out for a meal?'

The take-up he got on the second question was smaller than that he got on the first. David J. Girton's eating habits were expensive. Long training with a flexible BBC expense account had provided him with a compendious list of smart restaurants, which were beyond the means of most of his cast. Bernard Walton, and the others who could have afforded it, tended to duck the eating invitation. They were professionals, concentrating on the show. They'd be happy to go out for lavish meals between projects, or to celebrate high points of the current production — first night and so on — but they didn't aspire to them, as their director did, on a daily basis.

A good few of the cast, however, were happy to take up David J. Girton's invitation to 'a little drink' — particularly because he hadn't yet broken his old BBC habit of hurrying to the bar and buying the first round. So that was what happened on the day of the last London rehearsal for *Not On*

*Your Wife!* The director, keen to top up his own alcohol level, issued the customary 'Anyone fancy a little drink?', and most of the company were happy to take up his offer.

Bernard Walton was one of the exceptions. 'S-sorry,' he said, with the familiar and studied stutter which had been the dynamo of his comedy career. 'Got to get into the dickie bow for this AIDS charity do at the Shaftesbury.'

'I can't make it either, I'm afraid, David,' apologized the youngest member of the cast, Pippa Trewin, who played Louise. She was a pretty enough and perfectly competent young actress, though Charles had been surprised that she'd got a substantial part in such a major tour straight out of drama school.

He was even more surprised at that moment to see Bernard Walton give Pippa a discreet little wave and mouth, 'See you later, love.'

Maybe her casting wasn't such a surprise then, after all. Charles had known Bernard Walton for a very long time — he'd directed the young actor in his first major role, as Young Marlowe in *She Stoops to Conquer* — and in all that time Charles'd never heard the faintest whiff of sexual gossip about him.

19

In the relationship maelstrom that is the theatre, Bernard was one of the minority who had stayed locked into his original marriage. Indeed, it was a subject on which he frequently waxed boring in television chatshows and magazine interviews.

Charles's view had always been that Bernard was not that interested in sex. The all-consuming passions of the star's life were his career and, more recently, his desire to get a knighthood for 'charitable work and services to the theatre'. Any woman who could put up with his whingeing and worrying on all the time about those two subjects would have no difficulty in staying married to him.

But, thought Charles wryly, Bernard Walton wouldn't be the first star to have maintained a front of devoted domesticity and had a vibrantly active alternative sex-life going on. Nonetheless, the whispered words to Pippa Trewin did still seem out of character. Apart from anything else, dalliances with young actresses weren't recommended for an actor with his sights set on a knighthood.

Still, the conjectural infidelity of Bernard Walton wasn't Charles Paris's problem, and, besides, he was in no position to contemplate first-stone-casting. Charles's own sex-

20

life was currently moribund, and he was at that worrying stage of a man's life, his late fifties, when 'moribund' could easily become 'over'. Maybe he never would make love to a woman again. The current frostiness of his relationship with Frances, the woman to whom he was still technically married, offered little hope of a rapprochement, and there weren't currently any other contenders for the role of Charles Paris's bed-mate.

The only detail about the whole sad subject that gave him the occasional flicker of optimism was that, although nothing was actually happening, he hadn't lost the desire for something to happen. He still woke up randy in the mornings, and the flash of a leg, an image on the television, the glimpse of a woman on a poster, could still work their old, predictable, frustrating magic.

These were his thoughts as Charles Paris made his way through to the cloakroom at the end of rehearsal. The coat that he lifted off its hook felt lopsidedly heavy, and Charles remembered with relief that he'd got a half-bottle of Bell's whisky in the pocket. Not a full half-bottle, probably a half-full half-bottle, but it was still a reassuring presence. He had a sudden urge to feel the slight resistance of the metal cap turning in his hand, the touch of upturned glass against his lips, the burn of the liquor in his throat.

He looked around. He was alone in the cloakroom. Just a quick sip . . . ? But no. Someone might walk in, and there are certain reputations no actor wants to get in a company — particularly at the beginning of a three-month tour.

It wasn't as if he didn't need a pee, anyway. Charles slipped on his coat and went through into the Gents'. Once there, although the pressure was only on his bladder, he ignored the urinals in favour of a cubicle. He went in and locked the door.

Just one quick swig. To make him more relaxed when he joined the rest of the company.

Mm, God, it was good. He felt the whisky trickle down, performing its Midas touch, sending a golden glow right through his body. Mm, just one more. Lovely.

And a third. But that was it. Charles Paris knew when to stop. He firmly screwed down the cap on the bottle, thrust it deep into his coat pocket, and went off to join the rest of the company in the pub.

'Sorry, old boy. Didn't have time to get to the cash machine and it's my round.

Don't suppose you could sub me a tenner?'

'Of course.' Charles opened his wallet expansively. It was Thursday; he'd just been paid. 'Help yourself.'

'Well, I'll take twenty, just to be sure. But you'll have it back tomorrow, promise. If there's one thing I can't stand, it's being in debt to anyone.'

'No problem.' Charles was feeling in a generous mood. His Bell's level had been topped up by a double from David J. Girton's first round, and then a couple more. Now, ever the one to know how to moderate his drinking, Charles Paris was on the red wine. And that seemed to be slipping down a treat too. He was feeling really bloody good.

The beneficiary of his bountiful mood had taken the two ten-pound notes, folded them and stuck them firmly in his inside pocket, before handing the wallet back.

'You're a saint, Charles,' said Ransome George. He was one of those actors, of indeterminate age, who was never out of work. Though he was not the most intelligent or subtlest interpreter of a part, Ransome George's face was, quite literally, his fortune. It was a funny face, in repose a melancholy boxer dog, in animation an affronted bullfrog. He had only to appear on stage, or on a television screen, for the audience to start feeling indulgent, for them to experience the little tug of a smile at the corner of their lips.

He was also blessed with intuitive comic timing. Whatever the situation, some internal clock told him exactly how long to hold a pause, when to slam in quickly with his next line, when to extend the silence almost unbearably. And he never failed to catch the reward of a laugh.

That was all Ransome George could do. Whatever the part, whatever the play, the performance was identical. Whether the lines were spoken in Yorkshire, Cornish, Welsh, Scottish, Transylvanian — or an approximation to these, because he wasn't very good at accents — they would be delivered in exactly the same way. And they'd always get the laughs. That guarantee he carried with him made Ransome George — or 'Ran', as he was known to everyone in the business — an invaluable character to have in comedy sketches.

In a full-length play his value was less certain. Though a good comedy performer, Ran was not in truth much of an actor. He was good at individual moments, but couldn't lose his own personality in a character throughout the length of a play. This deficiency perhaps mattered less in farce than it would have done in more serious areas of the theatre, but Charles Paris was still quite surprised at Ransome George's casting in *Not On Your Wife!* Still, Ran seemed to have worked a lot with Bernard Walton over the years. Maybe the old pals' act, a phenomenon all too common in the theatre, had been once again in operation.

In *Not On Your Wife!* Ransome George was playing the part of Willie, the flamboyant (for 'flamboyant' in British farce scripts, always read 'gay stereotype') interior designer. He wasn't playing the part particularly gay — indeed he was delivering the Standard Mark One Ransome George performance — but the laughs were inevitably going to be there.

Whether Ran was in reality gay or not, Charles Paris did not know. But from the way the actor, boosted by the loan of twenty pounds, homed back in on the dishy young assistant stage manager, it seemed unlikely. Charles did notice, though, that the girl had just placed two full glasses on their table. It wasn't Ran's round yet.

Somewhere in the back of his mind came a recollection: he'd heard somewhere that Ransome George was surprisingly successful with women. In spite of his cartoon face and shapeless body, he could always make them laugh. And rumour had it he'd laughed his way into a good few beds over the years.

The thought threw a pale cast of melancholy over Charles, as he compared his own current sexless state. His eyes glazed over, looking out at, but not taking in, the bustle of the busy pub.

'Come on, it's not that bad,' a husky voice murmured in his ear.

'Sorry?' He turned to face Cookie Stone, the actress playing Gilly, who'd just moved across to sit beside him. Though not as cartoon-like as Ran's, Cookie's face too was perfect for comedy. A pert snub nose had difficulty separating two mischievous dark brown eyes, and her broad mouth seemed to contain more than the standard ration of teeth. But her body, Charles couldn't help noticing as she leant her pointed breasts towards him, was firm and trim.

He reckoned Cookie must be late thirties now, maybe a bit more, and, like Ran, she was never out of work. She'd started in her teens as the female stooge for television comedians, playing all those roles — secretaries, nurses, receptionists, shop assistants — that the sketches of the time demanded. And she'd always got the laughs by her mixture of sex and mischief. The body was undeniably sexy, but the jokey face — by no means traditionally beautiful — suggested another dimension to her character, an ironic awareness of the roles in which she found herself.

This quality had stood Cookie Stone in good stead when the priorities of comedy changed, when political correctness emerged as an issue, and women comedians started to take a more central role. That revolution had put out of business many of the pretty little things who'd formerly adorned television comedy. It was now unacceptable for a woman to be on screen simply because she was sexy, and for that to be the basis of an item's humour. But an actress who could look sexy while at the same time, by her expression, giving a post-modernist gloss to her sexiness, was worth her weight in gold. So there had been no blip in the career of Cookie Stone.

But her ranking in the comedy business hadn't changed. After a decade of playing stooge to a series of male comedians who commanded the lion's share of the show's funny lines (not to mention its budget), she now played stooge to a series of female comedians who commanded the lion's share of the show's funny lines (not to mention its budget). Cookie still had no power; she had simply changed bosses.

And, in a way, that was fair. Cookie Stone had no originating talent, but she was a very good mimic and a quick learner. She absorbed the comedy technique of everyone she worked with and, as a result, had become a consummately skilful comedy actress. Her every take, her every pause, her every intonation, had been copied from another performer, but her armoury of them was now so large, and her skill in selecting them so great, that she was almost indistinguishable from an actress of intuitive comedy skills.

'I was saying, Charles . . .' she continued, in a favourite voice, the humorous right-on feminist learnt from one of the first female stand-ups to do menstruation jokes on television, 'I was saying that, like, you really look as though you've just had a fax saying the world's about to end.'

'No. Rubbish. Someone just walked over my grave, that's all. You OK for a drink?'

Cookie raised a half-full glass of red. 'Cheers, I'm entirely OK, thank you,' she slurred, in the remembered voice of a comedian who'd killed himself with exhaust fumes after rather nasty tabloid allegations about rent boys.

They talked and had a couple more glasses of red wine, and then looked round and realized there was nobody they recognized left in the pub. The rest of the *Not On Your Wife!* company had all gone home, or on to eat. Maybe some of them, flushed with the success of the day's rehearsal and the fact that it was payday, had even gone to join David J. Girton at some smart restaurant.

Charles and Cookie could have had another drink, but it seemed the moment for him to say, 'You fancy eating something?' He wasn't sure whether he was hungry or not, but he knew some kind of blotting paper was a good idea.

Outside the pub, they swayed on the kerb. 'Where we going then, Daddy?' asked Cookie, in the voice of an American comedian who'd been given her own short-lived series at the moment when television had first fallen in love with female stand-ups.

'Erm . . .' A taxi drew up in obedience to Charles's wavering hand. 'I know.' He couldn't think of anywhere else. There was an Italian on Westbourne Grove, just round the corner from his tiny studio flat.

Inside the restaurant, he ordered a bottle of Chianti Classico. They also ordered some pasta — at least he was fairly sure it was pasta, though he had no recollection of eating it. Maybe it was one of those evenings when at the end of the meal impassive waiters had gathered up virtually untouched plates.

Charles did remember them ordering a few sambucas, though, and joking as they blew out the blue flames that rose from the top of their glasses. He remembered Cookie's head leant close to his across the table, her tongue constantly licking over her prominent teeth as she talked. And he remembered, in a fit of righteousness, ordering each of them a large espresso 'to sober up a bit'.

He also remembered listening with great concentration to Cookie Stone, though he was a little vague about what she actually said. He knew, however, that it was said in many different voices, that there was a lot about the actor's identity, and how every actor hid his or her true, snivelling, abject self under the comforting carapace of fictional characters, and how few men bothered to probe into what the real Cookie Stone was like, and, generally speaking, what bastards men were, and how all most of them wanted was just to get her back to their place for a quick shag.

And Charles remembered being very unthought that at some point during the events of the previous evening, he'd found a message from Frances on his answering machine. Surely that couldn't be true, surely that was just the guilt getting at him?

Even worse, though, was the fear that he'd actually phoned his wife back, just a quick call to establish contact, and that she'd said she wouldn't talk to him until he was sober.

No, that bit couldn't be true, he felt sure. It was just his mind providing another prompt of guilt to add to the muddy swirl of self-recrimination. But, hallucination or not, it wasn't a thought that improved his mood.

As it had transpired, in spite of his heroic rush to the station, Charles had just missed his train at Paddington and had to wait nearly a full hour for the 8.15. He'd hung mournfully about the concourse, clutching a copy of *The Times* he didn't feel up to reading, and wishing the owners of the privatized station had made more seats available. At one point he contemplated the rough remedy of a Full English Breakfast, but the smell of food as he entered the cafeteria brought nausea back to his throat and he had had to hurry out again.

The train had arrived in Bath on time, at 9.38, but there had been a queue for taxis and, as luck would have it, the driver Charles finally got seemed to be spending his first day in the city. The address of the studio was not familiar to him and, when they at last reached the relevant road, they had difficulty finding the right building. The studio was a recent conversion, and its name had not yet been put up outside.

As a result, instead of arriving in good time for a relaxed chat before the contractual ten o'clock start of recording, Charles had bumbled in at ten-twenty, panicked and deeply hungover. His producer said it really didn't matter, missing the train could have happened to anyone, but the girl who seemed to be looking after the technical side looked less than amused.

But then, if anyone was going to sympathize with Charles Paris's condition, his producer was that person. Mark Lear himself was certainly not unacquainted with the bottle. Charles had known him for years, and they had worked together when Mark was a BBC Radio producer of Further Education, a department which had later become known as 'Continuing Education' and no doubt gone through a whole raft of other name-changes in the years since.

Mark Lear had always been a licensed BBC malcontent, continually moaning derstanding and very sympathetic to Cookie, and saying she was right, yes, she was right, she'd really put her finger on it, and how if only men and women talked more, communicated more, then maybe there'd be a bit more understanding between them and they'd be able to break away from these old-fashioned stereotypes. Men and women were both people, after all, that was the important thing about what they were, people. Men and women were people.

He must also have paid the bill at some point, presumably with a credit card. He couldn't actually remember doing it, but the fact that he and Cookie were allowed to leave the restaurant suggested that the relevant transaction had somehow taken place.

For the life of him, he couldn't remember the conversation that must have ensued on the pavement outside the restaurant, the precise form of words — and who they were spoken by — which led to Cookie Stone going back to his place.

He must have been drunk, though, for that to have happened. To let someone else see the shambles of old newspapers and grubby clothes in which he lived, he must've had a few.

Charles had recollections of finding an

unopened bottle of Bell's at Hereford Road, and of opening it. He had recollections of charging a couple of glasses, then of moving a pile of newspapers and books off the bed, and of lying down on it with Cookie.

But of what happened next, he couldn't be exactly sure. Certainly, when he woke at three-fifteen, she was entirely naked. She lay on her back, breasts pointing firmly upwards, and snored nasally. Charles was wearing his socks and, somewhere round his shins, telescoped trousers and briefs.

But he didn't have time to explore further. His head was drumming, his throat was as dry as a desert of sandpaper, and he felt violently and urgently sick. He just managed to make it to the bathroom, where he threw up loudly and copiously into the toilet bowl.

Charles Paris finished the day, as he had begun it, with his trousers round his ankles, though this time it was not for professional reasons.

# Chapter Two

It wasn't good. It really wasn't good. The words swam in front of his eyes, and if there's one thing you don't want when you're being paid to read a book for audio cassette, it's the words swimming in front of your eyes.

In the not-inconsiderable annals of Charles Paris's hangovers, this one stood out. He'd never felt as bad as he did at that moment. He knew whenever he had a hangover he thought he'd never felt as bad as he did at that moment, but this was on a different scale. It really was.

Everything felt dreadful. His whole body ached. The joints, particularly knees and elbows, ached even more than the rest of his components. There was a pain and stiffness at the back of his neck that rendered him incapable of moving his head without moving the rest of his body too, like some awkward cardboard cut-out. The dryness in his mouth had moved on from sandpaper quality to the feeling of having been sand-blasted. His eyes stung as if he'd spent a couple of hours underwater in an overchlorinated pool. And his digestion felt seriously at risk. The jacuzzi of his stomach threatened to overflow at any moment, and without warning of which direction that overflow might take. His guts complained at their treatment with rumbles that wouldn't have sounded out of place in the third rinse of a dishwasher cycle. And a rumbling stomach doesn't help an audio book recording either.

He could have tolerated the sickness of his body, if his mind had not also been infected. While his mouth continued to pronounce the swimming words on the page, his mind seethed with self-hatred and re-crimination. Why on earth had he let himself get so drunk? He must've been aware of the way he was going, why hadn't he put a brake on it?

He was such a fool. A man in his late fifties behaving like a teenager at his first grown-up party. And it was hideously un-professional — the worst insult that can be levelled at an actor — for him to get so wasted the night before he was to start on a whole new area of work. Getting the contract to record an audio book could be a breakthrough into a different, and possibly lucrative, market; he mustn't screw it up.

At the bottom of all these anxieties, lurking like some evil predator in the depths of a murky pool, lay the question of what he'd said the night before. Worse than that, what he had *done* the night before.

Cookie Stone. What had happened between him and Cookie Stone? He knew the position in which they'd found themselves at three-fifteen, but what had been the precise sequence of events that had led up to that?

Various possibilities presented themselves. One — the most unlikely — was that they'd just gone to bed together for a cuddle, mutual support for two lonely people, and by agreement nothing else had happened. A second scenario — also, he feared, unlikely — was that they had enjoyed a long session of abandoned, passionate and satisfying love-making. The third — and the one towards which he was unwillingly inclining — was that they had prepared to make love, gone through all the soft-talking and the anticipatory blandishments, that they had started to make love, and then that he had proved incapable of completing the process, and fallen into a drunken stupor halfway through.

Charles had a horrible feeling that that

was what had happened, but his memory could offer him no help on the subject. His recollection of the previous night's events, after their departure from the Italian restaurant, was, to use the most generous adjective possible in the circumstances, hazy.

And there hadn't been much chance in the morning for Charles and Cookie to compare notes. He had woken in a sweat of panic at 6.33, suddenly aware that he was supposed to be catching the 7.15 train from Paddington to Bath for the day's recording. In the rush of his own dressing and incomplete ablutions, and of hurrying Cookie through her reduced morning ritual, there hadn't been any opportunity for an assessment — or more likely a post mortem — of the previous night's encounter. They had parted with their stale mouths joining in a dry kiss and a cheery 'See you Monday', but no mention had been made of any relationship in which they might be considered to be involved.

And, as so often after an unsatisfactory skirmish with a member of the opposite sex, all Charles could think about was his wife Frances. Though there seemed almost nothing now left between them, he still felt as if he had betrayed her. There was even, at the back of his mind, the appalling thought that at some point during the events of the previous evening, he'd found a message from Frances on his answering machine. Surely that couldn't be true, surely that was just the guilt getting at him?

Even worse, though, was the fear that he'd actually phoned his wife back, just a quick call to establish contact, and that she'd said she wouldn't talk to him until he was sober.

No, that bit couldn't be true, he felt sure. It was just his mind providing another prompt of guilt to add to the muddy swirl of self-recrimination. But, hallucination or not, it wasn't a thought that improved his mood.

As it had transpired, in spite of his heroic rush to the station, Charles had just missed his train at Paddington and had to wait nearly a full hour for the 8.15. He'd hung mournfully about the concourse, clutching a copy of *The Times* he didn't feel up to reading, and wishing the owners of the privatized station had made more seats available. At one point he contemplated the rough remedy of a Full English Breakfast, but the smell of food as he entered the cafeteria brought nausea back to his throat and he had had to hurry out again.

The train had arrived in Bath on time, at 9.38, but there had been a queue for taxis and, as luck would have it, the driver Charles finally got seemed to be spending his first day in the city. The address of the studio was not familiar to him and, when they at last reached the relevant road, they had difficulty finding the right building. The studio was a recent conversion, and its name had not yet been put up outside.

As a result, instead of arriving in good time for a relaxed chat before the contractual ten o'clock start of recording, Charles had bumbled in at ten-twenty, panicked and deeply hungover. His producer said it really didn't matter, missing the train could have happened to anyone, but the girl who seemed to be looking after the technical side looked less than amused.

But then, if anyone was going to sympathize with Charles Paris's condition, his producer was that person. Mark Lear himself was certainly not unacquainted with the bottle. Charles had known him for years, and they had worked together when Mark was a BBC Radio producer of Further Education, a department which had later become known as 'Continuing Education' and no doubt gone through a whole raft of other name-changes in the years since.

Mark Lear had always been a licensed BBC malcontent, continually moaning about the Corporation and asserting that he wasn't going to stay, that soon he would be 'out in the real world, doing my own thing'. Well, in the late 1980s, along with a great many other members of the BBC staff, he got his wish, though not perhaps in the way he would have wanted. Mark Lear had been offered an early retirement package that didn't carry the option of refusal, and at the age of fifty found himself being taken at his word and having the opportunity to 'do his own thing'.

The 'thing' he chose to do — or perhaps 'chose' is too positive a word to describe the way he drifted into it — was to set up an audio production company with its own tiny recording studios in Bath. It was an initiative Mark Lear could never have managed on his own. However much he banged on about BBC bureaucracy stifling his creativity, about his longing to shake the dust of the place off his heels and be his own boss, in reality he revelled in the cosiness of a big institution. Whether he'd had much initiative when he started his career was questionable, but twenty years in the Corporation had drained any he did have out of him. Mark Lear would never have started his own company without someone else to push him.

The person who had done the pushing was the girl behind the control panel in the studio that morning. Her name was Lisa Wilson, and two things about her relationship with Mark quickly became apparent. First, it was not exclusively professional. And, second, in their business venture she was at least an equal partner.

Charles reckoned he could piece together how Mark and Lisa had met. As a producer in the BBC, Mark Lear had always taken full advantage of the regular supply of attractive single girls who worked there, and his wife Vinnie had either remained in ignorance or, more likely, turned a blind eye to his serial infidelities. For many years, Mark had enjoyed a very convenient life-style, using the excuse of 'late bookings in the studio' to cover his philanderings, and always returning to the safety of the elegant Hampstead house which Vinnie's private income had bought them. The set-up was not one that Mark had ever had any need — or indeed desire — to alter.

The impetus for change, when it did come, came from Vinnie. She fell in love. She felt she'd done her duty by their three daughters, who were by then off at university, and for the first time in her life, Vinnie Lear behaved with total selfishness. She had no choice. The love she felt for her new man was unanswerably powerful. Within three months — in spite of Mark's self-justifying whingeing, in spite of their children's reactions, including the development of an eating disorder in the youngest, Claudia — the divorce had been finalized, the Hampstead house sold, and Vinnie had moved in with her new lover. Within another three months, Vinnie Lear, now insisting on being called 'Lavinia', had had her face and body expensively remodelled by plastic surgery, and remarried.

Mark Lear, for whom these events coincided with early retirement, spun reeling into a small flat in Pimlico. Once again, he'd achieved what had been long wished for. He'd said frequently to anyone who'd listen — and particularly to his sequence of young paramours — that what a free spirit like him really needed was 'my own pad, a bachelor place where I can just, you know, like, be myself'. And, in case this might raise in his listeners any inconvenient ideas of potential cohabitation, he would swiftly add, 'but of course, I couldn't do that, you know, because of the children'.

The reality of freedom, the realization that there were now no restrictions on his free spirit, did not prove to be quite the nirvana

41

Mark Lear had hoped for. No longer being in the BBC had reduced his supply of nubile young women. And those he did manage to lure out to Pimlico, though quite happy to have a bit of quick sex, proved less willing to listen to the witterings of a worried fifty-year-old — and deeply unwilling to provide any domestic back-up for him. Mark had been spoilt by living with Vinnie, and assumed that anyone vouchsafed the rich gift of his body would feel automatically obliged to reciprocate by doing his washing and cooking. But the single younger women he encountered in 1990s London were unaware of any such obligation.

It didn't take Mark Lear long to realize that, if he was going to find someone else to look after him, it would have to be in the context of another ongoing relationship. And it was around the time this message sank in that he met Lisa Wilson.

She was some twelve years younger, and had also worked in BBC Radio. She had never been on the staff — in the organization's changed climate almost everyone worked on short contracts — but Lisa had shown sufficient flair and energy to be in demand and be offered many such contracts. Her departure from the BBC had been voluntary. She genuinely wanted to set up her own business.

Since this decision coincided with the establishment of her relationship with Mark Lear, since he was an experienced producer, and since he had come out of his divorce with a lump sum from the sale of the house, it seemed logical for the two of them to set up in partnership.

Lisa had organized everything. She it was who had done the research and costings for the project, and who had made the economic decision that they'd do better out of London. She had found the premises in Bath, she had designed and overseen their conversion into studios. She had dealt with planning problems and building regulations. She had sorted out the insurance, checking quote against quote. She had arranged for the fixing of the security systems the insurance companies demanded — window-locks, dead-bolts on the outer doors — and on the studio and cubicle doors too, because valuable equipment might be stored in there.

It was Lisa Wilson too who had touted for work to keep the studios filled. She had selected where to place advertisements. She had had business cards and flyers printed. She had relentlessly followed up any contacts which might result in bookings.

And Mark, apart from the occasional whinge about moving out of London, had been content to be swept along in Lisa's wake. His skills, after all, were on the creative side of things; his sensitive mind couldn't be cluttered with managerial details.

But even in the studio, the environment in which Mark's skills were supposed to blossom, Lisa was taking the dominant role. When Charles arrived, Mark, who seemed to be nursing a hangover of his own, had been quite content to natter away for a while over a cup of coffee. It was Lisa who had pressed for them to start recording, pointing out that they only had two days to complete a full-length book.

The work in question was not one that Charles Paris would have read for anything other than money. It was entitled *Dark Promises*, and written by someone called Madeleine Eglantine, with the rest of whose oeuvre he was unfamiliar. The book was one of those standard-issue romances, in which the right man and woman meet in Chapter One, and are then kept apart for two hundred pages by misunderstandings and external circumstances, until being joyfully reunited, and presumably married, in the last chapter. Charles, who was of the view that everything necessary in the romantic genre had been achieved by *Jane Eyre* and *Wuthering Heights*, found it difficult to summon up much interest in the characters. The heroine, despite Madeleine Eglantine's constant assertions of how strong-willed and feisty she was, came across as totally insipid. And the hero, although there were frequent references to his 'struggles with his own demons', seemed plain dull. Nor could Charles find much good to say about the author's prose style.

Still, it was work, and work that could lead to other work. Lisa Wilson had organized a deal with a publisher to record a whole series of such romances. The audio book market was a growing one, and it would be handy for Charles to join that select list of not-very-famous but reliable actors who spend much of their time in the intimacy of small recording studios reading books out loud.

It was an opportunity, and Charles wished he was feeling less shitty as he faced that opportunity. He thanked God that he had actually done his homework on the book a few days before. If he'd left it till the train that morning, the text would have seemed more alien than it already did.

Even without the hangover, he wouldn't

have found it easy. As a bit of a writer himself, Charles found the book's style awkward, and kept wanting to change sentences to give them greater fluency. But he wasn't allowed to do that. Every time he deviated by a word from Madeleine Eglantine's text, Lisa Wilson would put down the talkback key from the control cubicle and say patiently, 'Sorry, can we go back on that?'

'But what I said was much better,' Charles had complained the first few times. 'I mean, it's not as if we're dealing with Shakespeare here, is it?'

'Sorry,' Lisa had responded firmly. 'We have to do the book as printed.'

'Oh, OK.' And Charles reread the unamended text.

What with these interruptions, and the fluffs caused by a tongue that seemed to be the wrong size for his mouth, and the retakes necessitated by intrusive stomach rumbles, the morning's reading made slow progress.

Charles hadn't realized how difficult it would be. He was an experienced actor, after all. But most of his work had involved other actors, whose performances his own could bounce off. Acting with others shared the burden; the maximum pressure was sometimes on one, sometimes on another.

46

But in that tiny, airless studio, he was on his own. It was just Charles Paris and Madeleine Eglantine. His concentration had to be total all the time.

In fact, the part of the proceedings Charles had found most difficult had arisen before they even started on Madeleine Eglantine's text. Once Lisa Wilson had checked Charles's voice level and made a few adjustments to the settings in the control cubicle, she had said, 'Can we start by doing the cassette numbering?'

'Sorry?'

'We have to get you to do the announcements that come at the beginning and end of each side. "Side One" — "End of Side One" — "Side Two" and so on.'

'Just that?'

'Mm. With this book you'll have to go up to "Side Twelve". Six cassettes, you see. If you could just do them all on the trot, leaving, like, a couple of seconds' pause between each announcement . . . ?'

Charles Paris chuckled, which was an unwise thing to do with a hangover like his. The chuckle seemed to shake together all the bits of him that hurt. Nevertheless, he managed to say, 'Well, that doesn't sound too difficult.'

'OK. Tape's rolling. In your own time.'

Charles left a silence and then intoned, 'Side One . . .'

His pause was interrupted by Lisa's voice on the talkback. 'No, sorry, can you do it again?'

'What was wrong with it?'

'Too much intonation.'

'Oh dear.'

'They should have no intonation at all. Just completely flat. No rhythm. Like the football results.'

Charles Paris tried again. 'Side One . . .'

'No, sorry. You're still making it sound like it means something.'

'Well, it does. It means "Side One".'

'Yes, but you're making it sound like "Side One" has some hidden significance.'

'OK. I will try to bleach the words of all significance. Is the tape still rolling?' Through the glass, Lisa Wilson's blonde head nodded. Pretty girl, thought Charles, I could envy Mark a bit of that. Even as he had the thought, came the recrimination. How on earth, after what had happened the night before, could he ever again find the nerve to have a sexual thought about any woman? 'Side One . . .'

'Sorry,' Lisa's voice broke in. 'Still sounds a bit actorish.'

Charles Paris found it very hard. He

sounded 'actorish' because he was an actor. And an actor is trained to give significance to words. To be asked to bleach them of all intonation and rhythm was to be asked to unlearn decades of technique.

He made another attempt. 'Side One . . .'

'Nearly,' said Lisa. 'Getting close. Just one more try and I think we'll be there.'

As Charles Paris struggled to get his tongue round Madeleine Eglantine's prose, he realized he was feeling worse. The hangover showed no signs of shifting. The pain across his eyebrows was intensifying.

Partly, it was the claustrophobia of his setting. The premises that Lisa Wilson had had converted into studios had been the ground floor of a corner shop. There were now, crammed into the space, a tiny reception, small sitting area, kitchenette, toilets and two recording studios. The larger could just about accommodate a small drama production or a musical group. It was walled with movable acoustic screens, which could be set up to muffle the recorded sound, or reversed to show a shiny surface which produced a more echoey or 'live' sound quality.

The other studio, in which Charles Paris was working, was little more than a cupboard, separated from its tiny control cubicle by thick double doors. There was just room inside for one chair, and a cloth-covered table with a cloth-covered bookrest on it. Beside this stood an anglepoise lamp, a jug of water and a glass. The studio's walls were heavily upholstered with dark sound-proofing material, which seemed to press down and take away more of the available space.

'It's very dead in here,' Lisa had said, when she first showed Charles inside. 'This is our dead room. That's what you want for an audio book. No ambient atmosphere. It makes the sound more intimate.'

As he read on, Charles was increasingly aware of how quickly intimacy could become claustrophobia. The narrow focus of light on the book intensified the feeling of encroaching darkness around him. The air he breathed felt stale and recycled.

'I'm sorry,' he said, about three-quarters of an hour into the session, after a particularly messy sequence of fluffs. 'Do you mind if I just come out and get a breath of air?'

'No, of course not,' said Lisa. 'Apologies, I should have thought. We try to open up the studio doors every half hour or so, but because we started so late, I forgot.' She pulled the two heavy doors open. Their draught-excluding strips hissed against the carpet. 'Come on, Charles, stretch your legs.' She shook her head in apology. 'Sorry. The air conditioning in there isn't working. Well, it is working, but we can't use it.'

'Oh?'

'Boring and technical, but they swore blind they'd installed a system that was completely silent. Sadly, as soon as we switched it on, it started to hum. Not very loud, but enough to come across on the tape. They should be here to sort it out tomorrow.' Lisa looked with sudden sharpness across to Mark. 'You did ring the engineers, didn't you?'

'What?'

'The engineers. To come and sort out this air conditioning.'

'Oh . . .' Mark said vaguely.

'*Did* you call them? Go on, Mark, *did* you?'

'Yes, of course I bloody called them! For Christ's sake, Lisa, stop treating me like a child.'

'So when are they coming?'

'Tomorrow. They're coming to-bloody-morrow!'

Charles Paris cleared his throat uneasily, and Lisa realized this wasn't the moment for a domestic row. 'Sorry, Charles. Would

51

you like a coffee or something?'

'Please.'

While Lisa went off to make the coffee, Mark Lear, who had hardly stirred from his chair all morning, grinned knowingly at his friend. 'Could do with something stronger than coffee, I dare say, couldn't you?'

'Well . . . I have got a little bit of a hangover this morning,' said Charles, with breathtaking understatement.

'Me too. Incidentally, sorry about the stuffiness. I'll put the air conditioning on now, to cool the studio down.' Mark Lear threw a switch. 'You see, it's all right so long as we're not actually trying to record. And, so long as we remember to open the studio doors every half hour or so, you'll be fine.' He chuckled. 'Basic rule of production — don't suffocate your artistes.'

Lisa returned with the coffee, and also a printed list on a laminated plastic sheet. 'Sandwiches,' she announced. 'If you say what you want, Charles, I'll ring through and then they'll deliver round lunchtime.'

'Oh, I think we'll go to the pub,' said Mark. 'It's so much easier.'

Lisa looked peeved, and spoke as if this was not a new argument. 'It may be easier, but it always takes longer, and we're already behind . . .'

'See how far we've got by one o'clock,' said Mark. 'If we've picked up a bit of time, we'll go to the pub.'

Maybe that wasn't the reason why the morning's second session of reading was more fluent than the first. Maybe Charles Paris was just getting into his stride. But the prospect of a drink was a real incentive.

Throughout the morning Lisa had given the orders, but as the hands of the studio clock approached one, it was Mark who said, 'OK, let's break it there. Well, we've done pretty well. Think we've earned lunch at the pub.' He turned defiantly to Lisa as he said the words, daring her to challenge him.

She didn't. She held back, and replied lightly, 'As you wish.'

'You coming?'

The blonde head shook. 'Got a few phone calls to do. And a bit of editing.' As Mark and Charles gathered up their coats, she couldn't help saying, 'Be sure you're back by two.'

'Of course,' said Mark. And then, with the slightest edge of irony, 'Of course, my dear.'

As a general rule, Charles Paris tried to avoid having a lunchtime drink when he was working, particularly working on something that required as much concentration as *Dark Promises*. But this time he wouldn't be having a drink for purely recreational reasons; it was a medical necessity. His system cried out for irrigation, and that had to be a pint of bitter.

As he felt the first mouthful go down, he knew his decision had been the right one. God, it made him feel better.

# Chapter Three

He was quite good. Really. At least he reckoned he was. Just a couple of pints, and two sandwiches to do the blotting-paper job. And it was only a few minutes after two — well, two-fifteen — when they got back to the studio.

But Lisa Wilson's face was unamused. It wore the kind of unamused look that, from primeval times, wives have perfected to greet husbands coming home later than they promised. Charles reflected that Mark Lear had maybe not landed so perfectly on his feet, after all. The attractions of a younger woman were presumably avid sex and blind adoration, not the cross-armed resentment of an aggrieved spouse.

'OK, straight through to the studio,' Lisa said brusquely. 'We're behind schedule.'

'Yes, just nip for a pee,' said Charles. He wasn't sure this was a good idea. A pee so soon after two pints of bitter could frequently be the precursor to a busy sequence of pees. Still, he did feel the need.

When he came back, Lisa was bringing Mark up to date on the phone calls she had made during the lunch break. 'I think you should follow up on it.'

'Yes, yes,' said Mark breezily.

'No, soon. I've found out that the market's there. I thought we'd agreed that you would do the follow-up on those kind of openings.'

'Yes, sure, sure.'

She lifted the cordless phone off its base and held it out to him, along with a business card. 'There's the number.'

'Yeah, I'm not going to do it right now.'

'Why not?'

'Because it's only half-past two. Everyone knows publishers don't get back from lunch till three.'

'You could leave a message.'

'Not on a Friday afternoon. They all go home early on a Friday. POETS. Piss Off Early — Tomorrow's Saturday.' He sniggered at the recollected BBC joke.

Lisa didn't share his amusement. 'I think you've got an outdated concept of how publishers work these days, Mark. It's a hard-nosed, accountable business, like everything else.' She waved the cordless phone in front of him. 'Come on, are you going to do it?'

'No,' he snapped. 'Will you kindly allow me to be the judge of how I conduct my own business!'

'*Our* business,' said Lisa. But she didn't press further. She put the phone back on its base, and they both seemed aware of Charles for the first time. Lisa answered the unintended interrogation in his expression. 'Possibility of more work,' she explained. 'A lot of publishers going multimedia. CD-ROMs.'

'Ah,' said Charles, to whom these expressions were vaguely familiar, but not subjects of which he had a full understanding.

'A lot of CD-ROM reference packages need an audio component,' she elaborated. 'Pronunciation dictionaries, that kind of thing.'

'Uh-uh,' said Charles, sounding as if he knew what she was talking about.

Lisa Wilson looked at her watch with a degree of exasperation. 'OK, we'd better get on.'

Charles was incarcerated back in the studio, which was quite pleasant at first because the air conditioning had been on throughout the lunch break. He set off again up the North Face of Madeleine Eglantine's prose. It was currently the Second World War that was keeping *Dark Promises'* perfectly matched lovers apart. Not only that, but the hero was also now at risk from the blandishments of a tempestuous Italian partisan beauty. Since the tempestuous Italian partisan beauty and the heroine seemed interchangeably wet, and the hero's dullness was unalleviated, Charles Paris still found it difficult to summon up much interest in the proceedings.

But the drink had helped. His body's individual components felt more as if they were part of some functioning whole, and the pain behind his eyes had lifted. There were a few fluffs arising from his reduced sense of inhibition, but not as many as there had been before lunch.

At least that was how the afternoon's recording started. After three-quarters of an hour, however, the alcohol was beginning to wear off, the air had grown stale, and Charles felt his energy flagging. The dull headache had returned, his tongue seemed again swollen and ungainly, Madeleine Eglantine's writing increasingly indigestible. As he stumbled to the end of a page on which there had been some dozen stops and starts, Lisa Wilson threw in the towel. 'I've got to change the reel. Take a coffee break there.'

'OK,' said Charles gratefully. 'And let me have some air, eh?'

'Sure. Let him out, Mark.' Lisa, preoccupied with the large reel-to-reel tape recorder, turned her back to the studio.

There was no response and Charles noticed, through the refraction of the double glass, that his friend had gone to sleep. Lisa spotted this at the same moment and, though Charles couldn't hear the words she actually used to wake Mark up, by a combination of lip-reading and simple deduction he managed to piece them together.

Mark Lear rose to his feet, stretching, and pulled open the double doors. 'Want to come out?' He twiddled the key of the door's dead-bolt, and asked inanely, 'Or would you rather I incarcerated you in there for good?'

'No, thanks,' said Charles, rising from his seat and going through into the relatively fresh air of the cubicle. He too stretched out his arms. 'Always worst bit of the day, early afternoon. That's when most of us are at our biorhythmically lowest.'

Lisa flashed a sharp look at Mark. 'With some people, it's hard to tell.'

Her partner ignored the gibe. 'Do you want a coffee, love?'

'Please.'

'Did you get a sandwich at lunch?'

'Wasn't time,' Lisa answered shortly, as

she reached for the telephone.

'You've got a good business partner there,' said Charles, when they were through in the sitting area and the kettle had been switched on.

'Oh, yes,' Mark agreed casually. 'I've always been lucky with my back-up.'

It was a splendidly dismissive remark, the kind that a BBC producer might often have made about his secretary. Charles wondered whether Mark was genuinely unaware that Lisa was doing all the work within their partnership. But maybe that was just a reflection of another old BBC tradition. There had always been plenty of producers whose offices had been run entirely by their secretaries, and it had been a point of honour that that fact was never acknowledged. Charles wondered idly how the balance of power operated in Mark and Lisa's personal relationship.

His head was now aching horribly again. His mouth was dry and the dryness permeated his body; parts of his anatomy seemed to grind unlubricated against other parts. Mark saw the hand Charles passed painfully across his brow and said, 'You need a top-up.'

'Hm?'

'Alcohol level. Dropping below critical.

Serious malfunction could result.'

The conspiratorial tone and the pseudo-scientific jargon made Mark Lear sound like a naughty schoolboy, and this image was reinforced when he showed Charles the half-bottle of Teacher's he had hidden in the cistern of the Gents' lavatory.

Mark took a long swig. 'Wonderful. Ideal storage place.' He winked. 'No ladies come in here, by definition, and the water keeps the whisky perfectly chilled.' He proffered the bottle to Charles. 'Go on, this'll pick you up.'

'I'm not sure that I should . . .' Apart from anything else, he was a Bell's man. He'd never really been that fond of Teacher's.

'Go on.'

Charles's hesitation went the way of most good intentions. And the injection of alcohol did give him a predictable lift. But something about the whole episode felt shabby. Two middle-aged men in the Gents', hiding from a woman to take illicit sips of booze . . . there wasn't much dignity in the scenario.

Of course, it put Mark in a worse light than it did him. Mark had actually set up this private cache of whisky to hide his drinking from his partner. Charles would never have done that. He didn't hide his drinking from anyone. But then, even as he had the thought, he realized that was probably only because he lived on his own. It's easy enough to be overt when you know there's no one watching. If he had been cohabiting with someone who monitored his every sip, he wondered how long it would be before he resorted to subterfuge. He had an uneasy recollection of a bit of covert swigging towards the end of the time when he and Frances had lived together.

Mark Lear led the way back to their coffees with a smug, got-away-with-it smile. He produced a packet of Extra-Strong Mints from a pocket, and popped one into his mouth. 'Hide the evidence, eh?' He grinned as he offered the packet across.

Charles felt uncomfortable. There was something too calculating in all this, too cunning. He knew he drank too much, but he felt there was a degree of spontaneity about his drinking. Surely his own approach had never been this cold-blooded . . . ? He did, nonetheless, take one of the Extra-Strong Mints.

Mark Lear grinned. 'Should keep us going till the end of the day's recording. The old "maintenance dose", eh?'

Charles resented the implication. He

didn't like the way Mark spoke of their two problems as if they were the same. Mark was clearly an alcoholic, who was in chemical need of a 'maintenance dose'. Whereas Charles, on the other hand . . . But he knew the exaggerated pique at his friend's words rose from a suspicion that they might be all too applicable to himself.

On his way back to the cubicle, Charles thought he caught a flash of suspicion in Lisa's face as she looked at her partner and Mark averted his eye. But the moment didn't last. Lisa had clearly been busy on the phone during their absence.

'I've talked to the publishers.'

'Oh yes?' Mark sounded Olympian, detached. He was glad to have staff to sort out the minutiae for him, and glad they kept him up to date with their progress.

'They're doing a version of a Thesaurus on CD-ROM and, yes, they are accepting tenders for the audio content.'

'That's good,' said Mark smugly, as if all his careful planning was about to come to fruition.

'I've fixed a meeting for Thursday afternoon. You'll be free to come, won't you?'

'Not sure,' Mark replied, with the air of a man in whose diary an empty space was an endangered rarity.

Lisa's lips pursed. 'Well, we'd better get on. Find out what new excitements *Dark Promises* has in store. Through you go, Charles. Afraid I'll have to switch off the air conditioning again.'

The last session of the recording was the most constructive of the day. Charles Paris was more fluent, he found the rhythms of Madeleine Eglantine's prose less alien, and a good few pages got safely recorded. Only in the last half-hour, after five-thirty, did his concentration go. Sheer tiredness took over. His voice became croaky, and the fluffs proliferated.

At ten to six, Lisa Wilson gave up the unequal struggle. 'OK, let's call that a wrap. Well done, Charles. Last bit was very good.'

'Thanks.' He acknowledged the compliment with a tired grin. But inside him was the lurking fear that the recording wouldn't have been so good without that mid-afternoon injection of alcohol. Had he really reached the stage when he needed a 'maintenance dose'?

As he went through into the cubicle, he ached all over, but it was a better ache than that brought on by the hangover. This was the tiredness of having achieved something.

'Only about twenty pages behind where

we should be,' said Lisa, with a hint of approbation in her voice. 'You picked up the pace quite a bit.'

'Well done,' Mark agreed. 'I'd say that deserves a drink.'

Charles saw the tiny spasm go through Lisa's face, as she bit back her instinctive response. She had been living with Mark long enough to know that direct confrontation wasn't the best way of dealing with him.

'You coming, love?' her partner asked, a slight tease in his voice, once again daring her to express disapproval.

'No,' she replied lightly. 'Got to do a Sainsbury's run when I finish in here.'

'OK. Well, if I'm not home when you get back, we'll still be in the Queen's Head.'

'Fine,' said Lisa Wilson, and only someone who, like Charles Paris, had witnessed her relationship with Mark throughout the day, would have known that what she meant was actually far from 'fine'.

'Happy coincidence.' Charles raised his glass, took a long swig and felt the warm glow of a second large Bell's irradiate his parched system. 'I mean, your studio being in Bath and our show opening in Bath.'

'What is the show? I know you told me, but I can't remember.' Mark Lear was also on the whisky, which he was downing as if the world's supplies were on the verge of exhaustion.

'*Not On Your Wife!*'

'Don't know it.'

'Well, you wouldn't. It's a new play. By Bill Blunden.'

'Oh.' The monosyllable contained all that snobbish resistance the playwright's work usually inspired in people with university educations. Bill Blunden may have been an audience-pleaser, but he didn't strike much of a chord among the intelligentsia. When, every now and then, Sunday newspaper reviewers took it into their heads to rehabilitate farce as an acceptable medium of entertainment, they would home in invariably on Feydeau, Pinero or perhaps Ben Travers. Bill Blunden was too ordinary, too mechanical; his plays were mere clockwork toys designed to entrap laughter. He would never attain intellectual respectability; his only comfort would have to remain the huge international royalties which his plays brought in.

'And you're touring it, Charles, is that right?'

'Mm, three months. Fortnight in Bath,

then single weeks. Bill Blunden always takes his shows on the road, works on them, does lots of rewrites, sharpens them up.'

'With a view to the West End?'

'Ultimately, yes. But some'll have three or four tours before he's happy with them.'

'So you haven't got a West End option in your contract?'

'Nothing so grand, no. They did check my availability for three months hence, but that's as far as it went.'

'Oh, right.' Mark Lear chuckled with sudden recollection. 'Checked with your agent, eh? I've just remembered, when we last worked together, you were with this incredibly inefficient agent . . . what was his name? Maurice Skellern, that's right. He was a kind of a joke throughout the whole business, the worst agent since records began.' Mark shook his head and chuckled again. 'Who represents you now?'

'Maurice Skellern,' Charles Paris replied.

'Oh.'

'I hope today was all right . . . ?' said Charles tentatively. 'I mean, the recording . . . ?'

'It was fine.'

'I felt awful, arriving so hungover and —'

'Don't worry, we've had many worse through the studio.'

'I didn't think the studio had been open that long.'

'Well, no, not through that studio, but when I was at the Beeb . . .' A hazy look came into Mark Lear's eyes. 'I remember once doing a play with Everard Austick, and he was virtually on an intravenous drip of gin.' The retired producer let out a little melancholy laugh. 'Good times we had, back in the old days . . .'

Charles could see what had happened. In Mark Lear's mind, the BBC, the institution he had spent all the time he worked there berating, had become a golden city in his recollection. Now he wasn't there, it was perfect. For Mark, perfection would always be somewhere he wasn't. Charles suspected that the same pattern obtained in his friend's private life too. While he had been with Vinnie, all his young girls on the side had represented the greener grass of happiness. And now he was with Lisa . . . Charles wondered where Mark's fantasies hovered now.

'No, but I hope the recording was all right. Lisa didn't seem very happy with what I was doing . . .' Charles ventured.

'Don't worry about Lisa. She gets very po-faced about the whole business. What she doesn't realize is that the creative process should be *fun*. She's always clock-watching and budget-watching . . . and number-of-drinks-watching. Do you think, if I'd had that kind of attitude, I'd ever have produced any of the great programmes I did when I was at the Beeb?'

Charles Paris was too polite to ask which 'great programmes', as Mark went on, 'No, creativity is a wild spirit. It's the untutored, the anarchic, the bohemian. That's what creates art — danger, risks being taken in the white heat of rehearsal — not a bunch of accountants poring over spreadsheets in offices.'

Charles searched for a safe, uncontroversial reaction, and came up with 'Hm.'

Mark Lear shook himself out of his 'misunderstood artist' mode. 'Right, same again, is it?'

'Maybe I should move on to the wine . . .'

'Time enough for wine. A couple more large Scotches first.'

Well, Charles comforted himself, it wasn't as if he hadn't worked hard. He'd earned some kind of reward. No, all things considered, his first day of reading an audio book hadn't been too bad. And *Dark Promises* by Madeleine Eglantine was by no means an easy read.

As for the hangover, well . . . that'd probably been mostly nerves. There was a definite pattern to these things. Charles's hangovers always seemed to be at their worst on days when he had something important to do. Days when he was relaxed, when he wasn't stressed, he could wake up feeling fine, however much of a skinful he'd had the night before. He never quite knew whether it was the challenge of a difficult day ahead that exacerbated the hangover, or whether his anxiety pushed him to drink more the night before such difficult days. Either way, he knew he was feeling better now.

It wasn't a bad achievement, actually, fitting in a couple of days' reading in the middle of the rehearsal schedule for a play. That was the kind of thing stars did. 'Doing a telly on that free Sunday before we open,' actors like Bernard Walton would say airily, while the rest of the cast would sit, shrouded in misery, thinking, 'There's no justice. The bugger's already being paid twenty times more than me for this show, *and* he's cleaning up with a quick telly as well.'

Charles Paris's current position wasn't quite on that financial scale, but it was still rather heart-warming. Mark Lear had specifically asked for him to do the reading of *Dark Promises*, and had been happy to fit the dates into the brief break in the *Not On Your Wife!* rehearsals when the show transferred from London to Bath. That was quite a novelty in Charles Paris's theatrical career — shoehorning bookings into a busy schedule, rather than planting tiny, distantly spaced oases of work into the arid wastes of his diary.

And he put from his mind the thought — no, the knowledge — that Mark had turned to him only because he was familiar, someone who wouldn't shake the boat, someone who was safe.

The third large Bell's was as welcome as its predecessors. Must watch it tonight, something in the recesses of Charles's mind mumbled, just moderate intake tonight — OK? But who was going to listen to a voice like that, when the alcohol tasted so good?

'Who's directing this tatty show of yours?'

'David J. Girton.'

'David J. Girton? From the Beeb?'

'Right.'

'Good Lord. Presumably he's left the old place?'

'No longer on staff. Gather he still goes back to work on individual projects on contract.'

Mark Lear let out a harsh laugh. ' "Individual projects on contract"? Oh, that's what they all say. It's the equivalent of that movie euphemism, "having a script in development", or "consulting" in advertising, or "wanting to spend more time with your family" if you're a politician. Means he's out on his ear.'

'No, David did say he was going back to produce another series of one of his long-running sitcoms next month. I think it's called *Neighbourhood Watch*.'

'Oh?' The news clearly pained Mark. It was all right so long as all his former colleagues were in the same boat, so long as they'd all been unceremoniously dumped, as he had. But he didn't like the idea that one of them was still reckoned to be of value to his former employer. The thought brought a new viciousness into his tone. 'He's a lucky bugger, that David J. Girton.'

'Oh?' Charles prompted innocently.

'Yes, a few years back he was extremely fortunate not to lose his job.'

'What happened?'

'Bit of financial fiddling.'

'But surely that was always common practice in the Beeb? I thought doing your expenses was one of the most purely creative parts of the job.'

'David's fiddling was on a rather bigger scale than that.' In response to Charles's interrogative expression, Mark was about to say more, but changed his mind. 'Let's just say, he was lucky to keep his job.'

'Ooh, you do know how to tease,' said Charles in the voice he'd used as the outrageously camp Gorringe in *Black Comedy* in Ipswich ('One of the best arguments for heterosexuality I've seen in a long time' — *Eastern Daily Press*).

'Who's in the cast then, apart from you?'

Mark Lear raised an eyebrow at the mention of Bernard Walton. 'He's quite a big name. They must have hopes for the West End if he's involved.'

'Oh yes, I should think Bernard's secure, but the rest of the company might change a bit on the way. Bill Blunden's shows have a reputation for touring with a cheapish cast, which gets more upmarket when the show "goes in".'

'So you think you might not stay the course?'

'I'd like to, obviously, but . . .'

'Hm.' Mark Lear nodded his head thoughtfully. 'Well, of course, Charles, you always have been a cheapish actor . . .' He seemed unaware that he might have said anything mildly offensive. 'And if Maurice Skellern's still your agent . . .' His grimace completed the sentence more effectively than any words could have done. 'Bernard Walton, though,' he went on. 'Well, you should be all right. He's definitely bums on seats, isn't he?'

'That's the idea. Though apparently the box office advance isn't as good as they were hoping for.'

'Probably pick up by word of mouth.'

'Maybe. You ever work with Bernard, Mark? I'm sure he did radio back in the early days.'

Mark Lear shook his head. 'No. I was first aware of him on the telly. That ITV sitcom . . . forget the name . . .'

'*What'll the Neighbours Say?*'

'That's the one. So who else have you got in the cast?'

Charles continued his run through the dramatic personae of *Not On Your Wife!* His friend reacted to the mention of Pippa Trewin.

'Do you know her, Mark? Have you worked with her?'

Mark shook his head in puzzlement.

'It's pretty unlikely you would have done, actually. She only finished drama school last year.'

'Hmm . . . No, I know the name in some connection, can't remember where from.'

Charles pointed to Mark's whisky glass.

'That rotting the old brain, is it?'

But his friend didn't respond to the jocularity in the question. 'Perhaps it is,' he replied slowly. 'Certainly there's a lot of stuff I don't remember these days. Not that it matters much. I'm not doing much these days that's *worth* remembering.' With an effort, he shook himself out of this melancholy downward spiral. 'You have that problem, Charles? The old memory? Can you still remember your lines?'

'Pretty well.' It was true. Memorizing lines was simply a matter of practice, and Charles hadn't lost the knack. When that facility went, then it really would be time to cut down on the booze.

Strange, he contemplated, how many of his thoughts these days finished with the phrase, 'then it really would be time to cut down on the booze'. If he ever actually screwed up a job because he was too drunk or too hungover to do it, then it really would be time to cut down on the booze. If he ever woke up somewhere and genuinely couldn't remember how he'd got there, then it really would be time to cut down on the booze. If he found he was consistently impotent, then it really would be time to cut down on the booze.

And yet he'd been close to all of those

situations. A harsh critic might say he'd been *in* all of those situations. The prospect of having to cut down on the booze was stalking Charles Paris, a looming, distant shadow on the horizon, but a shadow that was drawing closer all the time.

This sequence of reasoning always prompted the same two thoughts in Charles. First — but if I gave up the booze, it'd ruin my social life; everything I do in my leisure time involves drinking.

Second — *could* I actually give up the booze if I wanted to?

And, that particular evening, the two recurrent thoughts were joined by a third. What *did* happen between me and Cookie Stone on Thursday night?

Mark Lear continued asking Charles about the cast of *Not On Your Wife!* The other name that prompted a reaction from him was Ransome George.

'Old Ran. He still up to his old tricks?'

'Which tricks are those?'

'Borrowing money. Sponging. He always used to be entirely blatant about it.'

'Oh,' said Charles.

'Had a terrible reputation. You'd think everyone in the business must've heard about it, but he'd still always manage to find some innocent sucker to bum a fiver off.' Mark chuckled, shaking his head at the follies of humankind. 'There's one born every minute, isn't there?'

'Ah,' said Charles.

Mark Lear was caught by something in his tone and looked up sharply. 'He hasn't tried to touch you, has he? You haven't fallen for the old "left my wallet at home" guff, have you?'

'Good heavens, no,' said Charles.

Mark looked thoughtful, then chuckled again. 'Well, your company seems to have more than its fair share of skeletons in its cupboards.'

'What do you mean?'

'David J. Girton . . .' Mark mused, 'and Ransome George . . .'

'What? Do you know something bad about Ran? I mean, apart from the fact that he bums money off people and doesn't pay it back?'

'Oh, yes,' replied Mark, enjoying the power of telling his story at his own pace. 'Yes, I know something very considerably worse about Ransome George than that. Goes back to the early 1970s, I suppose . . .'

But suddenly the producer's manner changed. The slyly conspiratorial was replaced by the irresponsibly drunk. Charles followed Mark's eyeline to see that Lisa Wilson had just entered the bar. She looked stern, a mother come out on to the recreation ground to tell her son it was bedtime — and no arguments.

As if it was some ritual the two of them had been through many times before, Mark played up to the image. He whinged to Lisa like an eight-year-old about what a spoilsport she was, and how she wouldn't let him have a life of his own, and how he was a grown man, for God's sake, and at least Vinnie never treated him like —

'Well, I've got to be off, anyway,' said Charles. He didn't want to get caught in the crossfire of a domestic argument. 'Haven't checked in at my digs yet.'

'OK,' said Lisa. 'Ten sharp in the morning, for more *Dark Promises*.'

'Sure,' said Charles. 'I'll be there. Can't wait. You never know — tomorrow may be the day that either the heroine or the hero shows a spark of character . . .'

And he left Lisa Wilson to gather up her recalcitrant charge. Somehow, Charles reckoned that the minute he'd left, Mark Lear would turn all docile and follow her obediently home. But he also reckoned, once Mark had got home, that he would continue drinking.

★ ★ ★

Charles Paris's accommodation had been sorted out from London. The stage door of the Vanbrugh Theatre, Bath, kept a digs list, and he'd easily found a suitable landlady who had a vacancy for a couple of extra nights before most of the *Not On Your Wife!* company arrived.

She was a pale, anonymous woman — Charles Paris never seemed to end up with the larger-than-life, characterful landladies who people theatrical legend. The one in Bath was possessed of either a permanent sniff of disapproval, a bloodhound's nose for alcohol, or a bad cold. She showed him the room, which was fine, offered him an evening meal, which he declined, and directed him towards a late-opening supermarket, where he bought a chicken pie and, it has to be admitted, another half-bottle of Bell's.

By his standards, he didn't reckon he'd had that much, but the effects of alcohol are cumulative and, as he slipped, later than intended, into a drunken sleep, Charles Paris knew he'd have another hangover with which to face his second day of reading *Dark Promises* by Madeleine Eglantine.

His last thought, before he surrendered consciousness, was once again — What *did* happen between me and Cookie Stone?

# Chapter Four

Cookie Stone sidled up to him at the Vanbrugh Theatre in Bath on the Monday afternoon, and winked. 'I remember what you said on Thursday night.'

Charles Paris smiled weakly. He wished to God he did.

Fortunately, there wasn't much time for embarrassment. The rest of the day ahead promised to be too busy for reminiscence or recrimination. The cast of *Not On Your Wife!* was about to rehearse the play for the first time on set, and they all knew that, whatever standard the show had reached in the rehearsal room, on stage everything would be different.

The schedule for the next two days was tight. The get-in to build the set had happened on the Monday morning. (In the old days, Charles Paris reflected nostalgically, that would have taken place on the Sunday, but now prohibitive overtime rates made any theatre work on Sundays a rarity.) On the

Monday afternoon the lighting director would work out a basic lighting plot, to be tweaked and refined during the tech. run, which was scheduled to start at five, and to take as long as it took. Fortunately, *Not On Your Wife!* was not a complicated show from the technical point of view. The basic set of the two adjacent flats, once built, did not change throughout the play, and the lighting plot was a simple matter of switching between the two acting areas.

The Tuesday morning was to be reserved for final adjustments to the set and lights. The company would then be called at twelve o'clock for notes arising from the tech. run. At two-thirty they would start a full dress rehearsal, which everyone in the company knew would not be enough to drag the show back to the standard it had reached on the previous Thursday in London.

Then, on the Tuesday evening at seven-thirty, *Not On Your Wife!* would face its first-ever paying audience, amongst whom would be critics from the local press. This last detail, when announced, had distressed many of the cast — particularly Bernard Walton. The show, he argued, would be terribly rough on the Tuesday night. Give it a chance to run itself in for a couple of performances before admitting the press.

But for once the star didn't get his own way. The view of Parrott Fashion Productions, relayed through the company manager, was that, yes, the show might have rough edges, but, more important, they needed to get newspaper reviews as soon as possible. The *Western Daily Press*, as its title implied, came out every day, but Bath's other local newspapers had midweek deadlines. If their critics came any later than the Tuesday, the notices wouldn't make it into print until the Thursday week, by which time *Not On Your Wife!* would have only four more performances to do in Bath, before the whole caravan moved on to Norwich. The company manager apologized to Bernard Walton for this fact of life, but stood firm. The star might have total artistic control, but when it came to purely commercial considerations, he had to give way. Advance booking for the show wasn't as good as they'd hoped, and Parrott Fashion Productions insisted on a Tuesday press night.

It was clear on the Monday that the show's director was more than a little out of his depth. Though he'd got by all right in the rehearsal room, actually getting a play into a theatre presented different challenges to someone whose main experience had been in television. Up until that point in the production, David J. Girton had abnegated his directorial responsibilities to Bernard Walton and the rest of his cast. But the decisions he faced now were technical rather than artistic, and he needed someone else to whom he could abnegate these new burdens.

Luckily for David J. Girton, the perfect person on whom to offload all such matters was conveniently to hand. He was the company manager, the one who had explained to Bernard Walton the necessity of a Tuesday press night. His name was Tony Delaunay, and he had worked for Parrott Fashion Productions for years. He was small, with short blonded hair, and always dressed in a black suit which somehow gave the impression of being more casual than a suit.

Tony Delaunay had run more touring productions than most people — though obviously not David J. Girton — had had hot dinners. He was a creature of the theatre, who'd worked as a scene shifter while still at school. In his late teens, he'd tried to make it as an actor in a variety of low-budget London productions, before recognizing that his skills lay on the technical side. He had graduated through the ranks of assistant stage manager, deputy stage manager and stage manager to take on ever more responsibility. He could do lighting plots, he could build sets, he could pacify local stage crews, he could mollify furious designers and wardrobe mistresses, he could mediate between stingy managements and poverty-stricken actors. He had saved the bacon of Parrott Fashion Productions on more occasions than he cared to remember. He was the all-purpose theatrical Mr Fixit, and nothing surprised him.

So, effectively taking over the technical direction of a new Bill Blunden farce from a director whose main expertise was in television presented no problems to Tony Delaunay.

But he didn't crow. He didn't rub in the fact that the show's designated director was incompetent. Tony Delaunay had no ego; he was the ultimate pragmatist. *Not On Your Wife!* was due to open to a paying audience on the Tuesday night. Parrott Fashion Productions paid him to ensure that that happened, and Tony Delaunay would see that it did.

David J. Girton quickly recognized his good fortune in having the company manager there to do all his work for him, and arranged his own movements on the Mon-

day accordingly. Deciding, with some justi-
fication, that a director couldn't be of much
use during the get-in, he had appeared in
the Vanbrugh Theatre at noon to see how
things were proceeding. Comforted by the
fact that Tony Delaunay had everything in
hand, David J. Girton decided to slip away
for 'a little drink and a bite to eat'. And,
since he was in Bath, after a couple of 'little
drinks', he decided his lunch had better take
place at the Hole in the Wall restaurant.

After lunch, he felt so exhausted, he
slipped back to his hotel to put his feet up
for a few minutes. He didn't know much
about lighting, anyway. He'd only get under
the lighting director and Tony Delaunay's
feet if he was in the theatre. The art of
directing, after all, was the art of delegation.
Respect the individual skills of all the members of your team, and you become a well-
respected director. That had been David J.
Girton's approach in television, and it had
worked well enough for him there. It had
also perfectly suited his natural indolence.

When he returned to the Vanbrugh
Theatre, around four-thirty, he found that
Tony Delaunay and the lighting director had
finished their plotting, and that the entire
company was ready for the tech. run to
begin. David J. Girton gave them a few

rousing words of the 'Have a good show' variety, and allowed Tony Delaunay to start the run. Then, rather than slowing the process down by interfering — he had always prided himself on being a minimalist director — David J. Girton sat quietly at the back of the auditorium and watched the show unfold.

The run — in comparison to the majority of tech. runs — went very smoothly. That was of course down to Tony Delaunay. He managed the cast efficiently, speeding through easy sections of the text and bringing his meticulous concentration to bear on the play's more difficult moments. Observing all the required Equity breaks, he reached the final curtain just before nine o'clock in the evening. The cast members, who'd been fully prepared to work through into the small hours if necessary, were massively relieved.

As the final curtain fell, David J. Girton was seized by a late burst of energy. He strode down the auditorium from his perch at the back with an authoritative cry of, 'Could we have the house lights, please? And tabs up? All company remain on stage, please.'

The cast stayed obediently on stage. They'd all — with the possible exception of

Pippa Trewin — been through the process many times before. Tech. runs were a stage of a production which required infinite patience. There was no room for temperament or thespian ego. However many times you were asked to repeat something, however many notes you were given, you just put your head down and got on with it. So the *Not On Your Wife!* company remained on stage, ready for a long screed of directorial notes.

'Well . . .' said David J. Girton, with a bonhomous, avuncular smile, 'pats on the back all round, I'd say. Bloody well done, the lot of you. I've kept a pretty low profile today . . .' (that was something of an understatement) 'because I don't believe in interfering on the technical side. There are plenty of people around the studio — erm, around the theatre — who have their own very considerable skills, and I'm not the person to put my oar in and tell them what they should be doing. Pats on the back to all you technical chaps too, by the way.

'So all I want to say, really, is: Keep up the good work. Tough day tomorrow. We've got a dress rehearsal in the afternoon, and the call for that is . . . ?' He turned round helplessly to the company manager.

Tony Delaunay was, as ever, ready with

the relevant information. 'There's a company call scheduled for twelve for notes, and the dress rehearsal's two-thirty, so the "half" for that'll be one fifty-five.'

'Oh, well, I don't think we need the twelve o'clock call, do we? Seems a bit much to break into everyone's lunch hour.' There were a good few restaurants in Bath that David J. Girton hadn't tried yet.

But actors' stomachs are not their main priority when a show's about to open. 'I think we should stick with the twelve o'clock call,' said Bernard Walton. 'There are a couple of bits we need to run. That tablecloth biz in Act Two for a start . . .'

David J. Girton saw a potential lunch disappearing over the horizon. There was a serious risk he might have to make do with a sandwich. 'Do you really think we need to . . . ?'

'Yes,' said Tony Delaunay with unshakeable authority. 'Twelve o'clock call, as per schedule, for notes and the bits that need running.' He turned deferentially to the director. 'Anything else you want to say, David?'

'No, thanks. Just . . . all have a good night's sleep and see you at twelve tomorrow . . . that is, of course, unless anyone fancies going out now for a bite to eat?'

None of the cast did. They were tired, for one thing. Also, most of them were husbanding their touring allowance and didn't want to blue any of it so early into the schedule. Maybe after the first night, a company meal might be in order.

Before they all dispersed, Tony Delaunay, unthanked by the director for his super-human efforts during the day, but apparently unworried by the omission, shouted for attention. 'Sorry, just one more thing. Another call to add to your schedule. I've just been talking to Rob Parrott at Parrott Fashion, and he's not happy about the advance. Show like this ought to be getting more bums on seats in a town like Bath. So we'll be recording a commercial for local radio.'

He nipped an incipient murmur of grumbling in the bud. 'Of course, anyone who's involved will get paid. I'll talk to your agents.'

'When are we going to have to do this?' asked Bernard Walton truculently.

'Well, since we've got the matinee Wednesday, it'll have to be on Thursday some time. Won't involve all of you . . . obviously you, Bernard, and one other, I would imagine.'

'Oh, we do want a lot of voices involved.'

It was typical of David J. Girton that he should suddenly become assertive over a detail that didn't matter.

'Well, I don't think Parrott Fashion —'

But the director had got the bit between his teeth. 'Yes, Tony,' he went on self-importantly. 'We need a lot of voices for this commercial. I'll let people know who's going to be involved.'

Tony Delaunay betrayed only the slightest reaction of annoyance, clearly deciding that this was not something to take issue about in front of the entire company. 'OK. Anyway, just wanted to warn you about the commercial. I'll let you know more details as soon as we've sorted out a recording studio and that kind of stuff. Thanks. And I think we can break everyone there . . .' Tony Delaunay turned, with proper deference, to the director. 'If that's all right with you, David?'

David J. Girton, his brief moment of assertiveness past, looked up from his study of *The Good Food Guide*. 'What's that?'

'OK if we break them?'

'Sure, sure.'

'Right, that's it for today!' said Tony Delaunay. 'See you all at twelve tomorrow.'

The *Not On Your Wife!* company started to drift off into the wings. Charles Paris heard Bernard Walton saying to Pippa Trewin, 'So are they coming?'

'Hope to. I talked on the phone today.'

'Oh well, we must go out for a really good dinner, just the four of us.'

'That'd be lovely, Bernard.'

Once again, Charles was puzzled. Though there was certainly some relationship between the star and the ingenue, he still couldn't quite define it. But he had more pressing concerns on his mind; Ransome George was beside him as they crossed into the wings. 'Er, Ran, about that twenty quid . . .'

'Haven't forgotten about it, dear boy. Go to the cash point first thing in the morning.'

'Well, I'd be grateful if you could, because the thing is —'

'Don't you worry. First thing in the morning,' said Ransome George grandly and speeded up on the way to his dressing room.

Charles was about to follow, but suddenly found himself face to face with Cookie Stone. She grinned at him, and gave another wink. 'Wondered if you fancied going out for a "little drink" and "a bite to eat" . . .' She was a good mimic; she had caught David J. Girton's tone exactly. '. . . and whatever else is on offer?'

There was no ambiguity in the final

phrase. Charles Paris felt himself colouring, as he desperately tried to muster some excuse. 'Erm, maybe . . .' he said feebly. Then, with a brainwave, 'Just got to check something with Tony first.'

He found the company manager in the auditorium, talking on a mobile phone. Tony Delaunay raised a hand to acknowledge that he'd seen Charles, and continued his conversation. Its subject was guarantees and percentages; no doubt he was again talking to his boss at Parrott Fashion Productions.

'Yes?' he said, as he switched off his phone at the end of the call.

'Just a thought, Tony . . . Don't know whether you've got a studio sorted out for recording the radio commercial?'

'No, I was going to ask around. Why, have you got any ideas?'

'It's just I've been recording an audio book in a studio down here. It's run by some people I know. They've got the full setup, state-of-the-art technical stuff. I thought, if you hadn't got anywhere sorted . . .'

'Have you got their number? I'll call them. If they offer me a reasonable rate, then that'll be one less thing I have to sort out.' Charles handed across one of the newly printed cards that Lisa Wilson had given him at the end of the *Dark Promises* recording on the Saturday. 'Thanks.'

Charles reached the dressing room he shared with a couple of the other minor actors. There was no one else there, but his haven didn't remain secure for long. He heard a discreet tap on the door, and a 'Come in' admitted Cookie Stone.

'Ah,' said Charles. 'Hi.'

She leant her face forward, lips puckered over her prominent teeth, waiting to be kissed. He chickened out and planted a gentle peck on each cheek. If she felt any disappointment, she didn't show it. 'So, how about this evening then, Charles?'

'Love to,' he said, 'love to. Thing is . . . you know I was doing that audio book over the weekend?'

'You mentioned it, yes.'

'Well, there were a couple of retakes we didn't get round to — only tiny bits — but since we've finished earlier than expected this evening . . . well, I just rang through to the studio, and they're still there . . . so I'm going straight over now to get it sorted.'

'This time of night?'

He coloured. It did seem pretty unlikely. 'As I say, it's only a couple of tiny bits,' he floundered. 'And they're up against a tight deadline.'

He didn't sound very convincing, but Cookie Stone took his words at face value. 'OK. Very starry, though,' she observed with mock-deference. 'You fitting in bits of other work round the play schedule. Be off playing in charity Pro-Am golf tournaments next.'

'I don't see it. Even this audio book's not my usual style, I can assure you.' It was against Charles's nature to claim charisma he didn't possess, so he confided, 'I only got involved in this because Mark Lear —'

'Who?'

'Mark Lear. He's the producer. Why, do you know him?'

'No,' Cookie replied firmly. 'I've never heard of him.'

'Oh. Well, I've known him from way back. Old friends and confidants, know what I mean?'

'I suddenly understand why you're recording for him then. Jobs for the boys, as ever in the theatre?'

'That's it, I'm afraid.'

'Or jobs for the relatives,' said Cookie Stone, with sudden venom. 'That's the way to get on in this bloody business, get born into one of the great theatrical dynasties.'

Charles chuckled. 'Trouble is, that's one of those things we don't have a lot of control over, do we? Rest of us must just scratch a living the best we can, eh?' Cookie's expression was beginning to take on an amorous cast, so he cleared his throat and said quickly, 'Anyway, I thought it'd be easier to get these retakes done now, because we don't know how the schedule for the rest of the week's going to pan out, do we?'

'No, no, we don't,' Cookie agreed. She nodded, accepting the situation. 'Oh, well, make it another night, eh?'

'Sure,' said Charles, once again weak. Then, falling back on the traditional actor's defence of a funny voice, he assumed the one he'd used for *Every Man in His Humour* in Belfast ('Charles Paris seemed to have drifted in from another play' — *Plays and Players*). 'Make it another night,' he echoed.

Cookie Stone proffered her face to him again. This time he planted a kiss on the tip of her upturned nose. It was a kiss without attitude; it could have been an expression of deep affection, it could have been merely avuncular. 'See you in the morning,' said Cookie, and left the dressing room.

He didn't feel good about the glibness with which the lies had slipped out. It reminded him of times he'd lied to Frances. Lying never felt good, but the more readily the lie is accepted, the more of a heel its perpetrator feels. Cookie didn't matter to him — or at least he didn't think she mattered to him — so lying to her shouldn't cause him too much anguish, but he still didn't feel good about it.

The thought of Frances hurt like a jaw-deep toothache. In his brain remained a residue of the recollection that he'd rung her the night he'd got drunk with Cookie. Surely it couldn't be true. Cookie had been in the flat with him; he wouldn't have rung Frances with Cookie there, for God's sake, would he? But the thought remained, and it deterred him from ringing his wife again.

As if to give some kind of substance to the lies he'd palmed off on Cookie, Charles stopped at the stage door and dialled the number of Lisa and Mark's studio. Probably be no one there at that time of night, but if there was, better warn them that he'd given their names to Tony Delaunay.

Also, there was something in him that wanted to talk to Lisa Wilson. He couldn't have got off to a worse start, but he liked to think that, by the end of the *Dark Promises* recording, he had to some extent rescued himself in her estimation. In spite of the Friday night's drinking, his Saturday hangover had not been so bad (maybe supporting his theory that anxiety aggravated the condition), and on the second day he'd felt more at home in the world of audio book recording. He liked to think he'd completed his reading of Madeleine Eglantine's deathless work in a style that had been, at the very least, professional.

Certainly, at the end of the recording, Lisa Wilson had said, 'Well done. We must get you in to do another of these.' It could merely have been routine courtesy, but Charles liked to think there had been a bit more to the compliment.

There was another thing, too. He couldn't deny that, over the two days of close proximity, he had come to find Lisa Wilson increasingly attractive. He knew he shouldn't be thinking about women. The chaos of his relationship with Frances, the ill-defined nature of the one he had with Cookie Stone, the fact that Lisa was Mark's girl anyway, and the disaster-littered history of Charles Paris's emotional life should have stopped him from ever feeling another stirring of lust in any direction. But it hadn't.

'Hello?' Lisa answered. Given her character, it was no surprise that she should be working late.

'It's Charles Paris. I rang because I was talking to the company manager of our show and —'

'Tony Delaunay.'

'Yes. You mean he's been on to you already?'

'Mm.' Tony certainly didn't hang about; no doubt that was one of the reasons for his success as a company manager. 'Yes, we've fixed it.'

'To do the *Not On Your Wife!* radio commercial? Great.'

'He beat me down a bit on price . . .'

'No surprises there. He's a shrewd operator. Parrott Fashion Productions run a tight ship . . . which is the polite way of saying they're so mean that when they open their wallets moths fly out.'

'Still, it's new work,' said Lisa. 'Might lead to something else, you never know. Getting the studio used, anyway. So, many thanks for the introduction.'

'No problem. The cue came up and it seemed daft not to act on it.'

'Much appreciated.'

'Is Mark there?' asked Charles. He didn't particularly want to speak to Mark, but etiquette dictated that it was really Mark who was his friend, not Lisa.

'No, I'm just finishing up here. He's in the pub.'

'Ah.'

Charles thought he'd bleached the mono-syllable of all intonation, but Lisa still picked up on it. 'Yes, I must go and drag him out soon. Otherwise he won't be fit for anything tomorrow.'

'Mark always enjoyed a drink,' Charles observed uncontentiously.

'It's got beyond "enjoying".' There was bitter experience in Lisa Wilson's voice. 'I'm not sure that he does enjoy it now. He just goes on drinking, in a kind of blur of self-hatred. It seems to be part of some death-wish.'

'You're exaggerating,' said Charles lightly.

'I wish I was. My father was an alcoholic,' Lisa confided. 'I've seen it all happen be-fore. And I'm not enjoying going through it again.'

'Ah,' said Charles. There didn't seem a lot else to say.

Lisa Wilson sighed. 'Anyway, I'd better go and do my nagging-little-woman routine and extract Mark from the pub. Hm, I just hope he manages to keep off the stuff on Thursday.'

'Thursday?'

'That's when you're doing your radio commercial. I'm going to be in London, at this publishing meeting . . .'

'Oh yes, you mentioned it.'

'. . . so Mark will be in charge.'

'Come on, Lisa. He'll be fine. You're talking about a man who spent over twenty years producing radio programmes for the BBC.'

'I know,' she said gloomily, 'but I don't think you've any idea how much he's degenerated since they kicked him out.'

'I thought it was "voluntary redundancy" —'

'Kicked him out,' Lisa repeated. 'Mark's never really recovered from that. Totally knocked the stuffing out of him.'

Charles could only manage another 'ah.'

'Anyway, I must get on. Thanks again for mentioning us to Tony Delaunay.'

'No problem. See you, Lisa.'

' 'Bye.'

He put the phone down, feeling disproportionately sensitive. He'd said 'See you', and she'd only said ' 'Bye'. Did that mean she didn't want to see him? Did that mean her talk of further audio books had just been professional flannel?

Charles knew his reaction was ridiculous. He just felt exposed, nerve endings too near the surface of his skin. It was a combination of factors, the tensions of a play about to open . . . the ugliness of his relationship with Frances . . . the stupid situation he'd got himself into with Cookie . . . And Lisa Wilson's talk about Mark had raised the old worry about his own drinking.

His behaviour the previous week had been appalling, and the blame for it could be fairly and squarely attributed to alcohol. If he hadn't drunk so much, none of it would have happened. He must cut down.

But not quite yet. There was bound to be a pub on the way back to his digs.

Charles Paris was about to go out through the stage door, when he was surprised to hear voices coming from the Green Room. He thought all the company would have hurried off as soon as they could. He moved closer to the Green Room door.

He was even more surprised to hear that one of the voices belonged to Bernard Walton. 'Listen,' the star was saying, 'it's even more important at the moment that you keep quiet about the whole thing.'

'Don't worry,' Ransome George's voice cajoled lazily. 'No problem. I'll keep stumm.'

'The thing is, there's this guy who's going

to be around for the next couple of days, name of Curt Greenfield. He's writing a biography of me, and it would be very awkward if he found out anything that —'

'You have my word, Bernard. There's no danger I'll say a dickie bird.'

'Good.'

The star didn't sound totally reassured, so Ransome George went on, 'Listen, it's not in my interests, is it, Bernard? I don't want to spoil the arrangement we have at the moment. It's suiting us both fine, isn't it?'

'Well . . .' Bernard Walton wasn't convinced about that.

Ran chuckled. 'Well, it's suiting me fine. No, your secret is absolutely safe with me, Bernard. There's no way I want anyone sharing it. I'd be extremely miffed if I thought anyone was sharing it.' He dropped into a punch-drunk boxer's voice. 'In fact, I'd do a mischief to anyone I thought was trying to share it.'

'OK. Fine.' Bernard Walton sounded partially reassured. 'Well, look, I'd better be on my way . . .'

At the sound of movement, Charles Paris glided silently away from the Green-Room door. He didn't want to be caught eavesdropping.

Bizarre, though, what he had heard. There was now something else in his mind of which he couldn't make sense.

As he'd intended, Charles Paris found an anonymous pub on the way back to his digs. He started with a couple of large Bell's. After a busy day's technical rehearsal, he felt he'd earned those. Then he moved on to the wine, at some point interrupting the flow with an unmemorable portion of shepherd's pie. When 'last orders' were called, he had another large Bell's as a nightcap. And the half-bottle back at his digs still contained enough to drown him into sleep.

# Chapter Five

On the Tuesday, there was a lot of tension in the *Not On Your Wife!* company, and it rose to a crescendo in the break between the afternoon's dress rehearsal and the show's first performance at seven-thirty. It wasn't that the dress rehearsal had gone particularly badly; it was something else that was bugging people.

Every cast of every play that's ever been put on has been nervous of facing an audience for the first time, but the *Not On Your Wife!* company were suffering from an anxiety unique to the world of comedy. In the rehearsal period for most plays there are predictable fluctuations in company confidence. The day of the readthrough is always tense and tentative, with cast members insecure, sniffing round the unfamiliar, each masking his or her individual paranoia in standoffishness or forced joviality. In the next few days confidence usually builds. The company begins to bond, they get excited about the work they're doing, they start believing that they could be involved in a really major success.

The next downturn regularly occurs when they 'come off the book', because actors don't all learn their lines at the same rate. But once the text is firmly assimilated, there is another upswing. Yes, they are involved in something good; the show's really going to work. That mood is unfailingly dashed as soon as the company gets into the theatre and starts working on the actual set. That is why technical rehearsals are always so ghastly. But, as the best productions run up to the first night, there develops a nervous bubble of thrilled anticipation. The show's not ready, they need more rehearsal, but if everything comes together, if they have a following wind and a sympathetic audience, then it could be wonderful.

In comedy, while all of this regular pattern is followed through, the stakes are much, much higher. The play that seemed so hilarious at the readthrough, the play whose stage business frequently made the entire company collapse in hysterics during the early stages of rehearsal, becomes dull by familiarity. In the week before it opens, when all concentration is on the technical aspects of the production, the play seems about as funny as a bowl of cold sick. And, as the moment of first exposure to a paying audience approaches, the awful fear creeps into the mind of every company member: 'Suppose they don't find it funny at all? Suppose nobody laughs?'

There is no escape. The average 'straight' play with a couple of mildly humorous lines in it will be hailed by the critics as 'witty'; but when a show's billed as a 'comedy' or a 'farce', nothing less will suffice than continuous laughter. A farce company is so horribly exposed. Everyone has experienced the personal humiliation of telling a joke which gets no reaction.

Charles Paris had also had the personal experience of being in a farce whose audience would have got more laughs at a funeral. The show had been loosely adapted from some French original, under the title of *Look Out Behind You, Louise!* It had completed its three-week run in Newcastle to tiny and stony-faced audiences, before being finally put out of its misery. And it had elicited from the *Gateshead Gazette* the following notice: 'But for the word "farce" on the poster, I would have assumed the play to be a serious documentary about the casualties of "care in the community".'

It was *Look Out Behind You, Louise!* whose

dark shadow lurked in the back of Charles Paris's mind, as the first performance of Bill Blunden's new farce drew ever nearer. But each member of the company had his or her own comparable nightmare of failure. Privately, they all twitched with terror.

Generally speaking, the first night of *Not On Your Wife!* didn't go too badly. The play didn't get all the laughs it should have done, but it did get some laughs. There was something to build on.

And at least, for the company, that dreadful moment of presenting a comedy for the first time was past. They breathed a communal sigh of relief.

On the Thursday lunchtime, when Charles arrived at the studio, it looked as though Lisa Wilson's vigilance had been insufficient. Mark Lear was extremely drunk. He must have spent the morning taking continuous top-ups from the bottle in the Gents'. Charles hated to think how high Mark's 'maintenance dose' might be.

They had arranged on the phone that Charles should arrive before the other members of the *Not On Your Wife!* company involved in the commercial. It had been Mark's suggestion. 'Come round twelvish. We'll have a couple of pints before we do the recording.' The rest of the actors were called for two o'clock.

He had agreed to the earlier meeting because there had been a quality almost of desperation in Mark Lear's voice. Charles was determined, though, that, whatever Mark might do, he himself wouldn't drink. He had woken up in his digs that morning with yet another hangover, and there was a show to be done in the evening. He needed all his wits about him. Under the circumstances, it would have been deeply unprofessional for any actor to drink at lunchtime.

But somehow, once they were actually inside the Queen's Head, it all seemed less important. The very smell of the beer was heady and seductive. And Charles knew how much better a pint would make him feel. Just the one pint, mind, just to counter the morning's dehydration. Charles Paris knew when to stop.

Besides, Mark Lear needed him. The desperation Charles had heard on the phone was intensified in the flesh. Mark looked haggard and dispirited. To let a man in that condition drink alone would have been inhuman.

Charles got the first two pints and ordered sandwiches. After they had both taken greedy gulps from their glasses, he said,

'You don't look too good, Mark. Anything the matter?'

'You name it. Where shall I start?'

'Well, let's start with the most important. Will you be in a state to produce this commercial this afternoon?'

His question prompted anger. 'Of course I bloody will! What do you take me for, Charles? When I was at the Beeb, I'd do huge, elaborate, three-day productions and not draw a sober breath the whole time. And they were bloody good, bloody good programmes!'

'That's all right then,' said Charles soothingly. 'So that's not what's upsetting you?'

'No.'

'Which means it must be something else?' Mark Lear was silent. 'If talking about it's going to help . . . I'm happy to listen. If, on the other hand, you don't want to talk about it, that's entirely up to you.'

Of course Mark wanted to talk about it. He had never been much of a one for the stiff upper lip, for buttoning in his emotions. That wasn't his way. If he had a problem, then other people were bloody well going to hear about it. Mark Lear had always craved sympathy, ideally from a wide-eyed young girl, but when one of those wasn't available, anyone with open ears would do.

At that moment Charles Paris fitted the specification.

'Oh, I don't know, Charles, it's all such a bloody mess.'

'What is?'

'Everything. I mean, the way everything's gone wrong in the last couple of years. I'm out of the BBC . . .'

'Just as you always said you wanted to be.'

'I know, I know. But somehow it's different on the outside. And now I've lost Vinnie and the kids.'

'Again you always said you wanted freedom.'

'Yes, but I don't know . . . I just feel . . . I mean, I was never that great a father, but at least I had contact with them.'

'And now you don't see them at all?' suggested Charles, feeling an unexpectedly strong and sudden pang of guilt about his own daughter. When had he last seen Juliet? Or his grandchildren, come to that?

'No,' Mark replied. 'I suppose I should make the effort, but . . . well, the kids don't seem that interested in seeing me. They only hear Vinnie's side of things, obviously, but . . . anyway, two of them are off at university.'

'I thought all three of them were.'

'No, Claudia, the youngest . . . she's having some time out. She had this eating disorder . . . which I think was kind of started by us splitting up . . . so at the moment she's living with Vinnie and the new husband . . . though I can't imagine that makes her situation any less stressful. Oh, it's all such a bloody mess,' Mark repeated abjectly. 'I feel so guilty. Perhaps I should have stayed with Vinnie.'

'I gathered that wasn't an option.'

'Well . . . Maybe if I'd tried harder at the relationship?'

'It wouldn't have worked,' said Charles firmly. 'Vinnie is out of your life for good. And come on, cheer up. It's not as if you haven't got a rather good replacement. I wouldn't mind having . . .' He nearly said 'Lisa', but changed it to 'a girl like Lisa around. You're a lucky man.'

'I know, but . . .'

'But what?'

Mark Lear shook his head self-pityingly. 'It's just not working. I mean, it's not the same. I think she's had enough of me.'

'Anything particular make you say that?'

Mark grimaced. 'A girl like her . . . well, she's going to have had other boyfriends, isn't she . . . ?'

'I would assume so. She's very attractive.'

'. . . in the past.' Mark seemed not to be listening to what Charles said. 'Boyfriends in the past. She's talked about them, told me everything. There was this married man she had a long affair with . . . and quite a few others . . . in the past.' His eyes misted over as he picked away at the scab of his unhappiness. 'But how can I be sure they are all still in the past? How can I be sure she isn't still seeing them?'

'Mark, Lisa is living with you and has gone into partnership with you on the studios. Short of having your babies, I don't know what more she can do to express commitment.'

'No, but . . . I don't know. With her, sometimes I just feel so old. I mean, what woman's really going to want someone of my age?'

Mark had chosen the wrong person to put this question to. Perhaps it might have gone down well with one of his nubile totties; for Charles Paris it was too uncomfortably pertinent to his own situation.

'You've got Lisa,' he said brusquely. 'You're being given a second chance. If I were you, I'd be down on my knees thanking the Lord for His generosity.'

'Hmm.' Mark Lear's mood was too entrenched to be shifted so easily. 'I don't know, Charles . . . I just don't seem to have anything to look forward to . . . I can't really see the point of going on.'

'Oh, Mark, for God's sake . . . You're only fifty. You could have half your life still ahead of you.'

His friend shuddered. 'What a repellent thought.'

Charles continued trying to jolly Mark out of his gloom, but he recognized it was a hopeless task. Having been in that trough so frequently himself, Charles knew one could only wait for the mood to shift. And, though at the time he could never believe it would, ultimately it always did. Or, the depressive in him qualified pessimistically, it always had so far.

Mark Lear clearly didn't want to be shaken out of his gloom that day. He was in a bleak, self-destructive mood. Charles had only one more pint, but Mark kept ordering double Scotch chasers to go with his beer, and left the sandwiches untouched. As the hands of the clock approached two, he didn't have the air of a man capable of producing his hand from his pocket, let alone a radio commercial.

And one thing he said in the course of his maudlin ramblings stayed with Charles for the rest of the day. 'I feel afraid, actually

113

afraid. I don't know what it is, Charles, but I feel as though something awful's going to happen. I feel as if someone's out to get me.'

They got back from the Queen's Head a little after two, to find the other *Not On Your Wife!* actors waiting outside the studio. The atmosphere was scratchy. Since the beginning of the week their schedule had been punishing, and the previous day they'd done a matinee as well as an evening performance. The fact that they were being paid to do the radio commercial was not enough to raise their spirits, and the general mood was not improved when they realized that the man who let them into the studios was extremely drunk.

David J. Girton had won his point about having a lot of voices for the commercial. Though the expense involved went against all the penny-pinching instincts of Parrott Fashion Productions, it was an issue on which the director had proved surprisingly intransigent. Perhaps, finally recognizing that he wasn't having much influence on the actual production of *Not On Your Wife!*, he was determined to have his one moment of assertiveness over a detail.

As a result of his insistence, therefore, the

actors who had been called were Bernard Walton, Ransome George, Cookie Stone and Pippa Trewin. David J. Girton was also present, of course, though in a bad mood. He'd won his point about the number of actors, but had failed in his attempt to make the call later than two o'clock. As a result, he'd had to rush his lunch at Popjoy's to be there in time.

The mood of the assembled company went down another notch when they realized that Tony Delaunay was not present. The company manager it was who would be bringing the text of the commercial they were to record. That was being organized by the Parrott Fashion Productions office, and was to be faxed through to the Vanbrugh Theatre. But there had been some hitch at the London end, with the result that Tony Delaunay, who was never late for anything, was late.

The company members drooped around the studio, whose sitting area did not boast enough chairs to accommodate all of them, while Mark Lear stumbled about, trying to locate microphones and reels of tape. His antics and slurred speech did not inspire confidence. Charles wished to God Lisa Wilson was there; she'd have got everything sorted out within seconds.

There was a communal sigh of relief when Tony Delaunay came hurrying in, but it turned to a communal groan of exasperation when he announced that there were a couple of points in the script which still needed checking with Parrott Fashion Productions. He immediately dialled through to London. The actors looked even more bad-tempered, as Mark Lear continued to fumble around the studio.

'Hope we're not all going to be crammed into that little dead room of yours,' Charles said to Mark jovially, trying to lighten the atmosphere. He turned to the rest of the actors. 'Last time I was in there, there was no air at all; after half an hour I just couldn't breathe. It was some problem with the air conditioning.'

No one seemed particularly interested in what he was saying, but Mark responded, 'We're going to be in the big studio. Just as soon as I've got it all rigged up properly.'

'But the air conditioning in the little one has been fixed, hasn't it?'

'Not yet,' Mark responded tetchily. 'That's another bloody thing I've got to sort out.' And he blundered through the open door of the larger cubicle to stare hopelessly at the rows of switches, faders and jack plugs. For the first time, the anxiety struck

Charles that Mark might not actually know how to work the equipment. As a producer at the BBC, he would always have had a team of studio managers to sort out the technical minutiae for him; and from what Charles had seen, in their new studio Lisa Wilson dealt with that side of things. He began to regret his recommendation to Tony Delaunay.

And he felt very glad that the company manager was still on the phone to London. So far as the cast was concerned, the lack of a final script was what was preventing the recording from getting under way. They seemed not to have noticed that the studio wasn't yet properly rigged for them to start work.

Continuing his attempt to ease the atmosphere and doing his bit to help, Charles took orders for coffee and went off to fill the kettle.

Mark Lear tried to go through into the larger studio, but found it was still locked. He had some problem finding the key to the dead-bolts, but eventually managed to open the heavy double doors and go inside.

From over by the kettle Charles heard Bernard Walton's petulant drawl. 'Isn't it bloody typical? You work your guts out for weeks on a play, the whole complicated machinery runs like bloody clockwork, and then when you get to a minor detail — like this wretched radio commercial — it all screws up. I mean, why on earth did we have to come out to the bloody suburbs of Bath to record this thing, anyway? You'd have thought they could have found a studio nearer the centre. I wonder who was responsible for choosing this godforsaken hole?'

Charles kept quiet. In the corner of the room, Tony Delaunay continued to wrangle with the Parrott Fashion Productions office.

David J. Girton, still sour with lunch-withdrawal symptoms, looked across towards the studio, from which Mark was just emerging, and seemed to see him for the first time. 'Hey, you're Mark Lear, aren't you?'

'That's right.'

'David J. Girton.' He stretched out a hand. 'We met way back at the Beeb. I started in radio, before I went across to telly. Used to see you hanging round the Ariel Bar, didn't I?'

Mark Lear took the proffered hand and grinned slyly. 'I used to see *you* hanging round the Ariel Bar.'

'Gone, you know, that bar. Gone with all its memories of post-production celebra-

118

tions, failed seductions and drowned sorrows. That whole Langham block's back to being a hotel now.'

'I know,' said Mark. 'I've only been out of the Beeb eighteen months or so.'

'Oh, right. You couldn't stand the atmosphere under Chairman Birt either?'

'You could say that.'

'No, it's all changed.' David J. Girton shook his head mournfully. 'Old days, they used to say BBC top management was like a game of musical chairs, except when the music stopped, they added a chair rather than taking one away. Now, when the music stops, they take away two chairs, or three. Haven't seen blood-lettings on that scale since Stalin's purges.'

'You're still involved, though, I hear?' Mark Lear swayed slightly as he spoke, picking out his words with great concentration.

'Yes, I go back on contract from time to time. When they want a new series of *Neighbourhood Watch*. I know all the cast and the writer so well.'

'All right for some.'

'You haven't been asked back then?' asked David J. Girton smugly.

'Oh no. No, they're well and truly finished with me. Definite one-way ticket to the scrap-heap in my case.'

'Ah,' said the director. There didn't seem a lot else to say.

'Mind you . . .' A nostalgic glaze stole over Mark Lear's bloodshot eyes. 'I remember those times back at the BBC. Particularly the early days . . . You were left to your own devices then, just allowed to get on with things in your own way. Now there's a whole raft of middle management and accountants standing between the producer and any kind of real creativity.'

'Couldn't agree more.' David J. Girton grinned. 'Sounds like you're well out of it, Mark, old man.'

'Maybe.' For a moment Mark Lear was immobile, eyes still filmed with recollection. Then he lurched forward suddenly, as he continued, 'Sometimes think I should write a book about the Beeb as it was in those days. Yes, I think I should do it, tell a few home truths. Show the BBC . . . not like everyone presents it on all those bloody nostalgia programmes . . . like it really was . . . all the scams, all the fiddles, all the under-the-counter deals that went on. Shee, I remember some of the things I used to get involved in, moonlighting on other jobs . . . Of course, it all had to be terribly secret then, the BBC owned one's soul, it wasn't *nice* to work for commercial companies out-

120

side. Whereas now . . . your bonus is probably calculated according to how many other organizations you work for. Yes, I think I've got some interesting stories in me . . . You'd be surprised the unlikely things unlikely people got involved in. Some they certainly wouldn't want to be reminded of, I'm sure. Actually, the whole thing'd make a bloody good book . . . I can see the cover now . . . "Mark Lear takes the lid off the BBC in a way that —" '

He may have had further literary ambitions but he didn't get the chance to expatiate on them because at that moment, finally, Tony Delaunay put the phone down, and waved the precious Parrott Fashion-approved text for the radio commercial.

It was a simple enough forty-second spot, in which Bernard Walton expressed his view that *Not On Your Wife!* was the funniest play he'd ever been in, and the other cast members asked him questions about who else was in it, where it was on, and what the Vanbrugh Theatre's box office phone number was. Even though they were being paid, everyone except Bernard was rather miffed that they'd been dragged out for the recording. They'd each got such a tiny 'cough and a spit' in the commercial that they'd never be identified personally. One voice, any voice — even an anonymous voice like Charles Paris's — could have been used to read all Bernard Walton's feed-lines.

'Let's get this knocked on the head as quickly as possible,' said Tony Delaunay. 'I've got a lot to do, and I'm sure you all want a break before "the half".' The assembled company mumbled agreement. The company manager turned to David J. Girton. 'Will you be producing the recording, David?'

But the director's moment of assertiveness had passed, and given way once again to his customary languor. 'No, no,' he said rather grandly. 'I have complete faith in you, Tony.'

The company manager nodded, without comment, and turned to Mark. 'OK, through into the studio with them?'

'Sure.' Mark Lear moved clumsily across to hold back the double doors. His disoriented sullenness had suddenly given way to a kind of giggly euphoria. 'Through you come, my luvvies!' A few of the cast bridled — they didn't like being called 'luvvies' — but nobody said anything. 'Come on, into the studio! Let's commit this deathless piece of drama to tape!'

He looked piercingly at Cookie Stone as she passed through. 'I know you, don't I?

We've met before, haven't we?'

'I don't think so,' she replied.

'At the Beeb? Didn't you ever work for Continuing Education?'

'No.' Cookie dropped into a Brooklyn 'Broadway Babe' voice. 'I never got the breaks. From birth I was just a no-hoper. I never made it into Continuing Education.'

But by then Mark Lear had lost interest in Cookie, in favour of Pippa Trewin. Something of the old charm he'd focused on so many young women came back into his manner, as he murmured, 'And who are you?'

'Pippa Trewin.'

'Oh, *you're* Pippa Trewin,' he said. 'Well, well, well. I know all about you.' And he fixed her with a beady, challenging eye. The girl looked away, annoyance twitching at the corner of her mouth.

'Can we get on, please?' demanded Tony Delaunay from the control cubicle.

'Yes, of course.' Mark Lear stumbled through to join him. Tony put the talkback key down, and spoke through into the studio. 'All gather round the one mike, I imagine. OK, one run and we should be able to take it.'

They were cramped around the micro-

123

phone. A green light flicked on and Bernard Walton started speaking. Through the double glass, Charles could see Tony Delaunay and David J. Girton in the control cubicle, both looking confused. Tony turned to Mark Lear beside him. Their dumb show made it clear that no sound was coming through from the studio. Charles saw Mark turn helplessly to a bank of sockets and reach, without conviction, towards a jack plug.

In one seamlessly efficient movement, Tony Delaunay's hand swept up to a row of switches and adjusted them. 'OK, just give me a couple of words for level, Bernard,' his voice crackled through the talkback.

'From the minute the script of *Not On Your Wife!* arrived, I knew I was reading the funniest play that —'

'OK, fine.' Tony Delaunay's fingers flickered across the control desk, doing a little more fine tuning. Beside him, Mark Lear had sunk back into his chair, eyes almost closed, happy to surrender responsibility to the company manager. 'Give us a read and then we'll go for a take,' said Tony.

'Just a moment,' Bernard Walton objected.

'What is it?'

'This line: "the sauciest, sexiest, smuttiest show in town" . . .'

'What about it?' the talkback demanded.

'Can we lose "smuttiest"?'

'The text of the ad has been cleared with Rob Parrott. Not sure that we ought to make any changes.'

Bernard Walton was adamant. 'Look, I don't want my name associated with anything "smutty".'

'It's only a word, Bernard. It goes with "saucy" and "sexy".'

'No. "Saucy" and "sexy" are all right. "Smutty" is something else again. "Smutty" is unwholesome.'

'I don't think it's going to worry anyone.'

'Listen, Tony, I've lent my name to this new campaign for standards in television. To the Great British Public, Bernard Walton represents Family Values, the kind of entertainment you wouldn't be ashamed for your kids to see. Bernard Walton is not associated with anything "smutty".'

At this point Tony Delaunay's unfailing pragmatism once again took over. Rob Parrott might want the word "smuttiest" in the commercial, but Bernard Walton saw it as a potential threat to his knighthood. Persuading the recalcitrant star to include the word could take up valuable time. 'OK, lose

125

"smuttiest",' said the talkback. 'Do we need another word in there?'

'No, it'll flow all right with just "sauciest, sexiest show in town".'

'Right you are. OK, let's go for a read.'

Mark Lear lay slumped in the chair beside Tony Delaunay. He appeared to be asleep. Certainly he took no interest in what was being recorded in his studio.

The commercial was done in two takes. Tony Delaunay had got the small reel off the tape machine and left the building almost before the cast streamed back into the sitting area. 'Where's a phone?' demanded Bernard Walton. 'I need a cab.' He turned to Mark. 'Have you got a number for a taxi firm?'

Mark looked up blearily, and Charles was glad he'd noticed a printed card stuck on one of the notice boards. 'Here's one,' he said, handing it and the cordless phone across to Bernard.

'Hm . . .' David J. Girton stroked his hands down over his ample belly. 'Don't suppose anyone fancies a little drink? I noticed there was a pub that's open all day by the —'

'No,' Cookie replied shortly. 'We've got a show to do tonight. I'm off to my digs for half an hour's kip.' And, without a look or word to anyone, she left the building.

'Oh, for God's sake!' Bernard Walton slammed the aerial back into the phone with annoyance. 'Half a bloody hour for a cab! "In the middle of the school run rush," ' he mimicked. 'What do I care about bloody school runs? I'll see if I can find a cab on the street.'

And the star stumped out.

'Er, Ran,' Charles murmured. 'About that twenty quid . . .'

'Just off to the cash point now, dear boy.' And Ransome George too was suddenly gone.

'I should be off,' said Pippa Trewin. 'Meeting my agent for tea.'

David J. Girton chuckled. 'Oh, right. Mustn't keep the agent waiting, must we? Particularly when that agent's . . .' And he mentioned the name of one of the biggest in the business.

What is it with this girl Pippa Trewin, wondered Charles, as he watched her neatly and demurely leave the studio. She's had the best start in the business of any young actress I've ever heard of.

Now there were only the three of them left — Charles Paris, Mark Lear and David J. Girton. 'Well,' said the director diffidently, 'what *about* a little drink . . . ?'

127

He was preaching to the converted. Charles made a token remonstrance about having to do a show that night.

'Nonsense. Some of the best performances I've seen have come from people with a couple of drinks inside them. Freddie in *Neighbourhood Watch* gets through a whole bottle of white wine during every recording of the show.'

Oh well, thought Charles Paris, if the *director* says it's all right . . .

They had only a couple. Scotch this time for Charles, he didn't want to keep peeing during the performance. David J. Girton drank wine, forcing the Queen's Head to open a rather better bottle than their house red. Mark drank whisky, and drank it with a dull, silent determination.

Suddenly, after two drinks, he rose to his feet in a panic. 'Only left the bloody studio unlocked, haven't I? God, after all those provisos the insurance company made about security. See you,' he called back at them as he hurried out of the pub.

'It seems to me your friend has a bit of a drinking problem,' said David J. Girton sleekly, as he downed the remains of his second glass of Australian Shiraz. 'Another one?'

Charles looked up at the clock. It was twenty-five to four. Plenty of time to sober up before the show. 'Why not?' he said with a grin.

It was after four-thirty when they left the Queen's Head. Charles didn't reckon it was worth going back to his digs, so he shared a cab with David J. Girton into the Georgian splendours of the centre of Bath.

That night's performance was better. There were more laughs, and the whole show was more relaxed. Charles certainly felt his Aubrey had improved. Oh dear, was he reaching the point where he could only give of his best when he'd got a few drinks inside him?

One thing about the performance was interesting, though. In the Vanbrugh Theatre's audience that night was one of British theatre's most distinguished couples. The famous actress Patti Urquhart and her equally famous husband Julian Strange had come all the way from London to see *Not On Your Wife!* And what's more, afterwards they went out to dinner with Bernard Walton and Pippa Trewin.

# Chapter Six

'It's for you, Mr Paris.'

His landlady hadn't become any less anonymous as the week went by. Nor had she quite eradicated the sniff of disapproval with which she always approached him. There had been a slight thawing in her manner when he'd organized her two seats for the Thursday night (without mentioning that the advance at the box office had been disappointing and the performance was being heavily 'papered'); but any brownie points he might have gained there had been cancelled out by the hour at which he'd arrived back after the show.

Still, the call to the phone was a welcome distraction. Charles had decided that morning to go for the kill-or-cure option on his hangover and have the Full Breakfast his landlady offered. But, though Charles had started on the fry-up with commendable vigour, the further he got into it, the more his enthusiasm waned. There is something baleful in the expression of a congealing fried egg, and he didn't think he could face its reproaches much longer. He was glad to leave the egg's recriminations for the phone in the hall.

'Hello?'

'Charles, it's Lisa Wilson.'

'Oh, hi.' On the spur of the moment, he couldn't think of any reason for her call, but he was nonetheless pleased to hear from her. Could it be that his success with *Dark Promises* was to lead so soon to another booking? It didn't sound that way, though. There was something odd in her voice, a tension he had not heard before. Up till then in their dealings, Lisa Wilson had always been in complete control; now she sounded as if she was on the verge of some kind of emotional outburst.

She still hadn't responded to his 'Oh, hi.'

'What's the matter, Lisa?' he asked.

'It's Mark . . .' She gulped, and the sound could have been a sob.

'What about him?'

'He's dead.'

'What?'

'I got back from London this morning. I stayed over, you see.' She gulped again. 'He was in the studio.'

'Which one?'

131

'The one you used. The little dead room.'

'What'd happened to him?'

Now her sobbing was unrestrained. 'He'd . . . suffocated. I . . . I don't know exactly what happened . . . There was an empty whisky bottle in there with him. The doctor thinks he must've passed out from the booze. That's really why I was ringing, Charles . . . You were there to record the radio commercial, weren't you?'

'Yes.'

'Had Mark been drinking? He swore to me that he'd lay off the stuff, at least till the commercial was recorded, but . . . Had he been drinking when you saw him, Charles?'

It was impossible to deny that Mark Lear had been drinking, and drinking heavily.

'Oh, God.' Lisa's voice cracked in anguish. 'He must've passed out while he was in there, and been too insensible to wake up when there wasn't enough air. It's my fault. Just like it was with my father . . .' another huge sob welled up.

'What?'

'I let my father go out and drive when he'd had far too much to drink. He had a crash, hit a tree . . . He died three days later in hospital. God, I feel this is my fault too. If I hadn't stayed over in London, I'd

132

have found Mark in time. I could have pre-vented it.'

'You mustn't think like that, Lisa. You mustn't blame yourself. It just happened, that's all.'

There was unrestrained sobbing from the end of the phone. Then, with a great effort of will, Lisa Wilson regained control of herself. 'Charles, I want to see you, talk to you about it.'

'Sure. Where are you?'

'I'm at the studio now. There are police here, and ambulances, and all kinds of . . . I'll ring you, OK?'

'Yes.'

'I mean, it's quite possible the police will want to speak to you, anyway — you and the other people from the *Not On Your Wife!* company who were here yesterday after-noon.'

'Why? Is there any suspicion of foul play?'

There was an infinitesimal pause before she replied, 'No, I don't think so. But I guess they always check everything out. Have to, don't they? See if it's just an ac-cident . . . or I suppose . . .' she gulped again '. . . it could be suicide . . . or . . .'

She didn't complete the thought, but left it dangling, tantalizingly, in the air.

'I'm frightfully sorry,' said Charles. 'It's

an awful thing to have happened. You must be in shock.'

'Yes, I think I probably am a bit. Shock and guilt.'

'You have no reason to feel guilty.'

'Don't I? You don't know the half of it, Charles.' She let out a harsh laugh, which broke down into a sob.

'Just hang on in there, Lisa. Don't blame yourself. There was nothing you could have done. And, when things're a bit more sorted out, call me to fix a time to meet. Obviously we've got a show tonight . . . there'll be a matinee too on Saturday, but just leave a message with my landlady — OK?'

'OK. Thanks, Charles.'

He cleared his throat and then said, 'It may seem indelicate to ask, under the circumstances, but was your day in London good?'

'What?' she asked sharply.

'Your meeting with the publishers. Did you get the job?'

'Oh yes. Yes, we got the job.' Sobs once again threatened. 'Not that it actually seems very important now . . .'

'No, of course it doesn't. Look, I'm awfully sorry . . . You take care of yourself.'

'Sure.'

Back in the dining room, Charles's fried

134

egg looked even colder and more accusatory. He pushed the plate back. His landlady didn't say anything, but her look demanded an explanation.

'I'm sorry,' said Charles Paris. 'I've just had some bad news. A friend of mine's died.'

# Chapter Seven

As it turned out, Lisa and Charles didn't meet till the Sunday. By then, *Not On Your Wife!* had done another three performances, and the show was definitely getting better. The cast were more prepared for where the laughs were going to come, and their timing had improved considerably. The overall pace of the production had picked up, the audiences seemed to be enjoying themselves, and David J. Girton was very pleased with the way everything was going.

Bill Blunden, the playwright, was not so positive in his approval, but then it was not in his nature to be positive. He worked on his playscripts like a mechanic tuning a Formula One car engine. He tweaked here, he tightened there, he constantly dismantled, adjusted and rebuilt his creation. He'd watched every performance so far, making extensive notes about the audience's reaction to each line and each moment of comic business. And he'd been sitting up late in his hotel room, rewriting and reshaping the script. As yet, the cast had not been given any of the changes he was proposing to make, but there was a full company call scheduled for the Monday morning at eleven, and everyone had to be on standby for possible extra rehearsals during the second week of the Bath run.

Charles Paris's performances as Aubrey on the Friday and Saturday were workmanlike, but not inspired. He garnered the ration of laughs his part was allocated, but did not grow in comic stature as some of the other actors were beginning to. Charles was on automatic pilot for *Not On Your Wife!*; his mind was preoccupied with Mark Lear's death. The news of the tragedy had filtered through to the Vanbrugh Theatre, but prompted little reaction in the company.

For Charles Paris, though, the death had been a body-blow. Mark had never been a particularly close friend, but he was someone Charles had known for many years, and his sudden absence prompted gloomy reflections on human mortality. There was also a sense of shock. It was so recent. On the Thursday, Charles had been drinking with Mark at lunchtime; less than twenty-four hours later, the man was dead.

There were also uncomfortable parallels

to be drawn. Charles Paris didn't yet know the detailed circumstances of Mark's death, but there seemed little doubt that excessive drinking had played its part. There had been too many occasions in Charles's life, particularly recently, when, for the same reason, he hadn't been entirely in control of his actions. Mark Lear's death gave him a there-but-for-the-grace-of-God frisson. Charles Paris knew his own drinking was getting out of hand. He could all too easily have been the victim of a comparable accident.

His reaction to this realization, however, was not admirable. Instead of immediately cutting down on — or, ideally, completely cutting out — the booze, on the Friday and Saturday Charles actually drank more. It seemed that whisky was the only resource he had, the only palliative that could, however briefly, deaden the pain of the thoughts whirling around his head.

Also, he was into one of those cycles of cumulative drinking when the only way he could achieve all he had to was by continuous topping-up. The sequence of half-bottles of Bell's at his digs became a sequence of full bottles. On the Friday and Saturday nights — when he'd woken up at three, his thoughts too troubled for further sleep — he'd had recourse to the whisky. And he'd even taken a couple of solid slugs in the mornings before going down to face his landlady's breakfast.

Charles Paris knew he must stop, but he wasn't quite ready yet to do that. His current dosage was necessary, medicinal even. Wait till he was feeling a bit stronger, then he'd really take the drinking in hand.

The result of his mounting intake was that when, according to prearrangement with Lisa Wilson, he arrived at the studio at eleven o'clock on the Sunday morning, he was in the grips of another stinking hangover.

She too looked in a dreadful state, but presumably for different reasons. There were dark circles under her eyes, and her mouth was a thin line of tension.

Though he had never touched her before, it was instinctive for Charles to wrap an avuncular arm around her shoulders and put his lips to her cheek. She gave no sign of objecting.

'I'm sorry,' he said. 'You must have had a terrible couple of days.'

She grinned wryly. 'Known better. Would you like some coffee?'

'Please.' While she crossed to switch on the kettle, Charles looked around the studio space. 'No police tape or seals or anything like that. Does that mean they've finished their investigations?'

'I guess so,' she replied from the other side of the room. 'We'll find out for sure at the inquest, but they seemed fairly confident it was an accident . . . though one of them was asking about the possibilities of suicide.'

'Would you say Mark had a death-wish?'

She crossed to the table with two mugs of coffee. 'At times.'

'Yes.'

Something in Charles's intonation made her look up sharply. 'What do you mean? What did he say on Thursday?'

'Well . . . we had lunch in the Queen's Head.'

'He told me he wasn't going to drink.'

Charles shrugged. 'You said so on the phone. I'm sorry. At the time I didn't know he'd promised you to lay off.'

'No reason why you should have done. So what did he say?'

'He was just in a maudlin mood. Self-pitying. I'm sure you know what he could be like . . .' Lisa Wilson nodded with feeling. 'Well, Mark was saying that life was a mess and that kind of stuff. But I don't know that that would qualify as having a death-wish. I mean, he didn't talk about suicide

140

or . . . He was just gloomy, depressed if you like.'

'Hm . . .' Lisa fiddled with the handle of her coffee mug. Charles hadn't seen her in a state like this before. He suddenly realized it wasn't simply shock she was suffering from; she was actually nervous of something. Not of him, surely?

'Did Mark say anything about me?' Lisa asked diffidently.

'He did mention you, yes.'

'What did he say?'

'He implied that . . . that things weren't . . . Look, I'm sorry, the state of your relationship is none of my business. I —'

'What did he say?' she insisted.

'He, sort of, said that he was too old for you and that things weren't going too well.'

Lisa nodded her head slowly. 'Did he say anything about other men?'

'Other men?'

'Other boyfriends of mine.'

'Yes, he did, um . . . he said that you must have had other boyfriends in the past.'

'*And?*'

'And perhaps you still kept in touch with some of them.'

'Oh. Oh God.' Her blonde head sank down on to the table, and her shoulders shook with sobs. 'I should have come back.

141

I could have saved him. I shouldn't have stayed in London overnight.'

'Come on, Lisa, you had things to do. You were having that meeting with the publishers, trying to get work.'

She looked up at him, her eyes smudged with tears. 'My meeting with the publishers finished at five o'clock. I spent the rest of the evening — and the night — with an ex-boyfriend.'

'Ah. Did Mark know that was what you were doing?'

'Yes, otherwise he wouldn't have . . .' She recovered herself, and shook her head. 'I think he may have suspected.'

Charles nodded. That would certainly make sense of some of the things that had been said in the pub. 'But you can't blame yourself for that,' he urged. 'It was just bad luck that you were away when he passed out in the studio, just incredibly bad luck.'

She shook her blonde head decisively. 'No, it was more than bad luck.'

There was a silence. Charles's head was still drumming with a dull, low pain. He took a long swallow from his coffee. It had gone cold. Oh, he needed a drink.

Lisa Wilson sat up straight and flicked her head briskly from side to side, as if to flush out morbid thoughts. 'Incidentally, do you want some work, Charles?'

Her question got every actor's knee-jerk response. 'Yes.' Then, 'What? Not another finely chiselled literary gem from the deathless Madeleine Eglantine canon?'

'No. It's what I went to London about. This CD-ROM thing. The Thesaurus.'

'I remember you mentioning it. I didn't quite understand what it was about.' The advances of computers and the information revolution they had brought about had rather passed Charles by.

'A lot of CD-ROM reference works these days are multimedia,' Lisa explained patiently. 'So when you look up a word or phrase, you hear it as well as seeing it.'

'I think I'm with you so far.'

'Well, to get all those words and phrases so that they can be heard, someone has to record them.'

'And that's the contract you've got?'

'Exactly. Does recording that kind of thing appeal to you?'

'I am gobsmacked,' said Charles, 'chuffed, over the moon, delighted, ecstatic, jumping for joy, happy as Larry, glad all over, jumping for —'

'Yes, all right. You've got the idea. Well, the publishers need a whole Thesaurus recorded — and pretty damned quickly. I was

143

thinking . . . now your show's up and running, you'll be free during the days, won't you?'

'Most of the time, yes. May have the odd call for rewrites and extra rehearsal of bits and pieces, but basically I should be free.'

'Well, in that case, we should be able to get the whole lot recorded before you move on to . . . where's your next port of call?'

'Norwich.'

'Be good if we could get it all done, wouldn't it?'

'Yes,' said Charles, thinking of the money. 'How many words and phrases are there in a whole Thesaurus?'

'About a hundred thousand in this one.'

'Jesus,' said Charles Paris. 'And they all have to be spoken absolutely straight? No inflection, no vocal colouring?'

'None at all.' There was a gleam of amusement in her voice as she asked, 'Do you think you could do it, Charles?'

'Well, I could have a go.' He grimaced. 'Remember, though, you're dealing with someone who couldn't say, "Side One — End of Side One" without sounding "actorish".'

'Dead,' said Charles Paris into the microphone. Then he left a two-second pause, and went on, 'Deceased' — two-second pause — 'Defunct' — two-second pause — 'Died out' — two-second pause — 'Dead and gone' — two-second pause — 'Inert' — two-second pause — 'Lost and gone for ever' —

Lisa Wilson's voice came through the talkback before he completed the next two-second pause. 'No, I'm sorry, that had intonation in it.'

'What?'

' "Lost and gone for ever".'

'What kind of intonation?'

'Well, you were almost singing it.'

'*Singing* it?'

'Yes. Like in *Clementine*. "Thou art lost and gone for ever, dreadful sorry, Clementine." '

'Oh, sorry, yes. I wasn't aware I was doing it. It's something so deep and atavistic, it's almost impossible to get it out of my mind.'

'Well, you must *try*,' said Lisa's voice firmly.

'Yes, OK.'

They had started recording more or less straight away. For one thing, the publishers' deadline was tight, but also Lisa Wilson was in need of displacement activity. Work, any kind of work, might stop the repetitive churning of guilt and horror in her mind.

145

She'd quickly agreed an hourly rate with Charles and, as soon as she'd set up the small studio, they had started recording. They reckoned they could get an hour in before they broke for lunch.

It was still stuffy in the little dead room. Lisa had arranged for the air conditioning engineers to come the next day, and the police had offered no objection, which presumably confirmed that their investigations were at an end. But the airlessness in the studio cast a shadow over Charles. It did not allow him to forget that he was sitting in the very seat where Mark Lear had breathed his last.

Trying to blank that memory — and indeed all received memory — out of his mind, he once again pronounced, 'Lost and gone for ever.' He must've got it right, because there was no further interruption. 'Non-existent' — two-second pause — 'Obsolete' — two-second pause — 'Passed away' — two-second pause — 'Released' — two-second pause — 'Six feet under' — two-second pause — 'Dead as a dodo' — two-second pause — 'Dead as a doornail' — two-second pause — 'Dead as mutton' — two-second pause — 'Dead as —'

'No, sorry, Charles,' Lisa's voice broke in again. 'You're getting a rhythm to the words. You're making them sound like a catalogue.'

'Well, it's bloody difficult not to,' Charles Paris complained. 'Bloody hard — bloody tough — bloody arduous — bloody challenging — bloody problematic . . .'

They broke at one. 'Shall we go to the pub?' Charles suggested.

One look at Lisa's face told him it was a bad idea. 'Not if we're going to do any more recording this afternoon.'

'No, no, OK.' But, God, how his body screamed out for a quick injection of alcohol. 'Don't you drink at all, Lisa?'

She shook her head.

'Health reasons? Or don't you like the taste?'

'No. No, I like the taste all right. I like the taste very much indeed. Too much.'

'Ah.'

'I used to drink a lot, but then . . . I stopped.'

'Was that after your father was killed?'

She nodded. The recollection was still powerful enough to deprive her of words. 'Yes, I stopped then completely. I could see the way I was going. I didn't want history to repeat itself.'

'No. Was it easy to stop?'

She let out a harsh little laugh. 'Easy? No, it wasn't easy. It still isn't easy. Still, when I see people drinking on television, when I smell a glass of wine, when I . . . No, it's not easy.'

'Cohabiting with Mark can't have made it any less difficult.'

'True.' She grinned wryly. 'Mind you, compared to the other difficulties of cohabiting with Mark, the booze was kind of a detail.'

'Ah. So how did you give up? Just will-power? Or did you go to Alcoholics Anonymous or something like that?'

'No, I suppose it was just will-power. Well, I say "just will-power". Shock helped too.'

'Shock?'

She nodded. 'My father's death. We were very close. He did mean an enormous amount to me.'

'Presumably part of the appeal of someone like Mark? The older man?'

'I didn't have you down as an amateur psychologist, Charles.'

'No, well, most actors . . . it's kind of part of the job.'

'I didn't need Alcoholics Anonymous,' Lisa continued. 'When I'd seen how destructive the booze could be, when I'd seen what it'd done to my father . . . I didn't need any Twelve-Step programme. I was there in one step.'

'So presumably you tried to stop Mark drinking too?'

'Tried. Early on in our relationship, anyway.' She jutted out a rueful lower lip. 'Huh. I think I probably made it worse in his case. He drank more to get back at me.'

'What do you mean — "get back at you"?'

'Well, increasingly he kind of couldn't hold his own with me in the normal ways. I mean, the break-up of his marriage and being kicked out of the BBC . . . I didn't realize, when we first met, how much those two events had taken out of him. They'd totally destroyed his confidence. So, in our business venture here, I'm afraid Mark was really just a passenger.'

'That was rather the impression I got.'

'And then, in our private life . . .' She coloured. 'Well, I guess that wasn't very equal either, not after the first flush of meeting each other, anyway. And the booze was the one thing that Mark felt gave him a kind of power over me.'

'Power?'

'Yes. Constantly challenging me. Challenging me to have a go at him about it, to become the stereotype of the nagging little woman. And he knew how strong my taste for the stuff was too, so he was challenging me to keep off it. Yes, it was the only area in which Mark felt he had power over me.'

'Hm. If you don't mind my saying so, you don't paint a very rosy picture of your relationship.'

'No, Charles, I don't. It started, as many of these things do, quite romantically. There were warning signs, but I made that classic woman's mistake of recognizing certain qualities I didn't like about a man, and imagining that I could change them. Things didn't get really bad until we moved down here. I suppose I'd changed too. Over buying this place and getting it converted . . . well, somebody had to be assertive or nothing would have got done.'

'And that person wasn't Mark?'

'No. I made all the important decisions. I had to. So I guess he felt he was being even further marginalized. But I struggled on, trying to make the relationship work. We were in it together, I thought things would improve.' She sighed. 'But they didn't. They were never going to, so long as he went on drinking that much.'

Lisa shook her head in disbelief at what she was about to say. 'The awful thing is,

Charles, that when I realized Mark was dead
. . . along with all the shock and guilt and
everything else . . . a little bit of me was
actually relieved.'

'Ah.'

'It's a dreadful thing to say.'

'No. No, it's quite understandable.'

'And that bit of me — that disloyal, trai-
torous bit — was saying, "Now you've got
another chance. Now you've got the possibility of something in your life to look forward to." I'm sorry. I know it's an awful
thing to feel.'

'We don't have control over what we feel,
Lisa. I think it's very honest of you to admit
it.'

'Hm.' She sat back in her chair, somehow
eased by the confession, and looked piercingly into his eyes. He'd always thought hers
were blue, but this intense scrutiny revealed
them to be a pale, unusual grey.

'You drink too much, don't you, Charles?'
she said evenly.

'Well . . . Well, I suppose . . . I mean, I
do sometimes have rather heavy sessions
when I'm under pressure and go through
bouts of —'

'All the time,' said Lisa.

That almost made him angry. 'You've no
idea. You've no basis for saying that. We

met less than a week ago and —'

'I can tell,' she said.

There was no arguing with the certainty in her voice. 'Well, yes, all right, I probably do, but —'

'Why?'

'Oh, for God's sake, Lisa! You don't have to ask that question. You understand the compulsion. You know why people drink.'

'Maybe I do, in general terms, but why do *you* drink?'

'All right. I drink to . . . I drink to make life different.'

'Drink doesn't make life different.'

'I know. Nothing makes life different, but drink makes life *seem* different, and that seems to me the best deal that's on offer.'

'Is life so dreadful?'

'Most of the time I'd say, "yes".'

'And it hasn't occurred to you that it might be your attitude to life, the way you see life, that's actually dreadful? That life itself is entirely blameless?'

'That is possible, of course it is. However, the fact remains that I'm me, and I have only one way of seeing life.'

'And it looks better to you through the bottom of a glass of whisky?'

'Undoubtedly.'

Lisa Wilson shook her head in exasperation. 'But, Charles, just think how much of your time you *waste* by drinking.'

'It gets me through it,' he responded doggedly. 'Without the booze, life would just take so long.'

'Hm. And have you ever tried to give up? I mean, seriously tried?'

'I've tried to cut down from time to time. I've gone whole days without a drop,' he added virtuously.

'But never *really* tried?'

'If you mean by that, have I ever joined something like Alcoholics Anonymous, then the answer's no. I couldn't stand all those smug, self-righteous people swamping me with the patronizing zeal of the converted. No, thanks. If I decided to give up, I'd do it on my own.'

'But could you — ?'

'Actually, I heard this joke,' Charles interrupted, trying to lighten the atmosphere. ' "Friend of mine used to have a drinking problem, so he joined Alcoholics Anonymous. He still drinks, but under another name!" '

Lisa Wilson was not to be deflected by humour. 'Could you actually give up, Charles?'

'Give up booze? Of course I could.' His head was aching more than ever now. All he needed was a drink to melt away the pain. 'It's just that I don't want to,' he concluded.

She sat back, with a cynical curl to her lip.

'And what's that expression meant to mean, Lisa?'

'Just that I don't think you could give up.'

'Of course I could.'

'Yes?'

Her patent disbelief was beginning to annoy him. 'Yes, of course I bloody could! Just like that. All right, I won't have another drink till I leave Bath.'

As a smile of satisfaction spread over Lisa Wilson's face, one thought dominated Charles's mind. It was: Oh my God, what have I said?

'Good,' said Lisa quietly. Then she stood up. 'There's a corner shop along the road. They're open every day of the week, and do sandwiches and Cokes and all that stuff. Shall we grab some there to have for lunch?'

'Yes,' said Charles Paris, without enthusiasm. 'All right.'

They were again seated either side of the table, this time with their packets of sandwiches and their drinks. Lisa's bottle of mineral water was sparkling; Charles's was still — he found when he was recording that the fizzy stuff made his stomach rumble even more.

Lisa again seemed ill-at-ease, as she had done earlier in the day. It was as if there was something she had to say to him, and clearly it wasn't about the booze, because she'd already said that. Finally, after a long silence, the words burst out.

'Charles, when I came into the studio on the Friday morning, when I found Mark . . .'

'Yes?'

'There were a couple of things I didn't tell the police about . . .'

'What?'

'I told them I found Mark in the studio dead . . . which was true. And that I'd found the bottle of whisky in there with him. What I didn't tell them, though . . .' she was having difficulty in framing the words '. . . was that the door to the small studio had been locked.'

'Locked?'

She nodded. 'From the outside. The key was still in the bottom dead-bolt. I unlocked them both, then wiped the key with a handkerchief, and hung it up on the hook where it always goes. And I . . . didn't tell the police.'

'Why not?'

'I wasn't thinking. I was feeling guilty.' She looked into his eyes, wondering whether she dared confide in him. Deciding to take the risk, she went on, 'The man . . . the man I spent Thursday night with . . . he's married. I didn't want all that to come out.'

'But why should it have come out?'

'If I'd told the police everything, then, when they'd investigated, they couldn't have helped finding out.'

'Why? Was there something else that — ?'

'Also,' she interrupted him, 'other people maybe knew that things weren't too good between Mark and me . . . I suppose I was afraid that the police might have thought I had something to do with shutting him in, that I wanted to do away with him, that . . . I'm sorry, I wasn't thinking logically. It was very stupid of me.'

Charles Paris looked thoughtful. 'Don't worry about that,' he said. 'But this does change the situation, doesn't it?' Lisa Wilson nodded miserably. 'Because if you didn't lock him in . . .'

'Yes.'

156

'. . . then somebody else did . . .'

'I know.'

'. . . and that means that Mark Lear was murdered.'

# Chapter Eight

*After Louise has gone through into the bedroom, Aubrey triumphantly closes the door, and locks it. He pulls up his trousers and does them up, then crosses towards the French windows. As he does so, the lights dim in Louise and Ted's flat, and come up in Gilly and Bob's flat, where Gilly is just seeing Willie out.*

GILLY: And when my husband Bob comes back, you can try out your designs on him.

WILLIE (*very camply*): Don't tempt me.

*He goes out into the hall. Gilly turns back into the room to see Aubrey appearing on the balcony from behind the central partition. She rushes across to open the French windows.*

GILLY: Aubrey! I was worried you might have dropped off!

AUBREY: And I was worried *something* might have dropped off. I was in serious danger of joining the Brass Monkey Brigade out there.

GILLY (*putting her arms around him*): Don't worry about that, my darling. I'll soon have you up to scratch again.

AUBREY (*lasciviously*): It wasn't actually 'scratch' I was thinking of being up to, Gilly.

GILLY (*leading him towards the bedroom*): Ooh. Shall we get up to something else instead then? Now, where were we? Shall I just pick it up where I left off?

AUBREY (*enthusiastically*): Sounds good to me!

*They disappear into the bedroom. The door slams shut behind them. There is a moment's silence, then the doorbell is heard. It rings a second time. Gilly comes bustling out of the bedroom, followed by Aubrey. He once again has his trousers round his ankles.*

AUBREY: Oh no! The fates seem to be against us today! What am I getting myself into?

GILLY (*hustling him across to push him into a cupboard which stands against the central partition wall*): You're getting yourself into this cupboard, that's what you're doing!

*She closes the cupboard door on him, and hurries across to the door to the hall. The cupboard door opens, and Aubrey emerges, trying to pull his trousers up. As he gets out, he hears a banging noise from behind him. He turns and looks dubiously at the cupboard. There is a further banging noise. He realizes where it is coming from.*

AUBREY: Oh, no! It's Louise banging on the

bedroom door in the other flat!

GILLY (*heard from the hall*): No, do come in, Ted, by all means.

*Hearing the voices, Aubrey, still with his trousers round his ankles, hurries back into the cupboard. The banging sound from the other flat ceases. The cupboard doors close behind Aubrey, just as Gilly ushers Ted into the sitting room.*

GILLY: No, Ted, of course it's not inconvenient.

TED: I hope I didn't arrive when you'd got your hands full.

GILLY (*after a momentary take*): No, no, good Lord, no.

TED: It's a bit embarrassing . . .

GILLY: Well, yes, it is, I agree, but . . . (*realizing he's not talking about her situation*) Oh, is it, really?

TED: Yes, you see, I was worried you might have heard something.

*The sound of Louise knocking on the bedroom door of the adjacent flat is heard again.*

GILLY: No, no, I haven't heard anything.

*There is more loud knocking from Louise.*

TED: You're sure you haven't heard anything?

GILLY: Not a thing.

TED (*looking curiously at the cupboard which conceals Aubrey*): It's peculiar. I'd have sworn there was a banging noise coming

160

from that cupboard.

GILLY: From that cupboard? Nonsense!

*More loud knocking is heard from the adjacent flat. Gilly rises to her feet and hustles Ted through towards the bedroom.*

GILLY: No, the acoustics in these old flats are most peculiar. The sound seems to come from over there, but in fact it comes from over *here.* (*She pushes Ted through into the bedroom.*) You have a listen to that wall over there. Then you'll hear where the banging really comes from.

*Gilly closes the door behind Ted, and rushes across to let Aubrey out of the cupboard. He still has his trousers round his ankles.*

GILLY: You idiot, Aubrey! Why on earth were you making that knocking noise?

AUBREY: I wasn't!

GILLY: Yes, you were.

*There is once again a knocking sound from Louise's bedroom door.*

AUBREY: See!

GILLY (*looking curiously at the empty cupboard*): There's something most peculiar going on here.

AUBREY (*reaching down to pull up his trousers*): At least I'll be glad to get my trousers on.

*There is a sound from the hall of the front door being opened with a key.*

BOB (*from the hall, angrily*): Gilly! Gilly!

Where the hell are you, Gilly?

GILLY (*panicking*): Oh, my God, Aubrey! It's Bob! Quick, you hide under here!

*She lifts up the floor-length cloth that covers the dining table. Aubrey, still with his trousers round his ankles, scuttles underneath the table. Gilly drops the cloth to hide him, and is smoothing it down nonchalantly, when Bob comes storming in from the hall.*

BOB: Gilly! I have reason to believe that you are entertaining a lover here this afternoon!

GILLY: A lover, Bob? Me? Don't talk nonsense!

BOB: I know there's a man in here, and I'm going to find him!

*He looks furiously round the room for a hiding place. As he does so, the door from the bedroom opens, and Ted, looking slightly bewildered, comes into the sitting room.*

TED: About this banging, Gilly . . . I don't seem to be getting any.

BOB (*turning on his heel to face Ted*): Oh, my goodness, no! You, Ted! My best friend!

' "Well, you know what I think, Willie. When my husband Bob comes back, you can try out your designs on him." ' Bill Blunden read the line out at dictation speed, with all the animation of the Directory Enquiries electronic voice. 'Have you got that, Cookie?'

Cookie Stone nodded, her pencil completing the latest amendment to the already-much-amended script. The entire company had had an eleven o'clock call the morning after their first night at the Palace Theatre, Norwich. They all knew they'd been summoned for more rewrites, more tinkering, more fine-tuning from Bill Blunden.

Tony Delaunay sat at the back of the auditorium, silently watching what was going on. Now they were in Norwich, he was in charge of the show, officially as well as de facto. David J. Girton had returned to the BBC to start pre-production planning for the next series of his long-running sitcom, *Neighbourhood Watch*. He would reappear for the odd night on the tour, but his work as nominal director of *Not On Your Wife!* was — unless the show did ever make it into the West End — virtually finished.

'I just think the new line's got more rhythm,' said the playwright.

'OK.' Cookie was a professional; she'd been through this process many times before. She didn't pass judgement on the changes she was given, just learnt them and delivered them.

163

'Try it tonight. See what reaction you get.'

'Wilco, Bill. Roger and out,' she said in the voice of a Second World War ace.

'So it doesn't change your cue, Ran. Line's a bit longer, that's all.'

'Young Ms. Stone building up her part again,' said Ransome George, getting his laugh from the rest of the company. As usual, the line itself wasn't funny; but there was some alchemy in his timing and intonation.

'Then, Charles . . .'

Charles Paris looked up and tried to concentrate. He could no longer blame the booze for the fact that his mind kept wandering, but it did. It kept wandering back to Mark Lear and the circumstances of his death. It kept wandering back to the possibility — or even likelihood — that someone in the *Not On Your Wife!* company had caused that death.

'Yes, Bill?'

' "Brass Monkey Brigade" still not getting the laugh, is it?'

'No. I just wonder whether the audience is catching on to the reference. "Cold enough to freeze the balls off a brass monkey" . . . I mean, do people still use that expression?'

'I think they do,' said the playwright cautiously, 'but I've got another suggestion, anyway.'

'Oh, right. Good.'

'Try . . . "And I was worried *something* might have dropped off. And let me tell you — it's a long time since *I*'ve sung soprano!" and make sure you hit the "I". ". . . since *I*'ve sung soprano" — OK?'

'Do you really think that'll work any better?' asked Charles.

There was a rustle of reaction around the auditorium. This was bad form. Bill Blunden was the playwright, after all, he was the expert on farce. For a member of the company — except of course for Bernard Walton, who had star's privilege — to offer an opinion on a rewrite was simply not done.

But Bill Blunden didn't seem worried by the lapse of etiquette. 'Try it tonight,' he said evenly.

'OK,' said Charles, and caught a grin from Cookie Stone. That caused him a pang of guilt. She kept catching his eyes these days, as though they shared something other than the coincidence of appearing in the same theatre programme. In Bath she'd kept her distance, respecting his state of shock following Mark Lear's death. But now they were in Norwich, she seemed to be drawing closer to him again, spurred on perhaps by the memory of some intimacy of which he had no recollection.

'Then I think we can sharpen up the exit sequence to the bedroom,' Bill Blunden droned on. 'You and Cookie, Charles . . . If Aubrey makes his line: "It wasn't actually 'scratch' I was thinking of being up to, Gilly" . . . and then goes on: "Do you think we can still manage a little something?" . . . and, Cookie, as you lead him to the bedroom, you make your line simply: "Don't worry, it'll all soon be in hand!" '

'OK, love,' said Cookie. 'What, and cut the other lines?'

'Mm. And then, Charles, you just come back with: "Sounds good to me!" '

'Right you are,' said Charles. 'Sounds good to me!'

But it didn't really. Charles Paris didn't enjoy this constant juggling with innuendoes; he liked comedy that came out of character, rather than the mechanical deployment of double entendres. Still, Bill Blunden's international royalties showed that he was doing something right. British farce was a distinct subgenre of the theatre; and, whether Charles Paris liked the medium or not, it was one over which Bill Blunden had complete mastery.

'Now, Bernard . . .' the playwright continued, turning his focus towards the star, 'still not quite getting the boffo on ". . . got your hands full", are we?'

'No. Got a woofer at the last Saturday matinee in Bath, but then I did the face.'

'Hm, I think we can get it just with the line, actually . . .' said Bill Blunden.

'Not with the current line, we can't,' was Bernard Walton's tart response.

'No, I agree. So I've got a suggestion which may sort it out. After Gilly's cue: "No, Ted, of course it's not inconvenient" . . . try saying: "You weren't working, were you? I'd hate to have arrived when you were on the job." Try that.'

Bernard Walton grimaced. 'Bit contrived, isn't it? I mean, obviously I can get the laugh with an expression or a take, but I'd like to feel I was getting a bit more help from the line.'

'Try it tonight,' Bill Blunden wheedled. 'See if it gets the boffo tonight, eh?'

'Oh, all right,' said Bernard Walton. 'For want of anything better.'

'Now,' the playwright continued metronomically, 'still not getting as big a laugh on the word "banging" as we should be getting, are we?'

Charles Paris had reviewed the circumstances of Mark Lear's death on the train up to Norwich the Sunday afternoon after the Bath run finished. He'd talked a bit about it with Lisa Wilson during the preceding week, but they hadn't had much opportunity for detailed discussion. At the studio their days had been full; they'd been deeply involved in recording yet more Thesaurus words and phrases; and then he'd had to rush off to do the show in the evenings. The one night he had organized a ticket for Lisa to see *Not On Your Wife!*, though she'd come for a drink afterwards, they'd been joined by Cookie Stone and some other company members, so they couldn't talk about Mark's death, except in general terms.

The after-show drink had, incidentally, been a mineral water for Charles. Though he had deeply regretted the bold pledge he had given to Lisa, he had stuck to it.

His reasons had been mixed. For a start, the abstinence was the result of a long-held conviction that his drinking was getting out of hand; considerations of health alone suggested a cutback was in order.

Then there was the fact of Mark Lear's death. Whether he had died by accident or by murder, in either case alcohol had been a contributory factor. If he hadn't been so drunk, he would have been in a better condition to protect himself. His example loomed like a dark shadow over Charles. Mark Lear's death had been a warning, a final warning. Get your act together, Charles Paris, or you could be next.

Not drinking because of Mark's death also presented a horizon, something to work towards. *When* I've found out the truth of how Mark died, Charles comforted himself, *then* I'll allow myself to drink again. Somehow making the term of trial finite made it seem marginally more tolerable.

There was also Lisa, the fact that it was to Lisa that he had made his promise. The more Charles saw of her, the more he liked her. He didn't exactly have sexual ambitions in her direction — or if he did, he managed to convince himself they were inappropriate. She was his friend's girl, after all, currently traumatized by that friend's death. Charles Paris was far too old for her, anyway. Given the shattered state of his relationship with Frances — not to mention the totally undefined nature of his relationship with Cookie Stone — he was in no position to be entertaining any kind of sexual ambitions.

But it was the little spark of desire that kept him off the booze. If he hadn't fancied

Lisa Wilson, he could never have done it. Because it was hard. God, it was hard. That first Sunday had been awful, his hangover had screamed out for the relief of a little top-up. He'd survived the lunchtime — when Lisa was actually there, the danger of backsliding was very much less — but after they'd finished their recording session and he'd gone back alone to his digs, the pain had been almost intolerable. That Sunday evening had been one of the longest he had ever experienced.

The knowledge that there was a third of a bottle of Bell's sitting in the bottom of his wardrobe made the pain all the more excruciating. Just a little sip was all he wanted. Just one little sip, and then he'd screw the cap on again and put the bottle away.

But something in him knew the sipping wouldn't stop there. And something else in him managed to resist the urge. The reward for his abstinence was one of the best nights' sleep Charles Paris had had for years. So, but for the dark shadow cast by Mark Lear's death, Charles had faced the Monday ahead with more optimism than he could usually muster. He actually enjoyed — rather than just managing to get through — his landlady's breakfast.

But the two major alcoholic pressure

points of that day had occurred before and after the show. Before was not so difficult. The biorhythmic urge to have a drink between six and seven was diminished by the fact that he had a show to do. Though recently he had been slipping into the habit, the professional in Charles Paris knew that drinking before a performance was a bad thing. So getting through that night's *Not On Your Wife!* without alcohol had not been too arduous.

Not having any alcohol after the show, however, had been agonizing. There was no righteous reason not to drink then. He'd just done a performance, for God's sake! He'd given of himself in the role of Aubrey. He deserved a bloody drink! And everyone else in the company was going off to have a drink after the show. It would have been positively antisocial not to join them.

So he did join them and, somehow, with physical pain, he managed not to drink anything other than mineral water. Not wanting to admit the real reason for his abstinence, he invented a stomach upset to explain it away. The session in the pub was purgatory, but he managed to survive.

That wasn't the cure, though. If he'd imagined that, having cracked one night, he'd broken the back of the problem,

Charles Paris would have been wrong. It was still agony for him not to have a drink. The urge for a quick restorative injection of alcohol did not leave him. And, after that first blissful night, his old disrupted sleeping pattern reasserted itself. So it wasn't just the booze that kept him awake.

Still, Charles Paris thought to himself on the train to Norwich, I am managing. My health and my wallet must be feeling the benefit of not drinking. Perhaps my mind's clearer . . . ? Possibly I'm even giving a better performance as Aubrey . . . ?

But he wasn't entirely convinced. All he really knew about not drinking was the fact that he hated it.

It was to take his mind off the gnawing ache for a drink that Charles Paris had started reviewing the circumstances of Mark Lear's death.

On his mental video he reran the tape of the Thursday in the recording studio. If the death had been murder, then there were two significant moments during that afternoon. The first had been his own doing. It had been he, Charles Paris, who had drawn attention to the stuffiness of the small dead room and perhaps inadvertently suggested part of a murder method to the perpetrator. Mark's unlocking of the dead-bolts on the studio doors had supplied the other necessary element.

The other significant moment had arisen when Mark started on about the book he was going to write that would 'take the lid off the BBC'. At the time Charles had put this down as drunken rambling, but with hindsight he realized that Mark's words could have been seen as a challenge, and a challenge to one individual person in the studio. What was it he'd said exactly? 'You'd be surprised the unlikely things unlikely people got involved in. Some they certainly wouldn't want to be reminded of now, I'm sure.' If someone present that afternoon, someone with a dark secret connected with the BBC, had recognized the challenge that was being thrown out, then it was entirely possible they might have contemplated silencing Mark Lear for good.

Charles again went through the list of people who'd been present when Mark issued his ultimatum (if that was indeed what it had been). The list ran: Bernard Walton, David J. Girton, Tony Delaunay, Ransome George, Cookie Stone and Pippa Trewin. Which one of them had Mark Lear been threatening?

The person with the most obvious BBC connections had been David J. Girton —

and Mark had mentioned some financial malpractice that concerned the director. On the other hand, David J. Girton was the one person who couldn't have gone back to the studio to lock Mark Lear in the dead room. Any of the others might have done, but he had the perfect alibi: Charles Paris. He'd spent the afternoon drinking with Charles, and they'd shared a cab back to the Vanbrugh Theatre.

So it had to be one of the others. Once again, Charles concentrated on the list. Ransome George. Yes. As well as fingering David J. Girton, Mark had also implied that there was a skeleton in Ransome George's cupboard.

And then of course there was the strange fragment of conversation Charles had overheard between Ran and Bernard Walton in the Green Room after the Bath technical rehearsal. 'Your secret is absolutely safe with me.' That's what Ran had said. And then he'd gone on to imply that he'd be angry if anyone else knew about the secret.

There was something odd going on between Bernard Walton and Ransome George. And given the dearth of other candidates perhaps they'd have to be promoted to prime suspect status.

But what was the 'secret' they had mentioned? How was Charles going to find out more about their murky pasts? Gossip was what he needed, good old-fashioned dirty theatrical gossip.

By the time his train had reached Norwich, Charles had made a decision. He needed to ring his agent.

# Chapter Nine

'Maurice Skellern Artistes.'

'Maurice, it's Charles.'

'Long time no hear.'

Charles bit back the instinctive response — And whose fault is *that*, Maurice?, as his agent went on, 'So how you doing, Charles? Enjoying that tour I set up for you?'

'You didn't set it up for me. I was interviewed for it by Parrott Fashion Productions because Bernard Walton had mentioned my name. All you had to do was negotiate the contract. And then you accepted the first figures they mentioned without any argument. That is not my idea of "setting things up".'

'Don't be picky, Charles. Anyway, how's it going? It's the *Romeo and Juliet*, isn't it? And don't tell me, don't tell me — you're playing Friar Tuck.'

'I think Friar Lawrence is the character you have in mind, Maurice.'

'Oh well, same difference.'

'However, the show I'm in is not *Romeo and Juliet*. It's the first run of a new farce by Bill Blunden, entitled *Not On Your Wife!*'

'Yes, I knew that, Charles. Of course I knew that. I was only having a little joke with you.'

'Oh yes?' that Charles certainly didn't believe. 'All right then — test question. Where am I calling you from? Where've we got to in the tour?'

'Well, I . . . Look, honestly, Charles, without the contract in front of me, I'd find it very difficult to say. I mean, I suppose you imagine you're the only client I have to worry about all the time — and in a way I'm flattered that you think that, because it's a tribute to the kind of exclusive, personal service I'm giving you — but the fact remains that you're only one amongst many highly respected, highly valued clients. And if I could give you the chapter and verse of where every one of them is at any given moment . . . well, I tell you, Maurice Skellern's feats of memory would be in *The Guinness Book of Records*.'

The whole speech was so outrageously at odds with the truth that Charles Paris hadn't got the energy to start arguing. 'I'm in Norwich, Maurice,' he said dully.

'Yes, of course you are. Vanbrugh The-atre.'

'That's in Bath. That was last week. It's the Palace Theatre in Norwich.'

' 'Course it is. You know, Charles, what a lot of my clients do . . .'

'Hm?'

'. . . when they're on tour, they send me kind of itineraries . . . you know, week-by-week lists of digs where they're staying, contact numbers, that kind of thing.'

'Ah.'

'Or a lot of them have mobile phones. Do you have a mobile phone, Charles?'

'No, I don't.'

'Oh, you should. Wonderful invention, the mobile phone, for people in your profession, Charles. Means you need never be out of contact with your agent, never be out of the swim of the showbiz maelstrom.'

'I see. But since you never ring me, Maurice, I'm not quite sure what would be the point of my sending you itineraries . . . or of having a mobile phone, come to that.'

'No. No, well, right. For someone like you, Charles, I agree, it's probably not so important.' There was a silence, then the agent continued in an aggrieved voice, 'Incidentally, I hope you're not hassling me about more work, Charles. I've just set up this tour for you, there's no need to be greedy.'

'No, in fact, I wasn't ringing about work, Maurice. I was after some gossip.'

'Ooh.' Maurice Skellern's tone changed instantly. Its grudging note gave way to pure enthusiasm. 'Who d'you want to know about? Young Kenneth and his latest dalliance with — ?'

'No, Maurice. It's not current gossip. It's very old gossip. Possibly going back more than twenty years. Don't know if it'd be possible for you to track down something that long ago.'

'Wouldn't rule it out, Charles,' said his agent with quiet pride. 'I do have quite a network, you know.'

Though sadly not one to procure work for this particular client, Charles Paris thought.

'Who is it?' asked Maurice Skellern eagerly. 'Who do you want me to get the dirt on?'

'There are a couple of names — well, no, three, actually — and the connection is through the BBC — probably BBC radio — and, as I said, we could be talking twenty years ago . . .'

'What makes you think there's some dirt there?'

'A few things a friend of mine said. Mark Lear — sadly dead now. He used to be a producer in Continuing Education at the Beeb.'

'I remember the name.' Maurice's voice grew heavy with reproach. 'I seem to recall you once worked for Mark Lear, and tried to keep the fact from me. Tried, in fact, to cut out my commission . . .'

The accusation was left hanging in the air and, to his fury, Charles found himself feeling guilty. 'Yes, OK, well, it's the same guy I'm talking about. And the two I want the dirt on are someone who's now a television producer called David J. Girton . . .'

'Oh, I know him. Does *Neighbourhood Watch*, doesn't he?'

'That's right.'

'Yes, I've put quite a few of my clients up for parts in that.'

But never me, thought Charles resentfully. You never put me up for a part in it, did you? Still, making that kind of point to Maurice had never been worth the effort, so all he said was, 'I think we could be talking about when David was also working in radio. Some financial fiddle, maybe . . . ?'

'Leave it with me. If there's anything to find out, I'll find it out. You said there were three names?'

'One of the others is Ransome George.'

'Ah, dear old Ran.' Maurice Skellern let out the same affectionate chuckle that the actor's name prompted throughout the business. 'How is the old reprobate?'

'Much as ever, I gather.'

'Yes . . . The dirt you want on him isn't just the fact that he borrows money from everyone and never pays it back, is it? Because he's always had a reputation for that.'

'No, no, I'm sure what I'm after is something more serious.'

Maurice Skellern chuckled again. 'Ran's always been incorrigible on the old dosh-borrowing front. You'd think his reputation in the business would have preceded him and everyone would be forewarned, but, oh no, apparently he still manages to find the odd sucker who'll stump up a tenner.'

'Does he?' said Charles Paris shortly.

'OK. Leave it with me, Charles. I'll see what I can root out, and get back to you. Oh, you'd better give me a number where I can contact you in Bath.'

'Norwich.'

'In Norwich, right. You see, Charles, it would have helped if you'd given me a detailed itinerary . . . or had a mobile phone. Then I'd be able to get back to you whenever I wanted to.'

Yes, be nicer if you needed to do that because of work rather than gossip, thought Charles Paris. Then he remembered, 'Oh, I haven't told you the third name, have I, Maurice?'

'No, that's true.'

'Still talking round the same time. About twenty years ago, and with a radio connection, possibly through Mark Lear. It'd be in the very early days of this guy's career . . .'

'Who're we talking about?'

'Bernard Walton,' said Charles Paris.

'Why aren't you drinking?' asked Cookie.

They were sitting in an Italian restaurant near the stage door of the Palace Theatre. It was the Wednesday. They were well into the Norwich run of *Not On Your Wife!* They'd done a matinee that day as well as an evening performance. They deserved a treat.

'Oh, you know . . .' Charles replied casually, 'just seeing if I can do without.'

'And can you?'

'So far.' He grinned. Now he actually was alone again with Cookie Stone, it wasn't nearly as bad as he'd feared. He'd built up all these images of her rounding on him, accusing him of having behaved appallingly to her in London, but there had been none of that. She just seemed pleased to be with him; and he found her company strangely relaxing.

'Well, I hope you don't mind if I do.' She gave him a toothy grin and raised a glass of red. The candlelight from adjacent tables sparkled and refracted seductively through the wine.

'No, no. I'm not a proselytizing teetotaller or anything like that. I'm just having a rest from drinking myself.'

'But the attraction of having a drink's still there?'

'Oh yes,' Charles Paris replied, in one of the greatest understatements of his life. 'The attraction's still there.'

'This doesn't seem to be a very heavy-drinking company, does it?'

'No, maybe not. Mind you, old Ran was pretty far gone last night.'

'Really? Didn't know he was into the booze.'

'Well, last night he was. Came back to the cottage, you know, one I'm staying in with a couple of the stage management bods, and Ran was so far gone he had to stay the night.'

'Ah.' Cookie Stone's face took on a cynical twist, as her voice dropped into cartoon canary, 'Doing dat old twick, is he?'

'What old twick?'

She was instantly back into her normal voice. 'It's one he's used a good few times before, I gather. I bet he pulled it at somebody else's place on Monday night.'

'You've lost me.'

'What Ran does, Charles, when he's on tour, is to keep ending up in other people's digs. Sometimes he'll just leave it too late to get a taxi back; sometimes he'll do the too-much-booze routine — as he did with you; and on occasions he's been known to joke his way into young actresses' beds . . . all for the same reason.'

'Which is?'

'So that he doesn't have to pay for digs. He's managed to get through whole weeks without touching his touring allowance.'

'Really?'

'Oh yes, Charles. I'm afraid Ransome George is the original sponger. He knows all the wrinkles. And of course you know about the way he keeps borrowing money from people?'

'Heard something about it, yes.'

'Never pays it back, never has done.' Cookie chuckled. 'It's incredible, really, that someone with a reputation like that can still get away with it. You'd have thought there couldn't be a single person left in the business who didn't know about his little habit. And yet every production he's involved in, he still manages to find some dickhead who's stupid enough to lend him a fiver.'

'Really?' Charles was beginning to get sick of that particular litany. 'But, Cookie, you've never heard of anything really bad about Ran, have you?'

'How do you mean — "really bad"? I would imagine the dumbos who haven't got their money back reckon that's bad enough.'

'No, I meant anything . . . criminal?'

Cookie Stone shook her head. Her red hair brushed gently against her face. In the candlelight, her eyes didn't seem so close together, and her face softened into a kind of beauty.

Charles Paris lightened the tone of the conversation. Though Mark Lear's death remained on his mind, he didn't want to sound too inquisitorial. 'Quite a boring company all round, isn't it, actually? Boring company in a boring place.'

'Norwich?'

'Hm. Doesn't seem the hub of the universe to me. I have this theory that the most boring places in England are places that aren't on the way to anywhere. It's as if it's the pressure of knowing that the only people who go there are people who actually have to go *there*, rather than being on their way to somewhere else, that makes those places so dull. It's the same with bits of eastern Kent . . . and bits of Cornwall, I suppose . . . and, of course, all of Wales.'

Cookie grinned a crooked grin, and dropped into a husky Mae West voice. 'So, if you and I are in a boring place, I guess we're reduced to making our own entertainment, eh?'

Charles Paris wasn't quite sure whether or not this was a come-on, but to his surprise her words prompted a trickle of physical interest. He moved hastily on to less dangerous ground. 'No, I suppose what I meant about this company being boring is that none of them seem to have any dark secrets, do they?'

'Well, no dark secrets which aren't extremely badly kept dark secrets,' said Cookie.

He cocked his head interrogatively. 'Who're you talking about?'

'Let's say a young lady called Pippa Trewin . . .'

'What about her?'

'Oh, come on, Charles, you *know*.'

'I don't think I do.'

'Young actress fresh out of drama school,

186

gets a lead part in the new Bill Blunden farce, gets one of the best agents around, keeps having to rush off to see television casting directors about new series, movie casting directors about new movies . . . do you think that's just the result of her exceptional talent?'

'No. Well, if it were, it'd be a first in this business.'

'Exactly. All down to having the right contacts, isn't it?'

So his suspicions had been right. There *was* something going on between Bernard Walton and Pippa Trewin. There couldn't be any other reason why she was in the show. Charles would listen with new cynicism to the next interview in which Bernard waxed lyrical about the perfection and sanctity of his long-running marriage.

'Knowing the right people, that's what gets you ahead in this business.' Cookie Stone hadn't finished. A hobby-horse was being mounted. Her mouth contracted into a tight purse of resentment, as she went on, 'God, I've got more talent in my little finger than that kid, but do I get put up for the kind of parts she does? And, if I make it to an interview, am I the one who ends up being cast? Am I hell?'

'Oh, come on, who's ever pretended that

this business is fair?' Somehow it seemed only natural for Charles to reach out and stroke Cookie's hand as he gave this reassurance. His reward was a warm sparkle from her eyes. 'The people who make it, Cookie, are the ones who use every contact they've got. Like old Bernard himself. Do you know, I directed him in his first major stage role.'

'Did you?'

Charles nodded. 'Young Marlowe in *She Stoops* . . . Cardiff, way, way back.'

'Oh?' Cookie looked at him shrewdly. 'So is that why *you*'re in the show?'

'What do you mean?'

'We were talking about contacts. Are you in *Not On Your Wife!* because of the old pals' act with Bernard?'

'Oh, I don't think so.' But, even as he denied the allegation, Charles Paris had a recurrence of the nasty feeling that it might be true. It was Bernard Walton who'd suggested that Parrott Fashion Productions should see him for the part of Aubrey, so perhaps it was to Bernard that he owed his casting. Not the first time he'd had cause to be thankful in that direction. Charles wouldn't have minded if he thought Bernard Walton offered such gestures out of pure altruism, but they seemed to be made solely to provide an opportunity for the star to patronize his former mentor. At least, thank God, Charles thought, Bernard's already been done on *This Is Your Life*; there's no longer any danger of me being wheeled out as the unknown actor 'who was awfully influential in the early days of my career'.

'You know someone's writing a biography of Bernard?' said Cookie.

'Yes. I did hear it mentioned. Seems inconceivable, though. I wouldn't have thought Bernard had been around long enough to provide sufficient material.'

'Don't you believe it. Plenty of showbiz names to be dropped, I'm sure. And with the telly and stuff, there are a lot of punters out there who'd want to read that kind of book.'

'Have you heard if it's going to be a warts-and-all job, a proper exposé?'

Cookie Stone laughed away the idea. 'No way. *Authorized* biography, or near as dammit. Another stepping stone towards Bernard's knighthood, all carefully calculated, I bet. There'll be nothing in the book to sully the image of Showbusiness's Mr Squeaky-Clean.'

Mind you, thought Charles, the revelation of an affair with an actress young enough to be his daughter might sully the image of

Showbusiness's Mr Squeaky-Clean. Charles wondered if, by any chance, Mark Lear had known about that particular liaison.

Cookie had the wine bottle poised over her glass. 'I feel pretty selfish, sitting here slurping away on my own. Sure I can't tempt you, Charles?'

For a moment his resolve held. Then he pushed his glass forward. 'Oh well, just the one.'

Boring town though Norwich might be, it was a good place for theatrical digs. As well as some excellent inner-city addresses, the stage door list at the Palace Theatre also included a few in the countryside around. Charles Paris and his stage management friends were staying in one such, but it wasn't nearly as pretty as the tiny cottage outside which the taxi deposited him and Cookie Stone soon after midnight that evening. It was a crisp October night, and an early frost sparkled on the thatch.

'One of the nice things about touring,' she said in response to his expressions of admiration, 'is getting to stay in places you could never in a hundred years live in permanently.'

It was clear once they were inside the cottage that Cookie was a home-maker. All actors approach touring in different ways. Some see it as an opportunity to explore the countryside, taking advantage of their National Trust membership to visit sites of interest. Others use it to develop hobbies such as collecting books or antiques. Some fill their free afternoons catching up on films at the local cinemas; others wile them away in betting shops. Bridge-loving actors have been known, if they've found three like-minded people in the company, to spend an entire three months playing cards.

Some notice where they are and get a lot of feedback from the constant change of surroundings. For others, like Charles Paris, one place looks much like another.

And for him, touring always meant living out of a suitcase. Literally living out of a suitcase. Whether in digs or a rented house, away from home he made no pretence at personalizing his environment. (Mind you, the few people who'd seen his studio flat in Hereford Road would probably say he'd made no pretence at personalizing that environment either.) For Charles, touring meant one big suitcase, containing books, a bottle of Bell's (or at least it always had until his Lisa Wilson-inspired conversion) and three changes of clothes. While he was wearing one set, the other two remained, more or less folded, in the suitcase, except for their occasional — and not quite frequent enough — trips out to the launderette.

Cookie Stone, however, did not belong to that school of touring. The row of old production photographs on the cottage mantelpiece, the cuddly toys on the back of the sofa, the artfully scattered magazines on the coffee table, all showed her to be someone who enjoyed making any space her own. Maybe she was one of those actresses who was away so much, so often on tour or on location, that she had to take her home with her and stake her claim, set up her camp afresh, in each new setting. Or maybe she was just an old-fashioned homebody.

As soon as they were through the sitting-room door, Cookie had crossed to the drinks tray and lifted a bottle. 'It's Bell's, isn't it, Charles?'

'Well, back in the days when I was drinking . . . yes, it was Bell's.'

She shrugged. 'You've had half a bottle of red wine already tonight.'

'Mm.'

She held the bottle by its neck and let it sway gently from side to side. 'Up to you . . .'

Again his resolution was short-lived. 'Yes, I can't think of anything I'd like more.'

'Oh, I hope there's *something* you'd like more,' said Cookie, in a Marilyn Monroe little-girl voice, as she poured Scotch into two tumblers. 'How do you like it? With water or . . . ?'

'Ice, if it's convenient. Otherwise, on its own.'

'Ice is perfectly convenient.' Crossing towards the kitchen, Cookie Stone chucked over a box of matches. 'If you could just do the fire . . . ?'

The grate had been neatly laid. Shredded newspaper underneath kindling, lumps of coal and a log on top. As he put a match to the paper and watched orange shoots of flame lick upwards, Charles wondered if Cookie had a fire set in the cottage every night. Or was it only when she was expecting company?

She brought in the drinks, and they sat side by side on the sofa. 'Clink, clink,' said Cookie. They clinked their tumblers together.

Then Charles took a long swig of Bell's. God, he had missed it. God, it tasted wonderful.

He wasn't sure quite how they started touching, whether he moved first, whether she moved first. It didn't seem to matter; neither of them thought it was a bad idea.

'We're grown-ups, after all,' said Cookie, as they withdrew from their first long kiss. 'And it's not as if we haven't done this before.'

'No, for two people of our age to have got through life without having kissed anyone before would be pretty bizarre,' Charles agreed fatuously.

'I didn't mean "kiss anyone". I meant it's not as if we haven't done this *together* before.'

'No. Right.' He chuckled knowingly, but really wished he could remember exactly what they'd done before. How much they'd done before.

Still, this was no time for piecing together the past; his body was getting too interested in the present. His hand slid naturally down to the surprising firmness of Cookie's breast. 'You've got the body of a teenager,' he murmured into the soft redness of her hair.

'Oh God!' said Cookie in her best Hammer Horror troubled-heroine mode. 'We must find this teenager and give it back to her!'

'No, we mustn't.' Charles's hand was slipping down from the breast. 'First we must check all the bits are where they should be, to make sure we've got the right body.'

The fire's warmth was spreading now, and

their clothes seemed to slip away without embarrassment. Cookie let out a little gasp as Charles's hand found the soft centre of her. 'Do we want to go upstairs to the bedroom?' she murmured.

'Don't see the necessity. Very nice down here.'

They both chuckled at the double meaning. Her hands were doing their bit too. She held him just hard enough, stroked him just softly enough. She knew what she was doing.

'Oh, you're beautiful,' Charles mumbled, as the waves of pleasure mounted. 'Beautiful.'

Cookie contradicted him. 'No. I may be sexy, I may be attractive, I may have a good body, my face may "have character", but there's no way I'm beautiful.'

'Oh yes, you are,' said Charles Paris, as the imperatives of their bodies grew unanswerable. 'You're beautiful, Cookie Stone, you're beautiful!'

It was good. As they subsided into the nest of discarded clothing on the hearthrug and the firelight airbrushed away the blemishes of their bodies, both of them lazily untwitched.

The only tiny nagging question in Charles's mind remained: Was that the first time I've made love to her, or did it happen in London too?

'Well . . .' Cookie purred on a wave of fulfilment. 'That was better than the last time.'

A remark which, unfortunately, did not help clear up Charles Paris's confusion.

He felt good the next morning when he returned to his digs. The alcohol had left him with no hangover, and it was a long time since he'd had good sex — or any sex, if the truth be told.

Also there was a message at the digs for him to ring Maurice Skellern. Maybe he was getting closer to finding out who had murdered Mark Lear as well.

The only slight cloud on his horizon was the news from one of his fellow lodgers that, taking advantage of Charles Paris's absence, Ransome George had spent the previous night in his bed.

# Chapter Ten

'Nothing on Bernard Walton or David J. Girton yet . . .'

'Oh, well, thanks for trying, Maurice.'

'But give me time, give me time. I did get something on old Ran, though.'

'Ah.'

'I mean, his is a complete history of fiddles and not paying back money he's borrowed and all that stuff . . .'

'I know.'

Maurice chuckled down the phone. 'And I dare say nothing's changed in that department over the years. He's still finding idiots stupid enough to —'

'Yes, yes,' said Charles briskly. 'What've you actually got on him?'

'All right, all right. Let me get there. Notice, incidentally, Charles, that I haven't asked why you want this information. I've been very restrained.'

'Yes, and your restraint is much appreciated, but I'm sorry, I have to get off to the theatre shortly, so if you could just let me know what you've found out . . .'

'Of course. Now, the Mark Lear you mentioned, he had a lot of money, right?'

'His wife, Vinnie, had a lot of money, yes.'

'Hm . . . Well, I think some of it could have ended up in Ransome George's pocket.' Maurice Skellern let the information settle, saying nothing more, challenging Charles to prompt him. Charles resisted the temptation and let the silence extend itself until, with a disgruntled edge to his voice, Maurice went on, 'Ran got involved with some people who were making porn tapes . . .'

'Videos?'

'No, it was just audio tapes in those days. Ran may have started by acting in them, I don't know, but he certainly got involved in the business side too. Now the thing is, I've found out that certain BBC radio personnel were brought in to help produce the things . . .'

'And was Mark Lear one of them?'

'Can't be sure about that yet, but, if he was, that'd be your connection, wouldn't it?'

'Could be.' Charles was unable to hide the disappointment in his voice. He'd been hoping for more concrete information.

'It's also a fact, Charles, that some of the BBC people were encouraged, by Ransome George I think, to invest in the company that was making and marketing these tapes. And, when the inevitable happened, they lost their stakes.'

'By "the inevitable", you mean when the company went bust?'

'Exactly. As a lot of those seedy little operations did. Mind you, my information suggests that Ransome George himself may not have lost money. In fact, I'm pretty sure he creamed off quite a lot.'

'That would be in character. By the way, Maurice,' Charles asked curiously, 'where do you get your information from?'

'Ah, now I can't tell you that, can I?' The agent's voice was heavy with reproach. 'I just happen to have certain rather useful specific skills.'

Not for the first time, Charles wished Maurice's 'specific skills' included getting work for his clients. But all he actually said was, 'Well, thank you for that. Much appreciated.'

'I'm still working on it,' said Maurice. 'Still talking to people. I think it's quite possible I'll be able to tell you more soon . . . maybe definitely tie in Mark Lear's name with the porn tape company.'

'Be great if you could.'

'So where do I find you, if I need to get in touch?'

Charles Paris thought it inappropriate at that moment to pass further comment on an agent who didn't know where his clients were working. 'Leeds next week. But I'm going back to Bath on Sunday.'

'Really?' Maurice Skellern's antennae had instantly picked up the possibility of unpaid commission. 'You working and not telling me, Charles?'

'No, no, Maurice, of course not.' He chuckled, then lied, 'No, my visit to Bath is purely social.'

Despite Charles's complaint that Norwich wasn't on the way to anywhere, the city's train service was not bad. The 9.05 on the Sunday morning got into Liverpool Street at 10.58, giving him time to get round the Circle Line to Paddington and catch the 11.30 to Bath, where Lisa Wilson had arranged to meet him with her car at the station.

The early start had not gone down well with Cookie Stone. She had had in mind dinner after the show, bed and then a lazy waking up to Sunday papers and sex, the kind of indulgence that most established couples enjoyed. She was too much of a professional to argue against Charles's apology that he needed an early night on his own because he was working the next day, but she clearly didn't like it.

That reaction, which he couldn't keep out of his mind as he sat in the safety of the train from Norwich to London, was symptomatic of his relationship with Cookie. He had known from the start that he shouldn't have got involved there. Years of experience should have taught him the unwisdom of becoming entangled with anyone on a long tour, and the more time he spent with Cookie Stone, the more he realized how seriously he'd blundered by becoming entangled with her in particular.

It wasn't that he disliked Cookie. He was fond of her. She was enthusiastic and good at sex; she had a remarkably well-preserved body. And, even though her taste for funny voices could become wearying, she was entertaining company.

What was wrong with her, however, was the old performer's problem — insecurity. Charles, of all people, could sympathize with that. He'd been through every kind of angst about his talent as an actor and his adequacy as a human being. But in Cookie's case, the insecurity manifested itself in a particularly difficult way.

He didn't know her full history of previous relationships, but it seemed clear that at some point in her life she had been badly let down by a man — or, perhaps, at several points in her life she had been badly let down by several men.

This, coupled with the insecurity of a woman who'd grown up knowing she'd never be conventionally good-looking and always have to make her mark by personality, charm, vivacity or sex, left her as raw and vulnerable as a peeled shrimp. If only Charles Paris had known the rod he was making for his own back, he would never have called Cookie Stone 'beautiful'.

That was what had done it. A word he'd used in the heat of extreme physical urgency had fulfilled Cookie's lifelong dreams. It was the plot of every Barbra Streisand movie. At last, she thought, she'd met a man who found her beautiful, a man who really cared for her for herself.

In fact, Cookie Stone had fallen in love with Charles Paris.

He'd only realized this over the previous few days, and it had come as rather an unpleasant shock. For Cookie, though, the emotion was of longer standing, as she told him during one of her endless talkative times in bed when he'd rather have gone to sleep.

She'd fancied him from the moment she'd seen him at the *Not On Your Wife!* readthrough. 'And then of course,' she'd gone on, 'I knew things were going to be wonderful between us . . . after what happened that night in your flat in London.'

For Charles Paris, remarks like that weren't helpful. 'That night in your flat in London' remained a closed book to him, and however much he scoured his memory, it refused to give up its secrets.

He was left in one of those awkward situations, like having forgotten someone's name, not admitting to the fact straight away, and then getting so far into conversation with them that the admission that you didn't know who they were became insulting. Except with Cookie, it was worse than a name. To have forgotten someone's body, to have forgotten making love to someone, not even to be sure whether or not you *had* made love to them, now that was *really* insulting. And the longer Charles put off owning up to his uncertainty, the more potentially insulting it became.

Unfamiliarity with the circumstances of its commencement was not the only problem he had in his relationship with Cookie

Stone. Perhaps it was a hangover from the days when he'd still been cohabiting with Frances, but so far as affairs were concerned, Charles Paris's inclination was always to tick the box for 'No Publicity'. 'Why,' he had been heard to say speciously, 'do we want the whole world to know about something that's only important to *us*?'

Cookie, on the other hand, did want the whole world to know. Charles couldn't possibly have anticipated the weight of expectation she brought with her. All her previous disappointments had been cancelled, all her aspirations met, the moment he had called her 'beautiful'. Having quickly established that he was no longer in any meaningful sense married to Frances, Cookie could see no reason why they shouldn't shout their love from the rooftops.

At the very least she saw no reason why they shouldn't shout it to the assembled company of *Not On Your Wife!* Charles had managed so far to manufacture reasons why they should be discreet, but his fabrications couldn't last for ever. And the idea that any liaison could remain a secret for long in the gossip-machine of a touring theatre company was laughable. Besides, Cookie deeply wanted to tell everyone.

This threw Charles into an agony of awkwardness. It was not the first time in his life that he'd regretted a penis-driven impulse, but in the current case Cookie's galloping insecurity made the situation worse than ever. Any hint he gave to her that he was less than wholehearted in his commitment would throw her back into an anguish of rejection.

Cookie Stone's life was locked in a cycle of self-fulfilling prophecies. Charles Paris had started feeling he'd like to back out of the affair within forty-eight hours of its starting (and, so far as he was concerned, the starting point had occurred in Norwich), but even a man who had wanted the relationship to go the distance would have had his resolution tested by Cookie's constantly voiced anxieties.

'You don't really care about me,' she'd keep saying. 'You don't really think I'm beautiful. You're really just like all the other men, aren't you, only interested in the physical side, and when you lose interest in that then you'll lose interest in me. You don't really want this relationship to go anywhere.'

She repeated the litany so often that even someone madly in love with her might pretty soon start believing what she was saying.

And to someone like Charles Paris, who

was far from madly in love with her, what Cookie said was all too painfully accurate.

Oh, shit! Why on earth did he allow himself to get caught in these situations?

And he had another hangover, too.

It frequently happens that men in unsatisfactory physical relationships start to idealize women with whom they have platonic relationships, and that is exactly what Charles Paris ended up doing on the train from Norwich to London. He was really looking forward to seeing Lisa Wilson. It would be comforting to be with a woman he could just chat to naturally, without any of that confusing lust nonsense.

'Unfaithful,' Charles read without intonation, and left the statutory two-second pause. 'Perfidious' — two-second pause — 'faithless' — two-second pause — 'disloyal' — two-second pause — 'inconstant' — two-second pause — 'unprincipled' — two-second pause — 'double-dealing . . .'

This particular section of the Thesaurus was not doing anything to improve his mood, and he was relieved to hear Lisa Wilson's voice through the talkback saying, 'OK, got to the end of the reel. I should think you're pretty knackered. Shall we call it a day?'

'Please,' he said gratefully. The air conditioning in the studio was working now, but its atmosphere remained claustrophobic.

'Fancy a coffee?'

'And how!'

'Got anywhere?' asked Lisa, as they sat either side of the table over coffee and chocolate digestives.

'Got anywhere?' Charles echoed guiltily.

'I meant about Mark's murder.'

'Ah.'

'Because I kind of got the impression you were thinking about investigating it, Charles.'

He nodded. 'Yes. I've got to find out what really happened. You still haven't said anything to the police?'

She shook her head firmly. The blonde hair flurried and resettled. Natural blonde, Charles couldn't help thinking. Not like Cookie Stone's dyed red. And Lisa's face was innocent of make-up . . . unlike Cookie's, which never faced the day without a good half-hour of cosmetic concentration. Oh dear, thought Charles guiltily, once you admit the first hint of criticism, how quickly the floodgates open.

He didn't look forward to re-meeting Cookie in Leeds. He'd have to put an end to the affair as soon as possible. He'd have to fulfil all her gloomy prognostications, crush her like a snail without a shell, and show her that he, Charles Paris, was, like all men, just another shit.

And then, worse than that, for another two months he'd have to be with her on stage through all the ribald whackeries of *Not On Your Wife!*

Oh dear. One thing was certain, though. He'd never, ever get into a comparable situation again.

Charles had to drag himself out of his gloom to concentrate on what Lisa was saying. 'No, it's bad. I know I should say something to the police, but . . . well, I told you where I was the night Mark died.'

'The married man?'

'Yes, and . . . I don't know whether the marriage would survive if his wife found out.' She sighed. 'There are kids and everything.'

'Say no more.' He took a sip of coffee. 'You're right, though, Lisa, Mark's death has been nagging away at me. Still, I may be getting somewhere on it, I'm not sure. Tell me, did Mark ever talk to you about pornographic cassettes?'

'What, are you suggesting we needed naughty videos to spice up our sex-life?'

'No.'

'Actually, towards the end it could have done with a bit of spicing up,' she mused.

Charles didn't pick up on that, but went on, 'I'm talking about audio cassettes. Long time back, possibly as much as twenty years, Mark may have got himself involved in producing them.'

A spark came into Lisa Wilson's eye. 'Do you know, he did mention something about that. I've just remembered. Apparently, they used to use wet newspaper.'

'Wet newspaper?'

'Yes, for sexy sound effects. All the liquid sloshings about of sexual organs.'

'Good grief.'

She chuckled. 'Wonderful the things you learn how to do in the BBC, isn't it?'

'Remarkable,' Charles agreed. 'But did Mark mention any of the other people he was working with, you know, when he was producing these cassettes?'

'Don't think so. Can't recall any names. No, he just said he was moonlighting from the Beeb when he did it. In those days a BBC contract was totally exclusive. You weren't allowed to work for anyone outside.'

'Least of all if you were making porn cassettes.'

'Right.' Lisa fixed her grey eyes on his. 'Does that lead you somewhere — the fact that Mark was mixed up in the porn business?'

'Could do, yes. Ties in with something he said about moonlighting the afternoon he died. Yes, it could be very important.'

'Good. But you can't give me a name, say in which direction your suspicions are heading?'

Charles shook his head. 'Wouldn't be fair. Not till I've got a bit more information.'

'OK. I will wait on appropriate tenterhooks.' She reached across to the packet. 'Another chocolate digestive?'

'Why not? Who knows when I will eat again?'

'Are you going up to Leeds tonight?'

'No. I'll probably go back to London. The trains are fine in the morning. We've got a four o'clock call tomorrow, just to familiarize ourselves with the stage. No complete runthrough.'

'Ah. So you're not pushed for time?'

'No.'

There was a companionable silence, broken only by the munching of chocolate digestives. As Charles had anticipated on the train, it was comforting to be with a woman he could just chat to naturally. And, as for all that confusing lust nonsense . . . well, he couldn't deny there was a bit there, but thank God at that moment it wasn't relevant.

'So how're you managing without Mark?' he asked solicitously.

Lisa Wilson grimaced. 'Distressingly well. I'm afraid the feeling of relief has continued, and now I'm even ceasing to feel guilty about it.'

'Good.'

'Yes, I suppose so. Certainly a darned sight easier to run this place without Mark drifting aimlessly around all the time.'

'Hm. And . . . tell me if it's no business of mine . . . but is the affair with the married man still going on?'

'Good Lord, no.' Her hair spread outwards and reformed again as she dismissed the idea. 'No, that was really over a long time ago. Which was why it would have been so awful if it had come out at this point. I mean, there were times when it was very intense, when his wife would really have had something to worry about. But now . . . no. The heavy emotional bit had run its course. Our last encounter was just down to sex.'

'Ah. Right.'

'I'm afraid, you see . . .' she grimaced again as she chose her words '. . . sex between Mark and me had been more or less non-existent for some time . . . since we moved down here, I suppose. It was partly his confidence was shot to pieces and . . . well, the booze. He was drinking so much he just couldn't do it. And I'm afraid that wasn't good enough for me. I needed some physical attention. So I went back to a former lover for . . . what shall we call it? A quick fix? A quick service? I'm not proud of the fact, but that's what I needed at the time.'

Charles cleared his throat in a way that he hoped didn't sound embarrassed, and once again found himself transfixed by Lisa's grey stare. 'Apropos of nothing . . . how're you doing on the booze, Charles?'

'Ah . . . Well . . .'

'You promised me you'd give it up completely.'

'Yes, I know, I . . .'

'I see.' She sat back, letting out a long sigh of disappointment.

'Yup. 'Fraid I have backslid.' He fell back again on a funny voice — the one he'd used in an ill-fated play based on the career of John Wayne ('Thank God the Duke is dead and thus spared the knowledge that this sad travesty of his life has been perpetrated' — *South Wales Echo.*)

Lisa just looked at him. Charles found

her silent reproach more painful than if she had said something. 'I will try to get off it again, but . . . well, sometimes it's difficult.'

'Difficult, but worth doing. How long did you stay off?'

'Till last Wednesday.'

'Oh, terrific! Big deal!' Her voice was weighed down with sarcasm.

'It's a kind of occupational hazard in the theatre for —'

'Don't give me that crap! If you really wanted to stop, you could stop.'

'I know. I've proved it.'

'Proved it? Ten days? Come on. You've got to do better than that to convince me.'

'I think I could do better than that. I'm sure I could do better than that. But I don't think I could do it for ever.'

'Why not?'

'I don't know. Just "for ever" sounds so . . . final.'

'It is final.'

He shook his head ruefully. 'No, never going back on the booze . . . I'm afraid that's unthinkable.'

'Why?' asked Lisa.

'Well, I mean it's just . . . there are certain things, there are certain occasions, which one cannot imagine without a bit of alcoholic lubrication.'

'*One* cannot, or *you* cannot?'

'All right, *I* cannot.'

'Like?'

'Well, OK — sex. I mean, I cannot imagine going to bed with a woman without having had a few drinks first.'

'Why, are women that terrible?'

'No, no!' he said hastily, before noticing the twinkle in Lisa Wilson's eye. 'No, I suppose I mean it's just . . . I don't know, a matter of relaxation. A couple of drinks, a bit of . . . I guess for me drink has always been a part of foreplay.'

'The trouble is, that kind of foreplay can so easily mean there's no afterplay. As I found with Mark.'

'Yes, OK. I don't mean too much. I just mean a couple of drinks, to calm the atmosphere . . .'

'There are other forms of foreplay.'

'I know that.'

'And all those sex manuals and how-to-keep-your-man's-interest articles in women's magazines are always recommending that couples should try new forms of foreplay . . .'

'I know that too. There's a whole sequence in Bill Blunden's *Not On Your Wife!* on that very subject.'

Charles Paris found himself transfixed by

the steady gaze of Lisa Wilson's grey eyes, as she asked, 'Are you actually telling me, Charles, that you have never been to bed with a woman when you weren't drunk?'

'No, by no means. What I'm saying is that I can't recall having gone to bed with a woman without having had a couple of drinks beforehand.'

'Well, maybe you should try it one day. It'd be a new experience for you.'

He chuckled, shrugging the idea off. 'Yes, maybe I should.'

'How about today?'

For a moment he thought he'd misheard, but he hadn't. The even beam of her grey eyes was still focused on his face.

'Erm . . . well . . . nice idea,' he said lamely.

'Why not, Charles? We fancy each other, don't we?'

'Well, I fancy you, but I wasn't sure that —'

'Take it as read.'

'Good. Um . . . Thank you.'

'My pleasure.' She reached out and took his hand. 'At least I hope it will be.'

'I'll do my best,' said Charles. Then a sudden panic hit him. Suppose his best wasn't good enough? He'd managed all right with Cookie, but then Cookie was in love with him. Lisa Wilson was a younger woman, in her sexual prime, a woman of a different generation too, who probably had strong views on her sexual rights. He kept reading things in newspapers — even in *The Times*, for heaven's sake — about how assertive modern women had become in the bedroom. God, he needed a drink! That was why he needed a few drinks before sex, to take away performance anxieties.

One of Lisa's fingers was stroking the back of his hand. The action itself wasn't erotic, but the potential it implied was. He felt the reassurance of a stirring in his scrotum. Maybe she was right. Maybe it would be rather interesting to experience sex that hadn't been well marinated in alcohol.

'One thing . . .' said Lisa.

Oh dear, thought Charles. He had grown up in a generation for whom women saying 'One thing . . .' before sex usually presaged some mini-lecture on men not taking advantage, and women not being cheap, and commitment being terribly important, and other antaphrodisiac caveats.

'Yes?' he responded with foreboding.

'I don't want any commitment involved here. We're talking about physical pleasure, two people who fancy each other giving and receiving pleasure. No emotional entanglement — OK?'

What man had ever heard more heartwarming words? It was the ultimate masculine fantasy come true. 'OK,' Charles Paris agreed enthusiastically.

They went back to her flat. It was wonderful. Perhaps — heretical though the concept might be — it really was better without the booze.

When he left for the station early on the Monday morning, Charles Paris was more than a little in love with Lisa Wilson.

# Chapter Eleven

*As Louise goes through to the bedroom to change, the lights go down on Louise and Ted's flat, and up on Gilly and Bob's flat. Ted is sitting on the sofa with Nicky. He is embarrassed; she is all over him.*

NICKY: And I just think you're such a good man, Ted.

TED: Oh, really, it's nothing.

NICKY: No, but to agree to pretend to your friend's wife that your friend's mistress is your mistress . . . I don't know what you call a man who does that kind of thing.

TED: An idiot?

NICKY (*vindictively*): Mind you, it doesn't reflect very well on the friend, does it? So Bob's ashamed of me, is he?

TED: No, no, I think he just doesn't want Gilly to find out about you.

NICKY: But he told me he *did* want Gilly to find out about me. He said he wanted to have me out in the open . . .

TED: Really? Be a bit cold this time of the year.

NICKY (*not hearing what Ted said*): . . . but instead he actually wants to have me under wraps.

TED: Probably be warmer, wouldn't it?

NICKY (*furious*): Huh. Bob's a two-faced rotter. Still, two can play at that game. (*reaching for Ted's tie and drawing him towards her*) If he wants to tell people I'm your mistress, then I'd better become your mistress, hadn't I?

TED (*appalled*): What!

NICKY (*giving him a kiss on the lips and rising from the sofa*): Yes, you just give me a couple of minutes, Ted, and then come through to the bedroom — and I'll really have my revenge on Bob.

*She sets off towards the bedroom.*

TED (*weakly*): But, Nicky, wouldn't that just be using me as a sex-object?

NICKY (*as she goes through into the bedroom*): Yes! Any objections?

*As she goes off, Ted rises to his feet and stands irresolute.*

TED: Ooh-er.

*He decides his best defence is going to be escape, and hurries off towards the door to the hall. Just as he gets there, however, Gilly comes in from the hall, furiously angry. Ted backs away as she advances on him.*

GILLY: Do you know what I've found out about that slug of a husband of mine?

TED (*falling backwards on to the sofa*): No, no, I don't.

GILLY: That chit of a girl who he said was *your* mistress . . .

TED: Oh, no.

GILLY: . . . is actually *his* mistress.

TED (*weakly*): Really? Are you sure?

GILLY: What do you mean — am I sure? Surely you'd have noticed whether or not you had a mistress?

TED: Oh, I don't know. It's the kind of thing one could easily forget.

GILLY: If you think that, then you've clearly never had the right sort of mistress.

TED: I've never had any sort of mistress.

GILLY (*intrigued*): No? Goodness, Ted, your life must've been very dull.

TED (*miserably*): Yes — and I liked it that way!

GILLY (*furiously*): Ooh, Bob's made me so furious. (*She sits beside him on the sofa*) Do you know, I've half a mind . . .

TED: That's about all I seem to have at the moment.

GILLY (*thoughtfully*): . . . I've half a mind to get my own back on Bob — in the appropriate way.

TED (*with foreboding*): 'In the appropriate way'?

GILLY: Huh. Bob's a two-faced rotter. Still, two can play at that game. (*reaching for Ted's tie and drawing him towards her*) If he's saying you've got a mistress, then you'd better have a mistress, hadn't you?

TED (*appalled*): What!

GILLY (*giving him a kiss on the lips and rising from the sofa*): I'll just get us some champagne, Ted, and then we'll go through to the bedroom — and I'll really have my revenge on Bob.

*As she goes off into the kitchen, undoing her blouse, Ted rises to his feet and stands irresolute.*

TED: Ooh-er. Back home, I think.

*He turns to go out through the French windows. But as he opens them, Louise appears on the balcony in front of him, dressed in a sexy negligee. She comes into the room, closing the doors behind her.*

LOUISE: I knew you'd be here, Ted darling.

TED (*backing away and falling back on to the sofa*): What?

LOUISE: Ted, I've been reading this magazine article about putting the excitement back into your sex-life . . .

TED: Really? I'm not sure that my sex-life can cope with any more excitement.

LOUISE (*coming to sit lasciviously beside him*

*on the sofa*): . . . and it says that couples who've been together a long time should liven things up by making love at unexpected times in exciting new places . . .

TED: I'm quite happy with the boring old places, Louise darling.

LOUISE: (*taking hold of his tie and pulling him towards her*): I'd have thought a neighbour's flat was definitely an exciting new place.

*She suddenly reaches for the buckle of his belt, and starts to undo it. Ted struggles to get free.*

TED: Louise! Darling! I don't want to make a big thing of this.

LOUISE: I do — and, what's more, I seem to be succeeding.

*Ted manages to break free from her and stands in the middle of the room, clutching at his trouser-belt. Louise stands up, and throws off her negligee to reveal that she is dressed in sexy bra and pants.*

LOUISE: Ted, you don't always have to have a boring sex-life, you know.

TED: Ooh-er.

*At that moment Nicky appears from the bedroom door, dressed in sexy bra and pants. At the same time Gilly appears from the kitchen door, holding a bottle of champagne and also dressed in sexy bra and pants.*

LOUISE, GILLY AND NICKY (*all at the same*

*time*): Come on, Ted. I'm ready for you now.

TED: Ooh-er.

*He throws up his hands to his face. Unsupported, his trousers fall down around his ankles. The three women watch in amazement as he falls over backwards in a dead faint, as . . .*

*THE CURTAIN FALLS FOR THE END OF ACT ONE.*

'I'm still not happy about that "big thing" line,' Bernard Walton complained at the 're-writes call' on the second day of the Leeds run.

'It's getting the laugh,' Bill Blunden countered.

'Well, it isn't, actually. The laugh comes on Louise's line: "I do — and, what's more, I seem to be succeeding." '

'I'm sorry, Bernard. You can't have all the funny lines.'

This insinuation really offended the star's professionalism. 'I am not asking to have all the funny lines, Bill! I'm a team player, always have been. Ask anyone in the business, and they'll all tell you Bernard Walton works as part of an ensemble!'

The rest of the *Not On Your Wife!* company, who worked on stage every night getting no eye contact or feedback from

Bernard, might have questioned the accuracy of this, but none of them would have dared voice what Bill Blunden said next. 'I haven't seen much evidence of it. Your performance as Ted seems to me entirely self-centred. You're in a hermetically sealed little world of your own.'

'What the hell do you mean? How dare you, a mere writer, have the nerve to tell me — ?'

Tony Delaunay moved quickly to stem Bernard Walton's fury. The company manager was ever-present, ever-watchful, always ready to ease over any little difficulties the current Parrott Fashion production might encounter in its circuit of the country. 'Sorry, sorry, can we just cool it, please? Bernard, if you just say what your problem with the line is . . .'

'My problem with the line,' the star replied in a voice of icy restraint, 'is that it's been shoehorned into the script with no real logic and motivation, and that all it basically is is just a knob-joke. "I don't want to make a big thing of this." "I do — and, what's more, I seem to be succeeding." What is that about if it's not about an erection?'

'Of course it's about an erection,' said Bill Blunden. 'That's why it's getting the bloody laugh!'

'All right. Well, I suppose I'd rather be in a play that got its laughs from genuine wit and character, rather than from jokes about erections.'

This belittling of his playwriting skills was too much for Bill Blunden. 'Are you trying to tell me I don't know how to write comedy? Shall I tell you how many productions of my plays there were, world-wide, last year? Go on, you guess how many. You just try and have a bloody guess!'

'Look, let's not turn this into a shouting match,' Tony Delaunay eased in again, as ever smoothing the way, mollifying offended egos. 'Is your problem with the line itself, Bernard, or the fact that it's you who says it?'

'Well, all right. I suppose it is the fact that I'm involved in the exchange,' the star conceded. 'My audience doesn't expect to hear Bernard Walton doing primary school smut.'

'Sod *your* audience!' snapped Bill Blunden. 'Let's think about the play's audience, shall we, for a change?'

'No, no,' Tony Delaunay's conciliatory voice once again intervened. 'Bernard has got a point. He's the star of this show, his name's above the title, and people who come to see it have certain expectations because of his name. He shouldn't be having to deliver lines which are at odds with his public image.'

'Thank you, Tony.' Bernard Walton sat back, vindicated, but the playwright still looked unhappy, so the company manager continued his fence-mending.

'Look, Bill, Bernard has to be doing material he's comfortable with. He's a public figure who has been bold enough to take a stand against declining standards of decency in entertainment and —'

'Are you saying that *Not On Your Wife!*'s indecent?'

'No, Bill, no. I am not saying that. I am saying that Bernard's position is particularly sensitive at the moment, given the current national debate about moral responsibility in the arts — not to mention the fact that Bernard is currently having a biography written about him, so we don't want any adverse publicity. You know how the tabloids love the kind of "Anti-Porn Campaigner Spotted in Sex Club" type of story, and we —'

'Are you comparing my play to a sex club?'

'No, I'm not.'

'Oh, I see. You're just afraid this could prevent him from becoming *Sir* Bernard Walton, is that it?'

There was total silence in the theatre. Though everyone knew about the star's campaign for a knighthood, it was not a subject to be mentioned out loud. Bernard himself seemed about to make some response, but thought better of it. Needless to say, it was Tony Delaunay who defused the tension. 'All I'm saying, Bill, is that we have to be extra-cautious at the moment. Adverse publicity of any kind could affect our takings at the box office.'

This appeal to his wallet finally silenced the disgruntled playwright. The company manager continued, 'And don't forget, everyone, that our director's coming to see the show again this week. David'll be in Wednesday evening, so make sure that's a good one. Which reminds me . . . on the subject of Bernard's biography, the guy who's writing it . . .' He hesitated, trying to remember the name.

'Curt Greenfield,' Bernard Walton replied.

'That's right . . . Curt Greenfield. Some of you may have met him when he was in Bath. Anyway, he'll be up here in Leeds on Wednesday, tomorrow. He's going to be around the theatre to get some atmosphere stuff, background, you know. So can I remind you all of what I said when we started rehearsing — no unauthorized talking to the press about anything. If someone wants to interview you about the show, check it out with me first — OK? And the same goes for anyone talking to Curt Greenfield about Bernard.'

'Yes, so keep quiet about Bernard's secret past as a belly dancer — and his sex-change!' Ransome George shouted out.

As always, he got his laugh. Not wishing to appear as someone who couldn't take a joke, Bernard Walton allowed the sally a thin smile. But he didn't look very amused by it. Instead, he said in a tired, we-are-here-to-work-after-all type of voice, 'So, Bill, if you could think of a replacement for those couple of lines for Ted and Louise . . . I'd be most grateful.'

The playwright was struck by instant inspiration. 'How about Ted says: "Louise! Darling! I can't stick it out any longer", and Louise says, "Oh, I'm sure you can, Ted"?'

'It's still a knob-joke,' Bernard Walton objected.

When the meeting ended, the company drifted away. It was only twelve o'clock, and they weren't due back at the theatre till six fifty-five, the 'half' for that evening's performance. As they moved off, Charles heard

Bernard Walton saying to Pippa Trewin, 'Fun at the weekend, wasn't it?'

'Yes, really enjoyed it.'

'Heard any more about the film?'

'I've had a recall,' she replied excitedly. 'It's down to three girls now, my agent says. Going to see the producers again Thursday morning.'

'You'll walk it,' said Bernard Walton. 'Oh, and do give Dickie my best when you see him.'

Charles caught Cookie Stone's eye, and realized that she had heard the exchange as well. She grimaced. For her it was just another manifestation of the unfairness of a business in which it wasn't what you could do, it was who you knew.

For Charles, though, it had other potential meanings. Tony Delaunay's words about Bernard's image brought home to him again how damaging news of an affair with a girl barely out of her teens could be. But was the secret sufficiently important for the star to murder someone who threatened to expose it?

Charles noticed that Cookie Stone was still looking at him, and gave her a weak grin. The situation between them was far from resolved. After his magical night with Lisa, Charles Paris had arrived in Leeds full of the determination to make an immediate and final break with Cookie. He'd tell her she was a wonderful person and a great lover, and somewhere out there was the right person for her, and he was only sorry it wasn't him. He'd really enjoyed their time together, but now they'd have to think of it as no more than an enchanting interlude. It was over.

But seeing her in the flesh had made such directness impossible. He'd fudged around, using all the traditional vague masculine excuses for inadequate emotional commitment, phrases like 'taking a bit of time to adjust to things', 'needing a bit of space' and 'not wanting to rush things, letting the relationship find its own pace'.

And each time Cookie had asked him a direct question, like 'Do you mean this is the end for us?', he'd retreated from the hurt in her eyes and come up with some time-buying formula, such as 'No, no, of course not. Let's just see how things pan out.'

But he knew it was only a holding operation. At some point he'd have to grasp the nettle, and confront the inevitable unpleasantness. Still, he had so far managed to defer any actual sexual encounter between them in Leeds. Fortunately, Cookie was staying in a B & B with a rather old-fashioned landlady and Charles, as he confessed wryly, was staying with 'an old friend, someone who knows my wife . . . so you know, might be a bit awkward'. And then, feeble fool that he was, he'd lost any ground he might have gained there by saying, 'Still, always next week in Birmingham, isn't there?'

In fact, when he said he was staying with an 'old friend', he had been telling only half of the truth. Ruth was an old friend, but she'd never met Frances. And Ruth brought her own problems.

He'd been shocked, when he saw her, by how old she looked. It had been a good few years since they'd met, but surely not enough to justify the lines on her face, the thinness of her grey hair. Ruth's body had always been thin, but now the word was 'gaunt'. Her clothes hung uneasily about the jutting edges of her thighs and knees, shoulders and elbows.

He made no comment on her appearance, but she gave him one of her familiar sharp, cynical looks and said, 'A bit greyer, but I see it's the same old Charles Paris.'

'What does that mean?'

'It means you look the same — just ever

so slightly on the turn.'

'Thank you.'

'And it probably means you are the same. Still drinking too much?'

'I have been cutting down on that recently.'

She barked out a short, disbelieving laugh. 'Won't last. And I assume you're not back with the wife?'

'Well . . .'

'I see. Still juggling with a series of women, are you?'

At most times during recent years he could have denied the allegation hotly. But, given what had been happening the last couple of weeks . . . silence seemed the best option.

'I see,' she said again, in a tone of despair at the unerring predictability of humankind — or of mankind — or of Charles Paris, anyway. 'You're in this show with Bernard Walton?'

'That's right. *Not On Your Wife!*'

'He's good, Bernard Walton. Makes me laugh on the telly.'

'Mm. Well, of course, I can organize tickets for any night of the week you fancy.'

'Thanks. I'd enjoy that. Free most evenings these days, but I'll let you know.'

'Fine. Are you still working?'

'No, no, I stopped that.'

'Ah. And you aren't in any kind of, er, permanent . . . ?'

'Relationship?' That got the derisory laugh it deserved. Though there had been quite a few men in Ruth's life since her divorce from a central heating systems salesman, none had raised her opinion of the subspecies.

The look she fixed on him was as it had ever been, expecting nothing, because she knew that expectations with someone like Charles Paris could only lead to disappointments.

After the first performance in Leeds, Charles didn't have a drink with the company, and when he got back to Ruth's semi in Headingley, he saw that her bedroom light was on and the door ajar. On previous occasions those signs had been tantamount to an invitation, and he did hover on the landing for a nanosecond of indecision.

But no. God, no. His life was complicated enough at the moment. The last thing Charles needed was to start hurting someone else. He'd spent the previous night with Lisa. Then he'd had a rather sticky confrontation during the day with Cookie. And somewhere, lurking in the mists of guilt that filled his mind, was an indistinct image of Frances. Charles Paris went straight to his own bedroom.

'The Beeb was never very generous,' said David J. Girton. 'Almost mythic reputation for meanness, actually. All the comedians used to come on and say to the audiences, "I'm wearing my BBC suit today — small checks!" Boom-boom!'

He and Charles were in the theatre bar after the Wednesday night's performance. The director had managed to fit in a large dinner at the Queen's Hotel before the show, so all he was now in need of was a few 'little drinks'. He was on the red wine again, a Chilean Cabernet Sauvignon he'd got the barman to open specially. Very acceptable, David J. Girton had opined after the first sip. Charles Paris, who was sharing it with him, did not disagree.

'No,' the director went on, 'everyone was strapped for cash in those days, so, although it was deeply against BBC rules and potentially a sacking offence, a lot of moonlighting went on. Pop music was really booming, for one thing, and some of the Radio One stage managers made a very healthy living from producing commercial sessions for various bands.'

'And was Mark Lear into that?' Charles prompted.

'No, music was never really Mark's thing. All the stuff he produced was speech-based. Mind you, he got involved in his own un-official, don't-say-a-word, readies-in-the-back-pocket work as well.'

An interrogative movement of the head was all Charles needed to make David J. Girton continue. 'The porn industry was also expanding exponentially at the time. Mark got involved in producing dirty audio cassettes.'

Good to have it confirmed. Maurice had been getting very close to the truth. Might be bugger-all use as an agent, but the quality of his gossip was impeccable.

'And presumably, for that kind of work, Mark would have been paid a fee per session?'

'I assume so. As I said, readies in the back pocket. Nothing official, nothing that ever appeared on the old taxman's books, that's for sure.'

'No, of course not.' Charles took a long sip of red wine before remembering that he'd told Lisa he'd stay off the stuff. Oh well, too late to make changes that evening. And it was only wine, after all, not spirits. He went on, 'Tell me, David, I heard a rumour that Mark actually got involved in the management side of the porn tape business, put money into the company . . . Ring any bells?'

David J. Girton shook his head. 'No reason I would have heard if he had done, though.'

'No. You've no idea what other actors and actresses he might have been working with on these tapes, have you?'

'No idea. Anyone who was around at the time, I would imagine. Not many young actors would object to picking up the odd unofficial tenner for a quick session at the microphone, would they? And with that kind of stuff, there wasn't much danger of them ever being identified from their performances.'

'Why not?'

'Not many actual words involved, I would imagine. Lots of panting, groaning, and the odd grunt of "I'm coming!" Hardly Shakespeare.'

'No. Not to mention the wet newspapers.'

'Ah, you heard about that?' The director chuckled. 'Yes, Karen Cohen was telling me about that.'

'Karen Cohen?'

'Actress who's in *Neighbourhood Watch*. Don't you know her?'

'Know the name.'

'Well, she's a . . . what shall we say? She's a larger-than-life character. Larger than life in every way. Foul-mouthed, utterly disgusting, very funny. She's always telling us at rehearsal about her wicked past. I'm sure she makes half of it up, just to shock people, but it can be very entertaining. Anyway, she mentioned that wet newspaper thing. She says she did a lot of porn tapes back in the early 1970s — and I think she's probably telling the truth about that.'

'Well, could you ask her if she's got any names for other actors who were involved?'

'Sure.' David J. Girton looked at him with curiosity. And with something else as well. A caution, a guardedness, had come into his manner. 'Why do you want to know all this?' he asked. 'Are you writing the definitive history of moonlighting in the BBC?'

'No, no,' Charles came up with a quick lie. It was distressing how glibly he could sometimes lie. 'No, I was just talking to Mark's girlfriend about it. You remember — Lisa Wilson from the studio in Bath?'

'Didn't meet her.'

'No, no, of course you didn't. She wasn't there that Thursday afternoon. Anyway, she just wants to find out all she can about Mark's past. I suppose it's her way of coping with the bereavement.'

He felt marginally guilty about attributing these spurious motives to Lisa. On the other hand, in the cause of finding out how Mark died, she probably wouldn't mind.

David J. Girton's anxiety had passed. He'd decided that his own moonlighting wasn't the subject of Charles Paris's investigations. Relaxed, he chuckled at another recollection. 'Karen's very funny when she gets going on her days as a porn star. Because she did a lot of video work as well as the audio stuff. Featured in lots of little epics catering for those whose tastes run to the "bigger woman".'

'Ah.'

'Well, if you'd ever seen Karen, you'd know it was perfect casting.' He giggled. 'She said some of the "bigger men" she worked with were so fat she had difficulty actually finding their dicks, let alone doing anything with them!'

'And she's not ashamed of talking about that stuff?'

'You try and stop her. No, "shame" and "inhibition" are two words Karen Cohen just does not understand. She takes great delight in talking on chat-shows about the most intimate details of her life.'

'Whereas other actors might try to cast a

veil over some of the things they did just for the money?'

'Too true. Come on, Charles, I'm sure there must've been a few jobs in your past you wouldn't exactly boast about . . .'

'In my case, that's rather an under-statement, David.' Charles Paris tried to think which of the many had been absolutely the most embarrassing. Could it have been his performance as a burnt chip in an advertisement for cooking oil? Or his rendering of the role of a turd in an experimental work entitled *Sewer Fantasies* ('An evening of which I would like to flush away all memories' — *Time Out*). Charles wasn't even sure whether he'd boast about recording over a hundred thousand words and phrases for a Thesaurus on CD-ROM.

'And with those tapes that Mark Lear produced,' David J. Girton went on, 'there might be even more reason for the actors involved to keep quiet.'

'Why? Just because they were porn?'

'No, Charles, because they were gay porn.'

'Ah.'

# Chapter Twelve

'Maurice, I've now got information that definitely ties Mark Lear in with the audio porn cassettes.'

'Really?' Down the telephone his agent's voice sounded disgruntled. 'I was getting close to a result on that myself.'

'So if I can tie in the Ransome George strand, you know, prove that he got Mark Lear involved on the financial side . . .'

'Yes, all right, Charles. *If* you can do that, so what? How's that going to help you?'

'I'm not sure . . .'

He wasn't. All he knew was that Ransome George was now at the top of his list of suspects. Everything seemed to come back to Ransome George. First, there was his character, entirely amoral, out to get any money he could by any means.

Then there was the conversation Charles had overheard him having with Bernard Walton in Bath. Ran knew something that

Bernard wanted him to keep quiet, and Ran, presumably because of some financial arrangement with the star, also wanted to keep it quiet. If the challenge Mark Lear had thrown down in the studio threatened that cosy little set-up, then Ran was quite capable of using any means to neutralize that threat.

What the secret was that Ransome George and Bernard Walton shared, Charles didn't know. Bernard certainly couldn't have had anything to do with the porn tapes, because Mark had specifically denied ever working with him. But the tapes were the link between Mark and Ran.

Charles was confident that it would soon all be clear to him. Though he hadn't got the fine detail of motivations worked out yet, he felt certain that Ransome George had murdered Mark Lear.

'Maybe it'd make things easier,' he was aware of Maurice Skellern's voice going on, 'if you told me why you were trying to get this information.'

'Yes, yes, perhaps it . . . No, I'm sorry, Maurice. Have to keep quiet about it for the moment. I think I'd better talk to Ran.'

'All right, but when you're with him, just make sure you don't open your wallet.'

Maurice's laugh wheezed away at the hilarity of the idea.

'Yes, yes, all right, very funny. Anything on the other names I mentioned?'

'Nothing that ties them up with Mark Lear, no. David J. Girton may have been involved in some overnight expenses fiddles, but no worse than most BBC producers of the time got up to.'

'What about Bernard Walton?'

'Nobody's ever got anything on Bernard Walton — well, except for insincerity, egotism and being a workaholic. Anyway, all those just go with the territory of being a star. Otherwise, dear old Bernard remains Showbusiness's Mr Squeaky-Clean.'

'Never anything dubious on his sex-life?'

'Charles, the general view is that Bernard Walton doesn't have a sex-life, that he's so obsessive about his work Mrs Walton would get more action in a nunnery.'

'But they've got three children, haven't they?'

'Yes, and the consensus is that those three times were the only three times it's ever happened. I mean, I'm not one to spread gossip, but . . .'

Why is it that people say things like that, Charles wondered. Why do they say exactly the opposite of what they mean? Why do the shiftiest characters in the world always begin sentences with 'Honestly . . .' and 'Trust me . . .'?

But, as Maurice Skellern rambled on with more details about the supposed aridity of Bernard Walton's sex-life, Charles Paris was reminded of something else he had to check up on. He must find out precisely what place Pippa Trewin had in the star's life.

He finally located Ransome George in the pub near the stage door before the show that evening. He indicated Ran's gin and tonic glass. 'Another one of those?'

'If you're buying, Charles, I would be honoured.' He did it in his obsequious-funny voice. Had there been other people there to hear it, the line would have got its certain laugh.

They settled with their drinks. Instinctively, Charles had bought himself a large Bell's. It was only as he was carrying the glasses back to their table that he remembered his pledge to Lisa. Oh well, time enough. If he didn't drink on the Friday or Saturday, then when they met on the Sunday, he'd have survived nearly three days without booze.

Anyway, he was conducting an investigation. He had to relax the person he was pumping. If Ran noticed Charles wasn't on the Bell's, that might put him on his guard.

Even as he shaped these justifications, Charles Paris knew they were nothing more than the casuistry of the alcoholic. He raised his glass to Ran. 'Cheers.'

'Down the hatch.' Again, the timing and the voice were funny. It was difficult to consider someone who could be so consistently funny in connection with a murder enquiry. But then so impermeable was Ransome George's humorous defence that it was difficult at times to think of him as a human being, or to get near the real human being who must lurk somewhere in the middle of all the funny faces and funny voices.

'Was talking to my agent about poor old Mark Lear . . .' Charles began.

'Uh-uh.' Ran's reaction was entirely without attitude. He didn't sound anxious or guilty. He didn't sound anything. 'Who is your agent?'

'Maurice Skellern.'

Ransome George just giggled.

'Maurice used to know Mark way back in the early 1970s,' Charles lied. 'I gather you did some work for him back then . . . ?'

Ran didn't deny it. 'Odd little bits here and there, yes.'

'Agent mentioned something about some audio porn tapes . . .'

'So?'

'Do you remember making those?'

'Vaguely. I've done all kinds of stuff over the years. Never been out of work for more than the odd month.'

'Lucky you.'

'Partly luck. Partly grafting away, following up leads, making the right friends, you know how it is.'

'Oh yes. Were you actually involved in the production company that made the porn tapes?'

For the first time there was a wariness in Ransome George's eye. 'May have been. Why you asking?'

'To be quite honest, I think there was something funny about Mark Lear's death.'

'Funny?'

'Not to put too fine a point on it, I think someone may have helped him on his way.'

Ran nodded slowly, weighing the idea. 'I suppose it's possible. What's this got to do with the porn tapes?'

'Well, that afternoon Mark talked about writing a book, exposing things that went on in the BBC, or amongst people who had BBC connections . . . Do you remember?'

'Uh-uh.'

'And in retrospect I've come to the conclusion that what he was actually doing was
issuing a threat. He was saying he would
expose something he knew about someone.'

'Who?'

'That's what I don't know. Obviously
someone who was in the studio that afternoon.'

'Mm.' Ransome George caught his eye.
'You're not looking at me, are you? I never
worked for the BBC.'

'Not on the staff, I know, but you did the
odd radio as an actor.'

'Very few. Pretty quickly realized my face
was going to be my fortune and concentrated on the telly.'

Charles took another sip of his whisky. It
did taste good. The idea that he could ever
give the stuff up permanently seemed more
remote than ever. 'I've just a feeling, Ran,
that what happened to Mark is somehow
tied in with events at the BBC in the early
1970s.'

Ransome George shrugged, without much
interest in the subject. 'Maybe.'

'So I want to find out all the detail I can,
particularly about the time when Mark was
involved in producing those porn cassettes.'

'Well, good luck. I don't see that it has
anything to do with me.'

'You were involved in making those cassettes, so you could fill in a bit of the background.'

'Yes, possibly I could. Doesn't mean I will, though, does it?'

'Why not?'

Ran didn't answer that straight away. Instead, he asked, 'What kind of stuff do you want to know?'

'Anything. Everything. Names of the other actors involved, for a start.'

'It'll cost you.'

'What do you mean — it'll cost me?'

'I'd have thought the words were clear. We live in a consumer society. Most things have a price. Information's certainly a marketable commodity. I've got information you want. So, to get it, you're going to have to pay me.'

'How much?'

Ransome George stretched out a ruminative lower lip. 'Say five hundred quid per actor's name.'

'What? But I haven't got that kind of money.'

'Didn't think you had. Means you haven't got that kind of information either, doesn't it?'

Charles was too dumbfounded by this reaction to press his point. Instead, he said,

'Incidentally, Ran, talking of money . . . there's still the small matter of that twenty you borrowed from me on the last day of rehearsal in London.'

Ransome George looked up, his face full of shock and injured innocence. 'Oh, now come on, Charles . . .'

'What?'

'I paid you back that money when we were in Bath. Don't you remember, just before the first night? You were hurrying to your dressing room and I thrust a twenty into your hands.'

'I don't remember that.'

Ransome George hit his head with the heel of his palm in annoyance. 'Oh no, you must've left the note in the pocket of your costume. I bet one of those little sluts in Wardrobe nicked it.'

The awful thing was that, for a moment, Charles actually believed it. He'd under-estimated Ransome George as an actor.


'So what was it like directing Bernard Walton in his first major role?'

There was something creepy and slightly unwholesome about Curt Greenfield. He was late thirties, a showbiz journalist who'd developed a lucrative second string as a paste-and-scissors 'biographer to the stars'.

An uneven beard straggled round his chin. His clothes were sweatshirt, denim jacket, jeans and incongruously new-looking cowboy boots.

Curt Greenfield had no social graces, made no attempt at small talk. He hadn't offered coffee or a drink when Charles appeared in the theatre bar for the interview officially sanctioned and arranged by Tony Delaunay. All Curt Greenfield wanted was quick, quotable answers to his questions. Answers that could be shoved straight into his book with the minimum of editing.

'Well, he was quite inexperienced,' Charles replied, 'but he had got something.'

'Star quality?' asked Curt Greenfield, ever eager for the cliché.

'I wouldn't say that. More a stage presence. Even back then, when he was on stage, the audience found it difficult to concentrate on anyone else.'

Charles saw the biographer write down 'Star quality', then look up and ask, 'Why in particular did you cast him? What was it about Bernard that so impressed you?'

'Well, his stammer was certainly part of it.'

'So you'd say Bernard Walton's speech impediment, something which to many people might appear as an obstacle, in his case proved the springboard to stardom?'

'No, I'm not sure that I would say that,' said Charles, reluctant to have his views reduced to journalese.

Curt Greenfield ignored the objection. 'And was the Cardiff production when you first met him? You didn't know him as a child? You didn't know any of the Miles family or — ?'

'I met him first at the London auditions for that production of *She Stoops to Conquer*.'

'By which time he was already "Bernard Walton the actor"?'

'I suppose you could say that. He hadn't got much experience at that stage, but he had been around a bit.'

'Hmm . . .' Curt Greenfield didn't reckon any of that was worth writing down. His hopes for charming, winsome reminiscences of the star's boyhood were not to be realized. 'Anything else?' he asked restlessly. 'Any little anecdotes? Any stories that show what a popular member of the Cardiff company Bernard Walton was?'

'No, I can't think of any of those.'

The biographer shrugged. 'Oh well, if I put something like . . . "Bernard Walton's infectious high spirits made for a relaxed and convivial backstage atmosphere", that should cover it.'

'Not really. I think that'd give rather a misleading impression of —'

'And he's been generous to you over the years, I gather?'

'What do you mean?'

'Helping you out. Seeing you got the odd small part in shows he's been involved in. Not forgetting the lesser figures who helped him on the way up.'

'No, I wouldn't put it like that. I'd say —'

But Charles knew his protests were in vain. Curt Greenfield had arrived with his interview virtually written. Nothing that was actually said was going to change it.

The biographer closed his notebook with an air of finality. 'That's it. I'll see any quotes I use are attributed to you by name.'

'But will the words be what I actually said?'

Curt Greenfield looked at Charles in total incomprehension. He didn't understand the question. Then he sat back, with a reptilian expression, and said, 'By the way, you know what I'm writing about Bernard is, like, the official, authorized biography . . . ?'

'I got that impression. Be closer to a hagiography, I gather.'

'Mm?'

'A "hagiography" is the life of a saint.'

'Ah.'

'A biography devoid of criticism.'

'Oh, right, get your drift. I'm with you. And because it's that kind of book, that's why your nice camp little company manager . . . Tony . . . ?'

'Tony Delaunay,' Charles supplied.

'That's right. Well, that's why he's been so co-operative to me, setting up all these interviews. Anything that builds up Bernard Walton's image is presumably good for Mr Delaunay's business.'

'I guess so. Good for Parrott Fashion Productions.'

'On the other hand . . .' Curt Greenfield began slowly, 'if there's any other stuff you've got on Bernard Walton . . .'

'What kind of stuff?'

'Let's say stuff that's less flattering, less hagi . . . whatever you said, less "Lives of the Saints" stuff, eh? Well, I'd be interested to hear that too.'

'So you've taken a commission to write a book that's a whitewash, but in fact you're going to make it subversive, is that right?'

'No, no, Mr Paris. The book will be exactly what the publisher wants . . . and, incidentally, what Bernard Walton's management wants — they've put some money into the project too — but, while I'm doing all this research, while I'm meeting all the relevant people . . . well, if there's any dirt around on Bernard Walton, I've probably got a market for that too.'

'You'd sell it on anonymously?'

'Oh, you bet. So, if there is anything . . . ?'

Charles shook his head.

'I'd pay, if it's good. Ransome George gave me some good stuff.'

Suddenly Ran's remarks about paying for information began to make sense. 'What? What did he tell you?'

Curt Greenfield smiled an oleaginous smile. 'Now, come on, Mr Paris. I'm the one who paid for the information, not you.'

'Yes. Of course.'

'So if you have got any stories that might show the sainted Bernard Walton in less of a stained-glass window light, I'm very happy to discuss terms.'

'No, no, I don't think I've got anything,' Charles said distractedly. 'When did you talk to Ransome George? Yesterday?'

'No. I caught up with him when your show was in Bath. We had a very productive three hours of chat there one afternoon.'

'Which afternoon?'

'Erm . . . The Thursday, I think.'

'What time on the Thursday?'

'Three-thirty he came to my hotel.'

'It was just the two of you?'

'Yes. Well, most of the time. Tony Delaunay popped in . . . I don't know, half-past four, fivish, I suppose . . . just to see that everything was OK. He'd set up the interview, you see.'

'Hm. Can you be absolutely sure it was the Thursday?' asked Charles.

The biographer wrinkled his forehead. 'Fairly sure.'

'I mean, for instance, did Ransome George say he'd come from recording a radio commercial?'

'That's right. He did.'

Damn, thought Charles Paris. Because if Ransome George was in a hotel with Curt Greenfield telling tales out of school about Bernard Walton, then there was no way he could have been in a studio murdering Mark Lear.

It was something to do with Bernard. Charles kept coming back to that fact. His thoughts distracted him from whatever Cookie Stone was saying over dinner on the Saturday night after the show.

He shouldn't have been there with Cookie, anyway. Delaying the clean break, trying to let her down gently, wasn't going to work. It would only build up troubles for him later, because, from the bits of her

254

monologue he caught, Cookie Stone was still as deeply in love with Charles Paris as ever.

His mind homed back in on Bernard Walton. It must be some secret in the star's private life, something Mark Lear had found out about. But what? Well, he still hadn't fully investigated the Pippa Trewin connection. Maybe there had been company gossip on the subject . . . ? It was quite possible that he'd missed it. Charles Paris had incredibly unresponsive antennae for gossip.

'Cookie,' he said suddenly, 'about Pippa Trewin . . . ?'

Cookie Stone looked surprised. She had been in the middle of saying how wonderful it was to be with someone to whom you didn't have to explain everything, someone with whom you felt companionable enough to share silence, someone whose every thought you could anticipate . . . But she hadn't anticipated that Charles's thoughts would be currently centred on Pippa Trewin.

'What about her?'

'How long has her affair with Bernard Walton been going on?'

'*What!*' Cookie let out a screech that turned every head in the restaurant. Then, in an elaborate stage whisper, she went on,

'What on earth are you talking about, Charles?'

'Well, they seem to be very pally, they keep talking about mutual arrangements, they seem to see each other over the weekends . . . Apart from anything else, ask yourself: "Why is Pippa Trewin in the show, anyway?" '

'Pippa Trewin is in the show,' said Cookie Stone icily, 'because she has better contacts than anyone else in the business.'

'Yes, but Bernard must be getting some payback for —'

'Bernard Walton is her godfather.' The frost hadn't left Cookie's voice, as she went on. 'Her parents are Patti Urquhart and Julian Strange. That is why she's with a top agency, that is why she's got a fast track to television casting directors and movies. That is why her career is set fair, and why for the rest of her professional life she will continue to take parts that should be going to other, more talented, actresses who happen to have been born to different parents.'

'Oh,' said Charles Paris. 'I think I've been a bit stupid not to realize that earlier.'

God, that wasn't the only way he was stupid. As they left the restaurant, Cookie had said, 'I don't care about my bloody po-faced landlady. I'll never have to see the old bag again after tomorrow morning. Come back to my place.'

And like a fool, he had done so. He blamed the hurt in Cookie's eyes, which had been intensified by the furious sense of professional injustice their talk about Pippa Trewin had revived. But the only thing he could really blame was his own spinelessness.

And then, because of his tiredness, because of the prospect of seeing Lisa Wilson the next day, because of his confusion about Mark's death, Charles hadn't been very good in bed. And, although that was completely his fault, Cookie had blamed herself and started asking questions on 'Don't you love me any more? Have you stopped fancying me?' lines.

So, amidst all the recriminations and the angst, very little sleeping had taken place that night.

Charles's return to Ruth's house, early on the Sunday morning, to pick up his things, had exacerbated the feeling of being an emotional disaster area, unable to move in any direction without causing more pain.

Ruth didn't pass any comment on his overnight absence, but her expression didn't need words to back it up. All she said was:

'There was a message for you last night from a Lavinia Bradshaw. Wants you to ring her. Another of your women, I suppose?'

'Lavinia Bradshaw? I don't know anyone called Lavinia Bradshaw.'

'Oh no?' said Ruth, disbelieving.

'No, I don't. I really don't.'

He packed his bits in silence, and they almost parted in silence. But when he got to the door and looked back, Charles was astonished to see that Ruth was crying. Tears poured unchecked down her lined, grey face.

'What's the matter, love? What is it?' He put his arms around her, and felt the unnatural thinness of her body against his. 'What is it?'

'Oh, Charles, I just thought . . . you . . . I thought you, the eternally unreliable, eternally selfish, eternally randy . . . I thought you would . . . But now I'm too ugly and sick even for you to fancy me . . .'

She broke into a long wail. 'No, no,' he said, patting the sharp ridge of her shoulder. 'No, of course not. I just didn't think I should take advantage of you . . . I thought . . .'

There are some situations in which one can do nothing right. Charles Paris had been in a good few of them during his lifetime.

He'd been exercising restraint, trying to do the decent thing, and all the time Ruth had actually been *wanting* him to make love to her.

God, Charles Paris thought savagely on the train down to London, am I capable of doing *anything* that doesn't hurt someone?

# Chapter Thirteen

'End,' Charles Paris intoned, then left the required two-second pause, and went on, 'Ending' — two-second pause — 'Conclusion' — two-second pause — 'Finale' — two-second pause — 'Closure' — two-second pause — 'Curtain' — two-second pause — 'Termination' — two-second pause — 'Halt' — two-second pause — 'Payoff' — two-second pause — 'Last words — God, I wish they bloody were!' he concluded in exasperation.

Nothing came from the talkback. He looked up through the glass. Lisa Wilson's head was bowed. She showed no reaction to his lapse. Was she simply being professional, or was there actually a deterrent factor in her lack of response?

Charles focused his eyes back on the photocopied list of words, which swam before him. Even without his hangover, the task would have been hard. It was incredible how much concentration doing individual words demanded. The text of a play or a book at least had a logical sequence to it, there was a continuity of thought which could be followed through. With the Thesaurus, he had to start from scratch with each new word or phrase.

'Swansong,' he continued. Two-second pause. 'Coda' — two-second pause — 'Boundary' — two-second pause — 'Terminus' — two-second pause — 'Where the rainbow —'

He was suddenly and unexpectedly ambushed by giggles. 'I'm sorry, Lisa . . . It's just . . . "Where the rainbow ends" sounds so . . . I don't know, so showbiz!' Another burst of giggles ran through him. 'I mean . . . all the others are kind of doomy and dreary . . . and then suddenly you get to . . .' He dropped into a little Shirley Temple voice: ' "Where the rainbow ends"! Yippee! Yippee! "Somewhere, over the rainbow . . ." I'm sorry . . .'

He looked, through his uncontrollable tears of laughter, into the cubicle and saw, with relief, that Lisa was also incapacitated. Her eyes were streaming too.

'I'm sorry,' Charles managed to say again. 'It's just hysteria . . . It's like . . . like "gate fever" . . . you know, that thing long-term prisoners get when they're about to be released . . . A hundred thousand bloody words and phrases we've done . . . suddenly the end is actually in sight and I just . . .'

He broke down again. Lisa Wilson's voice came giggling through the speaker into the studio, 'You'll never make it to the end . . . It's like the horizon . . . the nearer you get to it, the further away it moves.'

'Or one of those classical myths . . . Who is it? Tantalus having the bunch of grapes constantly whipped away when his mouth gets near them . . . ?'

'Or Sisyphus pushing that bloody stone up the hill . . . ?'

'And watching it roll all the bloody way down again? Oh, I'm sorry, Lisa, I'm just completely gone . . . I can't do the next phrase. I literally cannot say the words, "Last g-g-g-g . . ." '

He went again. By the time Lisa's voice next came through the speaker, she had regained a degree of self-control. 'OK, Charles. Enough. The phrase is, "Last gasp".'

'Yes,' Charles Paris agreed soberly. 'Last g-g-g-g-g . . .'

And still he couldn't shape the word.

'Joke over,' Lisa's voice announced sternly. But, through the glass, Charles

could see her mouth was still twitching un-
controllably.

'Yes,' he said. With enormous concentration, he emptied his mind of everything,
bleached the words he had to say of all
meaning or connotation, and managed to
pronounce, 'Last gasp' — two-second pause
— 'Last lap' — two-second pause — 'Home
straight' — two-second pause — 'Last t-t-
t-t-' But this time it was the word 'trump'
that wouldn't come.

Once again the two of them had dissolved
into hopeless giggling.

'I can't believe it's all done,' said Charles
Paris, as he finally staggered out of the studio just before seven that evening.

'Well, it is.' Lisa indicated the high pile
of marked-up tape boxes. 'I've checked.
Every single word and phrase recorded. So,
in a few months' time, everyone who con-
sults that particular CD-ROM Thesaurus
will hear the dulcet tones of Charles Paris
wafting out of their computer's speakers.'

'Yes.' Charles hesitated before his admission. 'It seems somewhat late in the day for
me to ask this, Lisa, but what exactly is a
CD-ROM?'

'How long have you got?'

'Well . . .'

'Because I could give you an extended scientific description of the technology and potentialities of CD-ROMs, or I could just say they're a means of storing information which can be presented on a computer screen with illustrations in sound and pictures.'

'That'll do.' Charles reached out his arms behind him, joined his hands, and stretched. 'God, it really gets you in the small of the back, that kind of concentration.'

'Still, you can stop concentrating now. As I say, all done. Congratulations.'

'Thanks. Ooof.' He sank gratefully into a chair. 'Really calls for a drink, doesn't it?'

'I'll make us some coffee,' said Lisa Wilson tartly.

'The police have been round again,' she announced, when they were settled either side of the table, making inroads into another packet of chocolate digestives.

'Really?'

She pursed her lips. 'Still hasn't been an inquest yet. The first one was adjourned for a month, to give the police time to make more enquiries.'

'So we're not the only ones to suspect murder?'

'I'm not sure about that. I think they're

264

concentrating more on suicide.'

'Oh?'

'Well, you see, they don't know the one detail that we know — namely that the studio door was locked . . .'

'Because you haven't told them.'

'Exactly. But, if you rule that out as a consideration, then, given Mark's depressed mental state . . . suicide must look like a possibility. You know, he takes a bottle of Scotch, shuts himself into a space which he knows has no air supply . . .'

'But why's this suddenly come up now? I thought the police were satisfied at the time that it was an accident.'

'I don't think they'd made up their minds, but I reckon they'd have been happy to accept that explanation. No, someone has been stirring things up.'

'Who?'

'Who do you think?'

Charles shrugged. 'Search me.'

'Oh, come on, it's obvious. The widow.'

'Mark's ex? Vinnie?'

'Sure.'

'But I thought she'd given up all interest in him.'

'All interest in him as a human being, yes. But not all financial interest in trim.' In response to Charles's puzzled expression, she continued, 'Mark was heavily insured, and the beneficiaries of the insurance are his children. That situation wasn't changed by the divorce. I think his widow's view — not unreasonably — is that, since it was her money that paid all the premiums, she should ensure that her kids get what's due to them.'

'Ah. But if Mark was found to have committed suicide . . .'

Lisa Wilson nodded. '. . . then the insurance company wouldn't pay up. I reckon Mark's widow must've started making the claim, and then the insurance company — who, like all insurance companies, would do anything rather than actually shell out any money — became suspicious about the circumstances of his death. And I reckon they're the ones who've got the police taking another look at what happened.'

'That'd make sense. Has Vinnie talked to you about it?'

Lisa gave a firm shake of her blonde head. 'No. She wouldn't talk to me about anything. She may not have wanted Mark any more for herself, but she was damned if anyone else was going to have any rights in him.'

'So you never even met her?'

'No. And, of course, I've only heard

Mark's side of the story . . . but I do get the impression that she is one very strong-willed lady.'

'Yes, I suppose she always was. I didn't meet her that often, but she was strong, you're right. I think a lot of people who're born with money are strong. Of course, when I knew her, she was channelling all that strength into keeping the family together.'

'I gather she still is. Mark's no longer part of the equation — he ceased to be from the moment she walked out on him — but I think she'll still be ferocious in support of her offspring. The old "lioness with cubs" syndrome. Which is why she'll fight any suggestion that Mark committed suicide. She'd regard it as him having the last laugh on her — and there's no way she's going to allow that to happen.'

'No.'

'From everything I've heard about her,' said Lisa, 'she's a truly terrifying woman. I don't envy Mr Bradshaw.'

'Mr Bradshaw?'

'That's her new married name.'

'Of course! She's Lavinia Bradshaw.'

Lisa looked at him curiously. 'Yes. So . . . ?'

'It's just that a Lavinia Bradshaw has been

267

trying to make contact with me.'

'Ah. She's probably found out that you were here the afternoon Mark died. She'll want to see if she can get anything from you to scotch the suicide theory.'

'Well, I'll let you know what she says.'

'Thanks.' There was a silence. Lisa's grey eyes locked on to him, as her hand reached across and rested lightly on top of his. 'Talking of Scotch, Charles.'

'Hm . . . ?'

'How've you been doing this week?'

'On the booze front?' He grimaced wryly. 'Well, I cannot put my hand on my heart and say it's been a week of total abstinence.'

'Ah. Why not?'

'I'm sorry. I've had pressures and . . .'

'I see,' she said in a tone that meant: yes, she *saw*, but no, she didn't *approve*. She withdrew her hand from his.

'The thing is . . .'

'Don't worry, Charles.' She let out a little sigh of exasperation. 'You don't have to explain. Remember, I've lived with two alcoholics.'

'I'm not an alcoholic!'

Her grey eyes challenged him. 'No?'

'No. I can stop. I just . . .'

'. . . don't stop,' she supplied. 'Or at least not for long.'

'No . . . Well . . . I . . .'

Lisa Wilson stood up from the table. 'Which train are you getting back to London, Charles?'

He was dumbfounded, as all the carefully fostered fantasies of the previous week crumbled around him.

'Well, I wasn't sure that I was going back. I thought —'

'Charles,' said Lisa firmly. 'What happened last Sunday night was good. We both enjoyed it. It answered a need in both of us. But it was never intended to be the start of anything long-term.'

'No. I know that,' he said miserably.

'As I recall, I spelt out our "terms of engagement" at the time. No commitment, no emotional entanglement. And I also seem to recall that you were very keen to accept those terms.'

'They're the terms men have been trying to get from women since the race began.'

'Exactly. And also, generally speaking, the terms men have tried to impose on women since the race began . . .'

'All right. Possibly.'

'So you can't really complain when I act according to those terms, can you?'

'Look, are you making a political point

269

here? Is this part of some kind of feminist agenda that you — ?'

'No, Charles, it isn't. What I am saying is that what happened last week was very good —'

'But if it was so good —' he protested.

'It was what was needed at the time,' she steamrollered on. 'I enjoyed it, and it's a memory I will always treasure.'

'Me too.'

'Good. But it wasn't the start of anything. We lead different lives, we're very different people. What we're going to do shortly is part — with a big, friendly hug — and we'll certainly see each other again from time to time . . . but, so far as any physical relationship between us is concerned, that's over. Nice while it lasted, but not to be repeated. OK?'

'OK,' Charles agreed mournfully, and got out the little timetable of trains back to London.

Just before he left, as they were having their 'big, friendly hug', he asked, 'Lisa, if I hadn't had any booze during the week . . . ? I mean, is it because of the drinking?'

'No,' Lisa Wilson replied firmly. 'With you, the drinking's just a symptom of everything else.'

'Oh,' said Charles Paris. 'Right. Thank you.'

The digit '2' was glowing on his answering machine when he got back to Hereford Road. He replayed the messages.

The voice on the first was dauntingly upper class and authoritative. 'Charles, this is Lavinia Bradshaw. We met when I was married to Mark Lear. Could you get back to me urgently, please?' She gave a London number. 'I'm calling on Sunday morning, having, I gather, just missed you in Leeds. I'll be up till half-past eleven tonight, so could you get back to me? It's important that we meet before you leave for Birmingham tomorrow. Message ends.'

Yes, as Lisa Wilson had said, she was a very strong-willed woman. And she'd done her research on his movements; maybe she'd got all that detail from Maurice Skellern. When Charles had met Vinnie before, with Mark, it had always been on social occasions and perhaps then her ferocity had been masked. But now there was no gainsaying her. He'd have to call back. Besides, Lavinia Bradshaw might, unknowingly, hold the key to Mark Lear's murder.

Checking on his watch that it was only

just after eleven, he let the tape play on for the second message.

It was a full drama queen performance from Cookie Stone. 'Charles darling, I feel so miserable about last night, and about how we parted this morning. I just have to see you. I'm in Crouch End. It doesn't matter what time you get in, what time you receive this message . . . you just have to call me. You must.'

Oh, shit! thought Charles Paris. Why do I get myself into these situations? And why can't I get myself out of them with any kind of grace? He thought of the relative elegance with which he had just been dumped by Lisa Wilson. The rejection was still hurting, but he couldn't deny the fact that it had had style. Why couldn't he find within himself the skills to let down Cookie Stone in the same way?

He rang Lavinia Bradshaw. While he dithered about what time he would be leaving for Birmingham in the morning, she announced she'd be round at Hereford Road at nine-thirty. As on the recorded message, her tone of voice did not countenance the option of disagreement.

Then, for a full ten minutes Charles held firm. He checked through the flat and found there was a quarter-full half-bottle of Bell's.

He hadn't searched it out because he was going to drink it, just to assess the degree of temptation it offered. Because what Lisa had said to him had hurt. Charles Paris *could* stop drinking whenever he felt like it. It was just that he very rarely felt like it.

For a moment, he contemplated pouring the whisky down the sink, but that did seem an excessively melodramatic gesture. Also, that would be making things too easy. He had to prove to himself that he could keep off the booze, whatever temptations there were around him. Then, after . . . what? . . . a month . . . two months . . . six months . . . he could go back to Lisa Wilson and . . .

He knew that scenario would never be completed. The sexual relationship with Lisa was over. But he still wanted to keep off the booze. He'd been really offended by her saying that it was 'just a symptom of everything else'.

At the end of the ten minutes, Charles gave in and rang Cookie Stone. He was determined to be strong and sensible, to be supportive, but to leave her with no illusions about the true state of their relationship.

And he might have done all that, if she hadn't cried. Two minutes later, as he put the phone down, Charles realized he had agreed for Cookie Stone to come round to Hereford Road. God, he was an idiot!

She arrived within the half-hour, clutching a bottle of Glenfiddich. And although he managed to resist the whisky, Charles Paris didn't manage to resist Cookie Stone's body.

It was realizing the depth of her pain and her need that did for him, though he wasn't helped by her assertion, 'After all, this is where it all started.' For Charles Paris the obscurity which surrounded their first encounter had not lifted at all.

But he succumbed to Cookie's need for reassurance. 'You do really care for me, don't you? You understand the real me, don't you — not the flamboyant jokey front I present all the time? You really do find my body beautiful, don't you?'

And Charles — weak, weak Charles — supplied all the reassurances that his words and his body could provide.

And, with its own infuriating irony, his perfidious body conspired to dig the hole he was in even deeper, by performing exceptionally well.

# Chapter Fourteen

Charles woke up at quarter to seven in the morning, which meant that some sleeping must have taken place in the course of the night, but it didn't feel that way. He ached as though his body had been through the full cycle of an industrial carpet-cleaning machine, and the minute he showed signs of life, Cookie made him go through another spin.

Again, he was surprisingly effective, but his performance didn't give him the warm glow it might sometimes have done. Sex without love is never good, but sex without love with someone who's in love with you is worse, intensifying the accompanying guilt and self-hatred. Why is it, Charles pondered — not for the first time — that women so often identify sexual attention with love? In his experience, intense and continuous sexual activity was usually a sign of one partner trying to prove or justify something to the other. His most satisfactory physical relationships — like the one he and Frances had once shared — had involved a lot more stillness and stroking and cuddling than manic screwing.

The thought of his wife brought the inevitable pang of guilt, this time stronger than ever. He hadn't been strictly faithful to Frances since early on in their marriage, but he had rarely got himself into the kind of bedroom farce tangle he was in now. Cookie . . . Lisa . . . Ruth . . . What was he playing at? Was he going through some Final Benefit Night before the Eternal Safety Curtain crashed down and locked itself permanently in place?

One reason, Charles knew, why he made love with such avidity to Cookie Stone was that, for a while at least, it stopped her talking. But not for long. The most recent orgasm had hardly shuddered itself away, before she started up again. 'It worries me, Charles, that you sometimes seem so distracted when you're with me.'

'You shouldn't bother about that. It's what I'm like. I drift off. I lead a very full fantasy life, you know.'

If that had been intended as a joke, it was the wrong joke for the moment. Cookie's prominent teeth jutted forward ruefully, as she said, 'Full of other women, I bet.'

'No, no, of course not.'

'I bet it is. I do worry about you and other women . . .'

'You have no cause to. I mean, I still have a very strong bond with my wife, but . . .' Good idea to slip that in. Frances might prove a useful argument when the final breaking-off with Cookie eventually happened. 'I'm afraid the feeling I still have for my wife prevents me from committing myself fully to another woman . . .' he could say at the appropriate moment, then adding, '. . . even one as wonderful as you, Cookie.'

But, the minute he had the idea, he felt shabby. He did still care for Frances, but to use her as some kind of bargaining counter to get out of his other messy entanglements was disgusting.

Cookie's jealousy, however, had not been defused. 'I was worried about you and that woman in Bath.'

'Woman in Bath?' he echoed innocently.

'That woman . . . Lisa is it? . . . that you've been scurrying off every Sunday to do recordings with. At least, you *called* them recordings.'

Her tone was only half-joking, so Charles came in quickly, 'And you actually thought I was having a thing with her?'

'You might have been. You're so gor-

277

geous, Charles — at least, I find you so gorgeous — that I imagine every other woman in the world feels the same about you. That's what it's like when you're in love with someone . . . you're terrified that people are trying to steal them away from you.'

If Charles had needed any proof that he wasn't in love with Cookie Stone, that would have provided it. He was *dying* for someone to steal her away from him. He wanted nothing more than for some nice man, who really *did* think she was beautiful, who adored her for what she was, to come along and sweep her off her feet. If that were to happen, Charles Paris would not create any problems. He would do the decent thing, simply stand back and concede victory to the newcomer.

But he couldn't see it happening. He couldn't imagine the man had been born who could withstand her constant demands for reassurance. So deeply engrained was the self-doubt about her own attractiveness that all Cookie Stone's prophecies seemed doomed to self-fulfilment.

Still, there was one matter on which he could reassure her, without resorting to lies or half-truths. 'Cookie, I promise you that nothing happened between me and Lisa

Wilson yesterday. We like each other fine, but there is never any chance of it becoming a physical relationship in the future.'

Cookie seemed to accept his assertion — which was, to Charles's great regret, the absolute truth — and fortunately she did not enquire about any previous history. But, needless to say, reassurance on one detail did not allay all of Cookie's other anxieties. 'So what is it you're thinking about all the time, Charles, when you look as if you're not here?'

Oh God, he thought, can't I even have my thoughts to myself? Being with Cookie Stone in the real world was claustrophobic enough, without her setting up a monitoring post in his brain as well. But of course that was not what he said. Instead, he tried to fob her off with a half-truth. 'I am rather preoccupied at the moment. There's something I'm trying to find out the truth about. Something rather private.'

Many women in the world would have respected that hint, and discreetly withdrawn from further questioning. Cookie Stone was not amongst their number. 'What is it, Charles?'

'Well, something to do with . . . You remember that friend of mine who was running the studio in Bath . . . the one who was terribly drunk the afternoon we recorded the commercial . . . Mark Lear.'

'Lisa Thing's boyfriend?'

'That's right. Incidentally, he said he'd met you, didn't he?'

'Did he?'

'Yes. That afternoon. Don't you remember?'

She shook her head, making the hair rustle against his naked shoulder. 'Can't recall it. But you say he used to be BBC . . . ?'

'Yes. Radio. Continuing Education.'

'I probably got introduced to him in the Ariel Bar at some point. I used to do quite a bit of radio work when I started.'

'Hm.' Charles sighed. 'Well, Mark's death has, kind of, affected me. You know how upset I was in Bath. So I've been trying to find out what really happened there.'

'What, you think it might have been suicide?'

'Yes, or . . . who can tell?'

'You don't mean you think he might have been murdered, do you?'

'Well . . . I suppose it's a possibility.'

His words silenced Cookie Stone. Charles couldn't help thinking that if — heaven forbid — his relationship with her continued, he should bear that in mind. Maybe the mention of murder would always silence her. It'd certainly be less exhausting than having to make love to her all the time.

But the silence didn't last for long. 'Who would want to murder him, though?'

'I don't know. Someone who had a secret Mark knew about, and someone who so much didn't want that secret known that they were prepared to silence him for ever. If you remember, he did kind of issue a challenge that afternoon, that he was going to spill the beans about something.'

'Did he? I don't remember. I guess my mind's full of other things too.' Cookie had affected a throaty American voice, and pressed the length of her body against his. Oh God, thought Charles, not again.

But there was an 'again', and after it, out of sheer exhaustion, they both fell asleep.

They were woken by the peremptory buzzing of the entryphone. Charles looked at his watch. Half-past nine. Oh God! Vinnie! Lavinia Bradshaw!

He bustled Cookie into wakefulness. 'For heaven's sake, I've got someone coming to see me!'

'Another woman?' she asked, sleepy but already jealous.

'Yes, she is a woman, but not one that need cause you any anxiety. Please get some clothes on quickly! You've got to get out!'

Charles picked up the entryphone, but Cookie's rampant paranoia had not been appeased. 'She's coming here to your flat at half-past nine in the morning and it needn't cause me any anxiety? You really expect me to believe that, Charles?'

'Yes, I do. Now put some bloody clothes on!' He apologized into the entryphone. 'Sorry, sorry. Look, I'll be right down to let you in if you just wait —'

'But surely,' Lavinia Bradshaw's imperious tones crackled back, 'you can let me in by simply pressing the — ?' He cut her off, not without relish.

Shouting at Cookie, which he hadn't done before, had also proved an effective way of silencing her. Another one to bear in mind. She sat on the bed, resentfully pulling on tights, while Charles stumbled into his trousers.

The room looked a mess, fuggy with recent sex. He scrambled the bedspread inadequately over the twisted duvet, and threw open the window to let in cold air as an inadequate means of fumigation.

'Are you ready?' he pleaded once he'd pushed his feet into his shoes.

'Not quite.' Cookie seemed deliberately to have slowed down her dressing.

The entryphone buzzed again, seeming to echo the shrillness of Lavinia Bradshaw's tone.

'Look, I've got to go and let her in. I'll try and delay a bit on the doorstep, but you get down as soon as you can. When you see me, just kind of nod, you know, like you were somebody else living in the block.'

'I see. Still ashamed of me?' asked Cookie.

He countered the resentment in her voice by bellowing, 'Just do as you're bloody told! And I'll see you in Birmingham!'

Once again, the shouting silenced her. Charles crossed to plant a dry kiss on her pouting lips, checked he'd got his keys with him, and went down to open the front door.

'What the hell kept you?' demanded Lavinia Bradshaw.

She was expensively dressed, her image sharpened up considerably from the child-bound earth mother Charles recalled from their earlier meetings. Whatever her real age, plastic surgery had put her back firmly into her late thirties; and though the reddish-gold of her hair couldn't possibly be natural, it contrived to look natural.

'Sorry, Vinnie. I, er, um . . . sorry.'

'I didn't *wake* you, did I?' asked Lavinia Bradshaw, to whom the idea was entirely incongruous.

'Good heavens, no. I just, er . . .' Charles loomed aimlessly, blocking the doorway.

'Aren't you going to invite me in? It is quite cold out here.'

'Yes, sorry. I, erm . . .'

Still he hovered, preventing her entrance. Then he heard the welcome sound of footsteps behind him. He turned with relief to see a fully dressed Cookie tiptoeing demurely down the stairs.

She was not an actress for nothing. 'Good morning, Mr Paris,' she said without interest, as she passed him.

On the doorstep, Cookie came face to face with Mark Lear's widow. 'I know you, don't I?' said Lavinia Bradshaw.

'No, I don't think so,' replied Cookie Stone, before hurrying off down Hereford Road towards Westbourne Grove.

# Chapter Fifteen

When it came to sniffs of disapproval, Lavinia Bradshaw left Charles's Bath landlady standing. Sniffs of disapproval were what her face did best. Maybe the fining-down of plastic surgery had sharpened its ability, but Charles seemed to remember the Vinnie of old had a pretty good line in withering scorn.

That was certainly the expression with which she greeted the interior of his flat. The cold blast of early November air which came in through the window did not seem to have dispelled the stuffiness of recent body contact, merely spread it more evenly around the room.

Lavinia Bradshaw focused her disapproval on the window. 'I'm all in favour of fresh air, Charles, but there is a limit.'

'Yes, sorry, I . . .' He closed the window, sealing in the night's fustiness. 'Could I offer you a cup of coffee or — ?'

'No, thank you.' Lavinia Bradshaw's refusal may not have been prompted by the room's insalubrity, but that was certainly the way it came across.

'OK, fine.' He gestured to a chair for Lavinia. She looked at it dubiously. He hurried forward to remove a few weeks' shirts and socks. Very gingerly, Lavinia Bradshaw sat down, allowing her skirt minimum contact with the chair's doubtful surface. Charles perched with unconvincing insouciance on the edge of the bed. 'So what can I do for you?'

'Needless to say, it's about Mark. I've —'

'Oh, I hope you don't mind my interrupting, Vinnie . . .'

She clearly did. If her face hadn't already given him that information, he would have got it from the coldness with which she said, 'I'm no longer called "Vinnie". Everyone calls me "Lavinia" these days.'

'Oh, sorry. Lavinia. No, well, the thing is, before you start, just a quick question. That girl . . . that woman . . . who came down the stairs when I let you in —'

'Or seemed very unwilling to let me in, and kept me waiting on the doorstep.'

'Yes, yes, all right. I'm sorry about that. But that woman . . . you seemed to know her.'

'Well, I recognized her. We had met before.'

'And did Mark know her?'

'He'd met her too.' But she didn't want to be diverted. 'Charles, I'm not here to discuss passing acquaintances. I'm here to talk about Mark's death.'

'Yes, but —'

'Now let me tell you, I am not getting involved in this business for sentimental reasons. Once I finally left Mark, the only question in my mind was how on earth I'd managed to stay with him for so long. I put up with his drinking, his infidelities. I cooked for him, virtually brought up the children single-handed. Any debt I might have had to Mark I have paid over and over again.

'So I'm not raking through the sordid circumstances of his death for any reason other than the purely practical.' She then went on to confirm Lisa's assessment of the situation. Mark's life had been heavily insured, with a policy designed to benefit their children. But now the insurance company was kicking up a fuss, and had started the police reinvestigating what had caused her husband's death. 'Basically, they're suggesting it could have been suicide and, if it was, that invalidates the policy. I didn't pay out all that money in premiums not to get the payoff, so I'm determined to prove that

287

Mark didn't kill himself. Have you any reason to believe that he might have done, Charles?'

The direct question put him in a difficult position. Yes, Charles did have a reason to believe that Mark Lear hadn't killed himself, but only because he knew his friend to have been murdered. Lisa had found the door to the little dead room locked. So far she had been extremely unwilling to pass that information on to the police. For Charles to pass it on now to Lavinia Bradshaw might be regarded as a betrayal of Lisa, because he couldn't envisage Lavinia keeping quiet about it. She would ensure that the police's investigation was very quickly redirected.

'Come on, Charles!' Lavinia Bradshaw made him feel as if he was back at prep school, doing badly in one of Miss Pybus's quick-fire mental arithmetic tests. 'Apparently you were with Mark the afternoon he died. Did he say anything that could have led you to believe he was about to take his own life?'

'Well, he was severely depressed, and he was drinking heavily.'

Lavinia Bradshaw snorted. 'That is no surprise to me at all. I gather he'd pretty soon regretted setting up house in Bath with that slut.'

Charles resisted the temptation to come to Lisa Wilson's defence, as he went on, 'And yes, he did say things that could have been interpreted as expressing suicidal intentions. He said he felt old, he had nothing to look forward to, he couldn't see the point of going on.'

That prompted another derisive snort. In the course of their married life, Lavinia had heard Mark maundering on on similar lines far too often to take it seriously.

Charles endorsed her reaction. 'But though, quoted out of context, those words might have come from someone who was genuinely suicidal, you know and I know that Mark often said things like that.'

'Yes. And I always treated them with the contempt they deserved. Do you know, he even rang me that afternoon?'

'The afternoon he died?'

'Yes.'

'What did he say?'

'Oh, the usual maudlin rubbish. He was extremely drunk. He did all the nonsense about how we should never have split up, and how he still hoped we could get back together again, and how he loved me and the children, and how his life wasn't worth living without us. I'd heard it all many times before.'

'Did you tell the police about this?'

Lavinia Bradshaw was affronted by the suggestion. 'No, of course I didn't! They'd have immediately interpreted that as a sign that he was suicidal. Whereas, as you know, in his cups Mark was always saying things like that. And he didn't mean a word of them.'

'No. Probably not. I mean, of course — to play devil's advocate for a moment — there is always the Last Straw Syndrome to consider. He'd gone on saying that kind of stuff all his life, but eventually perhaps there came a point when the pressures on him were so great that —'

'Poppycock!' Lavinia Bradshaw snapped briskly. 'Mark was a shallow poseur. Like his emotions and his enthusiasms, his depressions were never more than skin-deep.'

It was chilling to hear the depth of resentment in her voice, a resentment that had been simmering away for more than twenty years of marriage.

'Well, I'm not so sure . . .' said Charles, trying to be loyal to his friend's memory, though rather afraid that she had assessed her ex-husband all too accurately.

'It's true!' Lavinia Bradshaw smoothed down her skirt, as if somehow to separate it from the contamination of Charles Paris's armchair. 'But is there anything else, Charles? Any actual proof you could bring forward to make it clear once and for all that Mark did not deliberately take his own life?'

'But if he didn't . . .' asked Charles cautiously, 'then how did he die?'

'Of drink and stupidity. He was so drunk when he went into the little studio that he passed out, and didn't wake up, even when he started to suffocate. It was an accident,' Lavinia Bradshaw announced with unarguable finality.

'Yes, quite possibly . . .'

'Everyone knows it was. It's only the bloody insurance company trying to duck out of its obligations, as usual. Come on, Charles. I told you. I need proof that my ex-husband didn't commit suicide.'

'Well, look . . .' he hedged, 'I can't actually supply that proof at the moment . . .'

'Oh, for heaven's sake!' Lavinia Bradshaw had no patience with such shilly-shallying.

'. . . but I can make a suggestion.'

'Then make it!'

'Yes, all right. Erm . . .' He had to phrase the next bit carefully. 'The person who found Mark's body was Lisa Wilson . . .'

'His latest bit of stuff.'

Charles didn't waste time taking issue

with the description. 'I should think if any-one knows the detail of what actually hap-pened to Mark, it'd be her.'

That seemed the fairest thing to do. Put the two women in contact and let them sort it out between them. If Lavinia Bradshaw was really determined to find out about her ex-husband's death, then she'd have to over-come her scruples and speak to his 'latest bit of stuff'. Whether or not Lisa Wilson would come across with the goods, admit she'd found the studio doors locked . . . well, that was up to her.

Charles thought the probability was that the two women would communicate, and Lisa would share all she knew. If they could overcome their instinctive antipathy, they'd recognize that co-operation was in both their interests. Lavinia Bradshaw was determined to secure her ex-husband's insurance money, and Lisa Wilson wanted to nail Mark's killer. Her attempts to achieve that with the help of Charles Paris having proved less than successful, she would probably be ready to try another approach.

They were two determined women. If they worked together, Charles didn't give much for the murderer's chances of escap-ing detection for ever.

Lavinia Bradshaw wasn't pleased by

Charles's suggestion. She had the feeling that he was holding something back, that he could tell her more. But, in spite of her fierce badgering, he didn't give in.

It was in the middle of the badgering that his phone rang. 'Excuse me,' said Charles and picked up the receiver. Lavinia Bradshaw's mouth went into a little moue of annoyance at the interruption.

'Charles, it's Maurice.'

'Ah, hello. Maurice, if you could make it quick . . .'

'What's this, Charles? Hurrying me off the phone? I might be ringing about a fabulous offer of a year's very lucrative work.'

'Are you?'

'No. As it happens, I'm not.'

'Well then, if you could make it quickish . . . I've got someone with me.'

'Oh, Charles. Another of your little lady friends, is it?'

'No. Well, it is a lady, but —'

'Say no more. My lips are sealed. Your secret is safe with me.'

'Maurice . . .' Charles was tired, and his patience was not inexhaustible. 'What is it you're calling about?'

'You may remember,' said Maurice Skellern with lofty dignity, 'that some time ago you asked me to find out about some gay porn tapes, produced by the late Mark Lear . . .'

'Yes, of course.'

'Well, I have been continuing my investigations into that matter, and I have found out the names of the actors who were involved.'

Maurice stopped dead. If there was one thing he loved doing, it was to dictate the pace of his revelations.

'Yes, Maurice, yes. Go on, tell me. Who?'

'A very interesting list of names it turns out to be . . .' the agent went on with infuriating slowness.

'I'm sure it does. Who are they, Maurice?'

Realizing that he had squeezed the last drop of potential melodrama out of the situation, Maurice gave Charles the names. And he was right. A very interesting list it did turn out to be.

When Charles had finished scribbling down the names, he said his grateful goodbyes and put the phone down. Lavinia Bradshaw looked extremely peeved at having been kept waiting so long. 'And that's really it, Charles, is it? You have nothing to tell me, except that I should get in touch with this Liza Wilson girl?' She deliberately pronounced the name wrong.

'Yes, 'fraid so.'

She snorted at the inadequacy of his information. 'Well, I'd better go. If you find out anything else, you've got my number.'

'Yes. If I do get anything, I'll certainly let you know. Then we can ensure that justice is done.'

Lavinia Bradshaw tossed her red-gold hair angrily. 'I don't give a damn about justice. I just want the insurance money.'

Charles Paris was seeing her off on the doorstep when another thought came to him. 'That phone call Mark made to you the afternoon he died . . .'

'Yes. What about it?'

'How did it end? Did you put the phone down on him?'

'No. I was about to, because I had to go out for a hairdresser's appointment. But in fact it was Mark who ended the conversation. He said he had to ring off because someone had just come into the studio.'

'Really? Did he say who that person was?'

'Now let me think . . .' Lavinia Bradshaw tried to piece the recollection together. 'He did call out, "Hello . . ." and then I think he said a name, but . . .'

'Try to remember. It could be very important.'

'Why?'

Suddenly Charles realized that, through

all her bluster, Lavinia Bradshaw was in fact not very bright. 'Because,' he explained, 'whoever it was was probably the last person to see Mark alive.'

'Yes, yes,' she said thoughtfully.

'And you haven't mentioned how the phone call ended to the police?'

'No, of course not, Charles. Really, you are dense. Suppose that person, whoever it was, got more of Mark's drunken ramblings of self-pity. Then they might have got the impression that he was suicidal.'

'That's true. Have the police actually talked to you about the phone call? Because presumably they could check who Mark did ring that day.'

'They haven't been in touch yet, no.' A sly look came into her eyes. 'And, if they are, I have a perfectly good cover story ready. Mark rang me to check what one of the girls wanted for her birthday.'

'Which of the girls?'

'Claudia. It was her birthday the next week.'

'Oh, is she the one who's ill? Mark mentioned —'

'Claudia is absolutely fine, thank you,' she said sharply. The slyness came back into her face, and was transformed into self-satisfaction as Lavinia Bradshaw went on,

'People about to commit suicide do not on the whole spend their last hours planning what they're going to give their children as birthday presents, do they?'

'No.'

The glee at her own cleverness gave way to a sudden recollection. 'Ooh, I've just remembered the name Mark said, the name of the person who'd come into the studio. It didn't mean anything to me.'

'No, but then you don't know any of the people who were doing the recording that afternoon.'

'That's true.'

'So tell me what Mark said. The name might mean something to me.'

She told him the name. It did mean something to Charles Paris.

'One other thing, Lavinia . . .' They had said their goodbyes and she had started off down Hereford Road.

'What now?' she asked crossly.

'That woman who was coming out of the house when you arrived . . .'

'What about her?'

'Where was it you and Mark met her?'

'It was in the hospital.'

'Hospital?'

'Private clinic, I should say. God, the prices they charge in those places! You pay out all that money in medical insurance, but they still have the nerve to —'

'I hope you don't mind my asking, Lavinia, but what were you in the clinic for?'

'No, I don't mind. Unlike some women, I'm very proud of my new body.'

'So you were in for plastic surgery?'

'That's right. Bags under the eyes, breasts, bum, the whole shooting match.'

'And Cookie — the woman we saw this morning — was in the clinic at the same time? And that's when Mark met her?'

'Yes. God knows why he bothered coming to see me. I'd made it abundantly clear by then that there was nothing left between us, but he insisted on turning up and whingeing away in the lounge for an hour or so.'

'And that woman was in the lounge at the same time?'

'Some of it, yes. I introduced them, you know, casually, the way one does.' She looked at her watch with irritation. 'I'm sorry, Charles, I really must be —'

'Just one more question, Lavinia . . . Do you happen to remember why Cookie — that woman — was actually in the clinic?'

She let out a harsh little laugh. 'Well, of course I remember. She was having the same as me.'

'Bags under the eyes, breasts, bum, the

whole shooting match?'

'Exactly,' said Lavinia Bradshaw, and set off briskly down Hereford Road.

# Chapter Sixteen

Before Charles left for Birmingham, he made a couple of phone calls. One was to Lisa Wilson to warn her that she might be contacted by Lavinia Bradshaw. He didn't spell out the details, but made it clear that she would have the option of telling Mark's ex-wife about the locked studio door. Whether she did or not was up to her.

Their conversation was civilized, even friendly. No one listening in would have detected that they'd ever been lovers, or that less than twenty-four hours previously one of them had announced they were no longer lovers.

Charles's second call was to the actors' union, Equity. He had a useful contact in the membership records there, who supplied him with the information he required.

By then, the confusions of the morning had not left Charles time to do as he'd intended and take the tour's dirty clothes to the launderette. Have to wait till Birmingham, he thought resignedly, as he scooped last week's dirty shirts, socks and underwear back into his suitcase (which felt uncomfortably light without its customary ballast of a Bell's bottle). By then he was so close to the train departure time, he had to take a cab to Euston.

He'd hoped to sleep for the hour and forty minutes of the train journey. He was utterly exhausted after the emotional upheavals of the previous few days — not to mention two virtually sleepless nights spent listening to Cookie Stone.

But sleep didn't come. His mind was too full. And, mostly, it was Cookie Stone who filled it.

A lot of details fell into place. The unusual firmness of her breasts, for a start. Charles Paris wondered whether, unwittingly, he'd recently had his first encounter with silicon.

But his other thoughts about Cookie Stone were more serious. She was an extraordinarily neurotic woman, of that there could not be any doubt. And she was deeply anxious about her attractiveness, or lack of it, to the opposite sex. She was also, regrettably, in love with Charles Paris.

He wondered just how deep Cookie's insecurities went, and what kinds of erratic behaviour they might drive her to. Finding out that she'd had plastic surgery fitted the overall picture, filled in a few more pieces in the jigsaw of her personality.

Except in cases of extreme deformity, the decision to have plastic surgery can never be a random one. The patient must be expecting some payback for the pain and inconvenience. In most cases, there must be some level of expectation that the transformation of the body will lead to some kind of transformation in the life. Lack of self-esteem, based on feelings of unattractiveness, the theory runs, will vanish when the external appearance has been adjusted.

And clearly it could work. For Lavinia Bradshaw, the plastic surgery of which she was so proud had been part of the reinvention of herself. Vinnie, wife of Mark Lear, the coping earth mother in droopy cardigans, had been transformed into Lavinia Bradshaw, designer clotheshorse, with a new body to complement her new lover.

But had Cookie Stone's transformation been so effective? From hints she'd dropped, Charles gathered Cookie's sex-life had been pretty inactive in the months before she met him. It was even likely that he was her first post-operation lover. Maybe for her, to have ensnared a lover — and a lover who called her 'beautiful' — was an endorsement of her decision to have the plastic surgery. It had worked!

But how would someone as deeply insecure as Cookie Stone react to the danger that her lover might find out what had happened? Did Charles believe that the body he evidently enjoyed making love to was the real thing? Would his discovery that it was in fact a patched-up, reconditioned body make him 'go off' her?

That was Cookie's greatest fear. That was the phrase that occurred most often in her monologues of self-doubt. 'Are you sure you haven't gone off me, Charles?' 'That hasn't made you go off me, has it, Charles?' 'You would say if you'd gone off me, wouldn't you, Charles?'

Yet again, Charles Paris asked himself the recurrent question: How on earth did I manage to get myself into this? How can I ever break it to someone who's paranoid that I'm about to go off her, that I was never really 'on' her in the first place?

And with this came the even darker, more uncomfortable question: What lengths would someone like Cookie Stone go to, to prevent her lover from finding out that she'd had plastic surgery?

Mark Lear had definitely recognized her that afternoon in the studio. At the time, he didn't seem to know where he recognized her *from*, but his words might have been enough to set Cookie's ever-present paranoia racing. And the challenges he was flinging out about uncovering people's secrets could have applied as much to her as to anyone else in the studio.

Charles didn't like the thought. So long as there were other possibilities to be considered, he'd rather not think it. But the thought wouldn't leave his mind, and troubled him all the way up to Birmingham.

He walked from New Street Station to the theatre. It was not so much that he needed the exercise — though he undoubtedly did — but that he wanted to compose his mind for the confrontation ahead. Now so many pieces of the puzzle had slotted into place, Charles Paris didn't want to screw up on the final details.

He felt very low. He didn't really notice the splendours of Birmingham city centre, so totally transformed since the last time he'd been there. He was too full of his own thoughts.

He passed a lot of pubs, most of which were open all day. The pull of a large Bell's was almost agonizingly strong, but he resisted it. After the confrontation, maybe

. . . after that night's show . . . after the end of the Birmingham run . . . then perhaps he'd have a drink. He knew that was how alcoholics had to think, one step at a time. Give yourself small targets, and try to meet them. Meet one target, and set up another one a little bit further away. And so on.

God, it was a boring prospect. But Charles Paris was determined to keep trying. What Lisa Wilson had said to him the night before had really hurt.

He stopped in a square, now dominated by a modern fountain above a large circular pool. He sat on the low wall of the pool and took out of his pocket the list of names he'd scribbled down that morning at Maurice Skellern's dictation. The names of the actors who'd been involved in the gay porn tapes Mark Lear had produced more than twenty years before.

There were six names. Henry Heaney. Stanley Murphy. Bernard Miles. Geoffrey Thomas. Robert Stephens. And Ransome George.

It was nearly three when he got to the theatre, a dead time on a day when the company weren't called till four-thirty. The set had been erected; the lighting plan — or rather the computer disks that contained it — had been installed. The theatre waited only for the cast to come, to hear a few notes on the slight differences of staging required by the new theatre. They would then do a leisurely walk-through of a couple of moments that might need minimal changes of blocking, probably have a brief break before the six fifty-five 'half', and at seven-thirty *Not On Your Wife!* would have yet another opening, this time hopefully to delight the good burghers of Birmingham. The tour had settled into a kind of rhythm.

Though the theatre was silent, Charles knew it was not unoccupied. Somewhere in unseen offices administrators would be at work. Backstage, final adjustments would be being made by the stage management. In the dressing rooms various actors would be going through their pre-performance rituals. Though it was one in a long sequence of them, this was still a kind of first night, and not even the most blasé of actors would have dared claim that he or she approached it with no nerves at all.

Charles Paris found the person he was looking for in the Green Room, sitting on a sofa, open copy of *Not On Your Wife!* on lap.

'Hi,' said Charles, and received a distracted answering 'Hi.'

'I've been looking for you.'

'Oh?'

'I wanted to have a word.'

'Uh-uh.'

'It's in relation to the death of Mark Lear.'

'Mark Lear?' But the puzzlement in the echo had been a bit contrived. The name was familiar.

'You remember . . . the drunk who produced that radio commercial in Bath.'

'Oh yes. Yes, with you.'

'The man who died that same day.'

'I heard about that. Terrible tragedy.' The response was automatic, uninterested.

'Some people,' Charles began slowly, 'are of the view that his death wasn't an accident . . .'

'Suicide, you mean? He certainly seemed in a pretty tense emotional state.'

'No, not suicide. Murder.'

'Really?'

'His girlfriend found the body the next morning. The doors to the studio he was in were locked.'

'Good heavens. Did she tell the police?'

'No. For reasons of her own, she didn't.'

'Oh.' Was Charles being hypersensitive to detect relief in the reaction?

'I'm pretty sure,' Charles went on, 'that Mark Lear was murdered . . .'

'If you say so.' A shrug, again uninterested.

'. . . by one of the people who was in the studio recording the commercial that afternoon.'

'What? Why, for God's sake? Most of us were meeting him for the first time that day.'

'No. In fact, Mark had met quite a few of us before, as it happened.'

'Really?'

'Being in the BBC, he'd worked with a lot of actors and actresses.'

'Ah. I didn't know he'd been in the BBC.'

Was that a straight lie? Charles didn't bother to investigate, but went on, 'He didn't do all his work for the BBC. Did a bit of moonlighting as well.'

'Really?'

'Yes. In particular, over twenty years ago, Mark Lear was involved in producing some pornographic audio tapes.'

'Was he?'

'Gay pornographic audio tapes.'

'I'm surprised there's a market for that kind of thing. I can understand people wanting videos, but —'

'There was a market then. Video hadn't really caught on in a big way.'

'Ah.'

'Anyway . . .' Charles Paris plunged boldly in. 'It's my belief that that afternoon in the studio, Mark Lear recognized some-body who'd worked on those tapes with him all that time ago. And when he said he was going to write a book exposing the things that went on in and around the BBC, that individual took it as a direct threat. He was so worried about his secret being exposed that, later in the afternoon, he returned to the studios, persuaded Mark Lear to go into the small dead room, perhaps even supplied him with a bottle of Scotch to take in there — and then locked the doors on him.'

'Interesting theory,' was all he got by way of response. 'I'm intrigued why you choose to tell me about it.'

'Because I'm convinced that you are the person who killed Mark Lear.'

'What? Oh, really!' The response was amused, rather than shocked. 'And what on earth gave you that idea?'

'Well, I asked myself who had most to lose by a revelation of what some might regard as a sordid past.' Charles took Maurice Skellern's list of names out of his pocket. 'I've a list here of the actors who were involved in recording the porn tapes. There's only one name here that appears on the *Not On Your Wife!* programme, and that person was definitely in the studio to hear Mark Lear make his threat.'

'Who are we talking about?'

'Ransome George.'

'For heaven's sake. Ran wouldn't worry about having done porn stuff. He'd glory in it. It's the kind of thing he'd dine out on.'

'I agree. I also happen to know that Ransome George has an alibi for the time of the murder. And that he has a very comfortable, ongoing blackmail system operating in connection with those audio tapes. So he was never going to upset the apple-cart, was he? No, Ran may be a creep and a blackmailer, but I've got to look for someone else in the role of murderer, haven't I?'

'So it would seem.'

'Going back to my question of who had most to lose . . . well, the obvious candidate was Bernard Walton.'

The figure on the sofa was silent.

'Because the situation for someone like Bernard Walton is different from old Ran's. It matters rather more what a *star* did in the past — particularly when that star is currently involved in a high-profile campaign to turn the tide of violence and smut in the media.'

Still not a sound from the sofa.

'Yes, the name "Bernard Walton" would definitely be of interest to the tabloids, wouldn't it? "Mr Squeaky-Clean in Gay Sex Revelation".'

'Working on a gay sex tape doesn't necessarily mean someone's gay,' came an objection from the sofa.

'I agree. God, you don't have to tell me — of all people — to what subterranean depths of work an impoverished actor will sink. But the average tabloid reader doesn't know much about the world of the theatre. Probably tends not to be very imaginative, either. For the average tabloid reader, the news that a well-known public figure once took part in a gay porn recording . . . well, it's the kind of dirt that sticks. Wouldn't do a popular figure any good at all. Certainly rule out the chances of a knighthood — and could also have a nasty effect on the box office of any show they might be involved in.'

The figure on the sofa had reverted to sullen silence.

'So I think it would have been very definitely worth keeping that particular secret quiet . . . even if keeping it quiet necessitated the murder of one drunken old has-been. Better surely that Mark Lear should die than that the precious image of Bernard Walton should be sullied.'

'I'm not denying or confirming what you

311

suggest,' the accused said lightly, 'but I'd be very interested to know how you'd set about proving your allegations.'

That was indeed the problem. Charles felt sure he was right, but the evidence remained extremely thin on the ground. Still, no need to let his quarry know that. 'Mark Lear was on the phone to his ex-wife when you came into the studio that afternoon. She heard him greet you by name.'

This revelation produced a moment of discomfiture, but it soon passed.

'You're going to need more than that.'

'Maybe.'

'Assuming . . .' again the voice was light, almost teasing. 'Assuming there was any truth in what you're saying, can I ask what put you on to me?'

'I wasn't sure till this morning, when I got the list of names of people who'd been involved in the porn recordings. Then I asked myself: Who actually had most to lose if the truth came out? And I looked at the names, and two stuck out like sore thumbs.'

'Which two?'

'Bernard Miles and Robert Stephens. Both very big names in the theatre at the time those recordings were made. Bernard Miles was running the Mermaid, and I think Robert Stephens was still married to Maggie

Smith. He was half of the golden couple of British theatre. There is no way, at that stage of Robert Stephens's career — or of Bernard Miles's career — that either of them would have been involved in recording pornographic audio cassettes. So there was only one conclusion possible. If it wasn't the famous Bernard Miles and the famous Robert Stephens, then it must have been another Bernard Miles and another Robert Stephens.

'Now, the making of porn cassettes is a pretty hole-in-the-corner business. No names billed on the outside of the pack . . . young actors, new to the business, paid off in cash . . . so Equity rules wouldn't have applied. But in the professional theatre it'd be different. And I'm sure I don't need to remind you of that basic Equity rule, that an actor's name is his stock-in-trade. You can't have two Equity members with the same name. So if your parents christen you Anthony Hopkins, or Ian McKellen, and you want to be an actor . . . bad luck, sunshine, it's already been bagged — you have to change your name.

'The same would have applied twenty years ago if you had been christened Bernard Miles or Robert Stephens. Ordinary enough names, nothing wrong with them as names, but sadly there were actors who'd already laid claim to them.' No response from the sofa. 'It was Curt Greenfield who told me that Bernard Walton's family name was Miles. I didn't realize the significance of the information at the time. It was only this morning when I got this list that I realized, in his early days, when he was trying to get a foothold in the business, Bernard Walton would still have been known as "Bernard Miles". So the name had to be changed.'

There was a sullen 'Yes' from the sofa.

'Only a small change, in that case. Just the surname. Whereas you changed "Robert Stephens" into something a little bit more exotic, didn't you?'

'Yes,' said Tony Delaunay. 'I did.'

At that moment further revelations were deferred by the crackle of a voice from the tannoy. 'Could Tony Delaunay come up to the lighting gallery, please? We've got a bit of a problem.'

The company manager rose lithely from the Green Room sofa. 'Well, if they've got a problem, I'd better go and sort it out,' he said, redefining his raison d'être. Wherever there was a problem on the show, it was a point of honour for him to sort it out. His loyalty to Parrott Fashion Productions was total, but there was also the issue of his own self-esteem. Tony Delaunay prided himself on being equal to any challenge that his work might throw up. And, if that challenge was the threat of adverse publicity to the star of *Not On Your Wife!*, and a resultant diminution of box office takings, then Tony Delaunay would have regarded it as a point of honour for him to sort that out too.

He stopped at the door and, looking back sardonically at Charles Paris, said, 'Still be very interested to know how you propose to prove the allegations you've just made.' He grinned infuriatingly and, with a brisk shake of his shoulders, spelled out the reason why he had murdered Mark Lear. 'Can't hang about, though. The show must go on, love.'

# Chapter Seventeen

Charles Paris's frustration was intense. He knew he was right. Tony Delaunay had virtually admitted he was right. And yet, as the company manager had so enjoyed telling him, Charles had no proof.

The unattractive prospect loomed of two more months touring *Not On Your Wife!*, with Tony Delaunay's impudent smile constantly reminding him of his powerlessness. Throughout the Birmingham week Charles fumed. Apart from anything else, he felt such a sense of anti-climax. He had psyched himself up for the encounter, had had his confrontation with the murderer, and yet at the end of it seemed no further advanced. The whole situation was infuriating.

Charles's fury did not, however, arise from a righteous sense of justice cheated. Mark Lear's death seemed less shocking with the passage of time, even perhaps — given the direction in which his friend had seemed to be heading — a merciful release.

It was hard to imagine Mark undergoing the kind of total character change which would have been needed for him to start enjoying life again.

But, whatever his victim's prospects had been, Tony Delaunay was still a murderer. And some atavistic instinct in Charles Paris told him that murderers shouldn't be allowed to get away with their crimes.

All through the Birmingham week, one thought dominated Charles's mind. There must be some way of nailing the bastard.

An idea came to him on the Sunday between Birmingham and Brighton. Back at Hereford Road, he had been greeted by his accumulated post, piled carelessly on a hall shelf by the various Amazonian Swedish girls who occupied the other flats.

There wasn't much of interest. There was very rarely much of interest in Charles Paris's post. He was a lax correspondent, and there's a basic rule that, if you don't send out many letters, you don't get many replies. Nor was his career sufficiently busy to generate a great deal of professional correspondence.

So most of what Charles did get was junk mail. Finance companies, apparently ignorant of his appalling repayment record, kept trying to issue him with new credit cards. Book clubs attempted to lure him into their webs with offers of 50p hardbacks. Insurance companies earnestly asked him, 'What would happen if you were suddenly unable to work?' Since Charles's answer to this was: 'It would be par for the course, my career's always been like that', all such communications tended to get filed in his wastepaper basket.

And then of course there were the bills. Charles Paris had a system with bills. He would pile them up on the mantelpiece of his room until the majority were red, then suddenly indulge in a cathartic orgy of payment, closing his mind to the cheques' combined and simultaneous impact on his beleaguered bank account.

It was a bill, however, which suggested another approach to the problem of Tony Delaunay. It was Charles Paris's telephone bill.

Telephone bills still had a slight air of novelty for him. For many years Charles's sole means of communication with the outside world had been the payphone on the landing at Hereford Road. But that had vanished in the refurbishment which had turned a houseful of 'bedsitters' into a houseful of 'studio flats'. So, along with facing considerably increased rent demands, Charles had also been forced into organizing himself a phone line. An answering machine quickly followed, and he was no longer reliant on the erratic message service of the Swedish girls. Charles Paris had at last put a tentative toe into the waters of modern technology, and he was repeatedly astonished at how he'd ever managed to conduct his life without it.

He didn't reckon he used the phone that much, but every time a bill arrived it was still a nasty shock. On this occasion, however, the size of the sum owing wasn't what struck him. It was the fact that his bill was itemized.

There is no defence against that list of figures. The total demanded may seem outrageous, but when one sees every transaction laid out in such detail, argument becomes impossible.

Itemized bills, Charles had decided, must have had a profound influence on the nation's morals. Together with the 'last number redial' facility and the '1471' method of monitoring the most recent incoming call, itemized bills must have severely clipped the wings of the average adulterer.

But it wasn't moral considerations that

were uppermost in Charles's mind at that moment. He realized that an itemized phone bill might help him to reconstruct Mark Lear's last hours.

Charles looked at his watch. It was early on the Sunday afternoon. Though he had spent a night at her flat, Lisa Wilson had never volunteered her home phone number to him, but Charles thought it was worth trying the studio. Lisa seemed prepared to work every hour there was to get her business up and running.

Sure enough, she was there, doing some tape editing. She didn't sound particularly surprised to hear from him — or indeed particularly interested.

Charles leapt straight in. 'Lisa, I've been thinking about the phone . . .'

'What?'

'The phone calls Mark made on the afternoon he died.'

There was a sudden change in her tone. 'How did you know?' she asked sharply.

Charles was bewildered. 'What?'

'How did you work it out?'

'Well,' he floundered, 'it just seemed kind of logical . . . that we know he used the phone and . . .'

'And do you think I should tell the police?'

'Erm . . .'

'I mean, if I didn't tell them that the doors were locked, I can't really tell them about the phone either.'

'What about the phone?' he asked helplessly.

But Lisa Wilson was so caught up in her own thoughts, she imagined Charles knew more than he did. 'The fact that I found the cordless phone in the little dead room with him.'

'And you moved it?'

'I had to.'

'Why?'

'1471.'

'Mm?'

'I checked "1471" on the phone.' A sob came into her voice. 'And the last number Mark had dialled . . . probably when he was dying . . . was the number of the married man who . . .'

'The one you spent the night with?'

'Yes.' Her voice was taut with pain. 'I'd told him all about this guy . . . you know, when Mark and I started going out together . . . so he knew the name. I didn't know he'd got the phone number. He must've copied it out of my address book . . . and when he was dying, that was the last number . . . He must've known I was deceiving him . . . He must've been trying to contact me . . .'

She was too upset to say any more. Charles asked gently, 'And did he get through? Did he talk to . . . your friend?'

'No. The guy's a writer. The number's the office where he works. He wasn't there. Mark must've got the answering machine.'

'But, so far as you know, he didn't leave a message?'

'No. I'd have heard.'

'Hm. So you took the phone out of the studio, and put it back on its base, so that the police wouldn't get on to . . . your friend?'

'Yes. And I dialled another number, so that the "1471" wouldn't give it away.'

'But the police would still be able to find out what calls he made. It's all logged somewhere.'

'I know. I wasn't thinking very clearly. I'd just found Mark dead. I was feeling so guilty . . .'

'And the calls'd be on your itemized phone bill, anyway.'

'Right. Of course they would.'

'Have you had a phone bill recently? I mean, a phone bill that covers the day Mark died?'

'Yes. One came last week. I didn't check it. I didn't think . . .'

'Have you got it there? Look for calls after three-thirty.'

'Mm.' There was a rustling of papers. 'I never thought of looking at this.' After a moment's silence, she announced, 'He only made three calls after three-thirty that day.'

'And the last one was to your friend?'

'Yes. That was at 17:02. For under a minute. He must've just listened to the ansaphone message and hung up.'

'When were the other calls?'

'One at 15:42.'

'And that was presumably to . . .' Charles reeled off Lavinia Bradshaw's number.

'Yes. That lasted six minutes, twelve seconds . . .'

'And was interrupted by the murderer coming into the studio.'

'Was it? Charles, how do you know — ?'

'Don't worry, I'll explain in a moment. What was the third call?'

'That was at 16:37. It lasted twelve minutes, nine seconds.'

'And what was the number?'

'It was the same one.'

'What, you mean — your friend?'

'No, Charles. It was another call to his ex-wife.'

'Really?' said Charles Paris.

The Bradshaws' house was in Blackheath, large and imposing. Lavinia's second husband also had money. Pooling their resources had made for a very lavish life-style indeed. The husband was away on business that weekend, but Lavinia was quite happy for Charles Paris to come round. 'Anything that's going to help get this wretched insurance business sorted out,' she said when he rang her. But no, she hadn't yet got round to talking to Lisa Wilson. It was clearly not a task she relished, though her greed would probably not allow it to be deferred for ever.

The sitting room into which she ushered him demonstrated the impersonal luxury that only an interior designer can bring to a house. It seemed to be for demonstration purposes only, too neat ever to be lived in by real human beings. The curtains billowed too lavishly; the cushions were scattered too artlessly; the gas flames licked too politely around the unchanging ceramic lumps of coal.

It was late afternoon. Lavinia Bradshaw offered him tea or coffee, but nothing stronger. Charles declined.

'I want to check about the phone calls Mark made the afternoon he died.'

'Well, I told you. He rang me, and maundered on as usual. All that self-pitying non-sense.'

'And then he was interrupted by the arrival of Tony Delaunay.'

'Tony somebody, certainly. He definitely said "Tony". Perhaps you should talk to this Tony.'

'I have talked to him.'

'And did he say anything that proved it wasn't suicide?'

'Erm . . . Well . . .' Charles had to remind himself that Lavinia knew nothing of the suspicions of murder. He would have to edit what he said carefully. 'Before we go on to that, could I just check about the phone calls?'

'Phone calls? There was only one. I had to go out to the hairdresser's. I had an appointment at four.'

'Mark called this number again at four thirty-seven.'

'Well, I wasn't here. He certainly didn't talk to me again.'

'He talked to somebody for twelve minutes and nine seconds.'

The line of Lavinia Bradshaw's mouth hardened. 'Oh, did he?' She rose briskly from the sofa, 'I'll go and get her.'

The girl looked ghastly. The loose print

dress, worn undoubtedly on her mother's orders to obscure the precise outlines of her body, perversely had the opposite effect. It drew attention to the matchstick thinness of her legs, the disproportionate swellings of her joints. In the same way, the thick Alice band, intended to cover her hair, simply drew attention to its sparseness.

'This is Claudia.'

'Hello. I'm Charles Paris.'

The girl looked at him without interest. She seemed preoccupied. Her eyes were unfocused, but had a glint of deviousness in them.

'Claudia darling, sit down.'

She obeyed, placing herself gingerly on the edge of an armchair, as if her skin was not thick enough to cushion her against the hardness of its upholstery.

'Claudia, did you talk to Daddy on the phone the afternoon he died?'

The girl moved her head round slowly to look at her mother, but said nothing.

'Claudia, I asked you a question.' Still silence. 'Come on, darling, this is important. Important for you. It might affect whether or not you get the money from Daddy's insurance.'

The girl's gaunt face took on a slight sneer at the mention of money. Her mother was predictably stung by the reaction. 'Claudia! I've had enough of this nonsense! I've been very tolerant over the last months, let you do your own thing, indulge all your silly faddishness . . . but this is something important. You must tell us whether or not you spoke to Daddy on the afternoon he died!'

'It really would help if you could tell us,' said Charles, more softly.

The skull-like face turned from its mother towards Charles Paris, and fixed the same look of challenging contempt on him.

Lavinia Bradshaw rose to her feet in fury. 'Claudia! Will you please do as you're told!'

The girl raised thin arms to wrap around her body, but it was not a gesture of fear. The sleeve on her dress slipped down to reveal the narrow straight line of her forearm and the ugly knob of an elbow.

'Claudia!'

'Do you think perhaps I could speak to her on her own?' asked Charles Paris gently.

'Why didn't you tell her, Claudia?'

'Because she's not interested. She didn't care about Daddy at all.'

From the moment that Lavinia had stomped huffily out of the room, the girl had made no difficulty about answering

Charles's questions. Her silence — and probably her anorexia too — was a weapon in a private battle with her mother. She didn't need to deploy it against anyone else.

'Some people might take the view . . .' Charles started cautiously, 'that her attitude was justified . . . that your father didn't treat your mother very well.'

'I don't care how he treated her. He was always nice to me. But once she'd walked out, she wouldn't let us see him. The other two didn't mind, but . . .'

'Did you try to get to see him?'

'It was difficult . . . being away at university and . . . He didn't get in touch much. And I was worried . . . I didn't know whether he wanted to see me.'

'And was that . . . I mean, when they split up . . . was that when you started to get ill?'

'I'm not ill,' said Claudia Lear, with total conviction. 'I'm fine.'

'Well, when you started to lose weight . . . ?'

'Maybe.' She shrugged. Then she let out a little laugh. 'Mummy's livid about it, you know. To match her new, tarted-up image, what she wants her daughters to be is three perfectly groomed designer accessories.' She opened out her skeletal arms, and said with a note of triumph, 'Well, she can't take me anywhere, can she?'

'No. Going back to what I was saying, Claudia . . .'

'Hm?'

'Why didn't you tell your mother about your father's call?'

'Because it was nothing to do with her. All she cares about is this bloody insurance. Daddy wasn't a person for her, just a means of getting some more money.'

'So, if you did have proof that he didn't commit suicide, you wouldn't tell your mother about it?'

'Why should I? Let her sweat. I hope she doesn't get the insurance money.'

'It's not her you'd be doing out of it, though. It'd be you and your sisters.'

The bony shoulders shrugged. 'Who cares? We'll get plenty of money one day.' She chuckled. 'I don't mind paying a bit to see Mummy pissed off.'

'And do your sisters share your view?'

'God knows. I doubt it. They're a couple of mercenary bitches, just like Mummy.'

'Hm . . . And when your father rang you, Claudia, that afternoon, would you say he sounded suicidal?'

'No. If he had, I'd have told everyone. Mummy would've been really furious.'

'So how did he sound?'

Claudia Lear drew her thin lips together as she tried to think of the right word. 'Kind of . . . resigned, I think.'

'Resigned to the fact that he was going to die?'

'Maybe, but he didn't say that. I mean, he was very drunk and sleepy, so it was difficult to say exactly what he meant.' She looked at Charles with sudden pride. 'He did say he loved me, though.'

'I'm sure he loved you, Claudia.'

'Yes.' She nodded with quiet satisfaction.

'So . . . what exactly did he say?'

'Well, he rambled, but . . . He said he'd got himself into something he couldn't get out of . . . that he was locked in . . .'

' "Locked in"? He did actually use the expression "locked in"?'

'Yes. I suppose he meant some business thing he'd got involved in . . .'

'What else did he say? Did he mention anyone by name?'

'Tony. He mentioned someone called Tony. Tony . . . Delaney?'

'Delaunay.'

'Yes, that's right. He said: "Tony Delaunay's got me locked into this, and there's no way out." ' A nostalgic smile came to the girl's thin lips. 'And then he said he loved me.'

# Chapter Eighteen

*Inspector Cruttenden looks with amazement at Nicky, then back at Bob and Gilly.*

INSPECTOR CRUTTENDEN: But let me get this straight. (*He points at Bob.*) If you're not having an affair with this young lady, Nicky, who are you having an affair with?

*Bob looks round the stage in desperation. He looks hopefully at Willie.*

WILLIE: No, no, you can't be having an affair with me. (*He smiles winsomely at Ted.*) I'm having an affair with Ted.

TED: No, you're not. This whole thing's a ghastly misunderstanding.

WILLIE (*taking his hand*): Don't you worry your pretty little head about it.

TED: Ooh-er.

INSPECTOR CRUTTENDEN (*to Bob*): So who are you having an affair with?

BOB: Erm . . . (*brainwave*) I'm having an affair with Ted too.

WILLIE (*slapping Ted's face*): You two-timing slut!

TED: Ooh-er.

WILLIE (*turning on Bob*): And you're no better, you . . . (*slapping Bob's face*) . . . you Judas!

*During the ensuing dialogue, Ted creeps away to hide out of sight under the table, which he approaches from behind.*

LOUISE: Look, for heaven's sake, can we get some sense into all this, please! Ted is my husband . . .

INSPECTOR CRUTTENDEN (*taking out his notebook to make notes*): Right.

GILLY: And Bob is my husband . . .

INSPECTOR CRUTTENDEN (*making a note*): Right.

LOUISE (*turning to look at Nicky*): And Nicky is . . .

GILLY (*also turning to look at Nicky*): Yes, Nicky is . . .

INSPECTOR CRUTTENDEN: Come on, the young lady must be somebody's mistress.

LOUISE: Yes, yes, she's . . . erm . . .

GILLY: I say, you wouldn't like her to be your mistress, would you, Inspector?

INSPECTOR CRUTTENDEN (*looking lasciviously at Nicky and really attracted by the idea*): Well, I wouldn't say no. Wouldn't mind a bit of . . . (*recovering himself and going back into his mournful mode*) No, I am very happily married to Mrs Cruttenden. Worse luck.

(*turning beadily on Louise and Gilly*) Now come on — who's this young lady's lover?

*Suddenly, as if goosed from behind, Aubrey shoots out from under the tablecloth, where he has been hidden since Act One. He still has his trousers round his ankles.*

AUBREY: Ooof!

GILLY AND LOUISE (*triumphantly turning to point at Aubrey*): He is!

*During the ensuing dialogue, Ted emerges from beneath the table. Pulling the tablecloth over him as if it can make him disappear, he tiptoes towards the French windows.*

AUBREY: What am I?

GILLY (*pointing to Nicky*): You're this young lady's lover.

AUBREY: Am I? (*looking at Nicky and very much liking what he sees*) Fwoor! You know I've always fancied the younger woman.

NICKY (*looking at Aubrey and very much liking what she sees*): And I've always fancied the older man.

*They go into a clinch.*

GILLY (*beaming at Inspector Cruttenden*): So everything's turned out all right.

LOUISE (*also beaming at Inspector Cruttenden*): Yes, and you can go back to the station.

INSPECTOR CRUTTENDEN: Yes. (*He turns to go to the front door, then suddenly stops and has a thought. He turns back.*) Except . . .

GILLY: Except what?

INSPECTOR CRUTTENDEN: I came here looking for an escaped convict . . .

LOUISE: Ginger Little.

INSPECTOR CRUTTENDEN: That's right . . . who is known to be in this vicinity, dressed as an Arab terrorist.

LOUISE: Oh yes.

*By this point, Ted has just reached the French windows, and is about to open them. With the tablecloth over his head, he does indeed look like an Arab terrorist.*

GILLY (*pointing at him*): Look, there he is!

*Ted tries to escape, as the rest of the cast chase him round the stage. He trips, and all the rest of the cast pile up on top of him in a breathless heap. Ted's head is covered with the tablecloth. There is a moment's silence, then Ted lifts up the edge of the tablecloth and looks out at the audience.*

TED: Ooh-er.

*THE CURTAIN FALLS FOR THE END OF THE PLAY.*


That was the fifth ending they'd tried. They'd introduced it for the Brighton week, which followed on from Birmingham. It didn't work any better than the previous four endings. Bill Blunden, however, was not disheartened. He knew his plays took a long time to get right. If *Not On Your Wife!* didn't come together this time round, he was quite reconciled to the thought of its doing another tour the following year.

For Charles Paris, the continuation of the tour was not relaxing. Though he'd spelled out in considerable detail to Cookie Stone that their relationship wasn't working and needed to end, she seemed unable to take this idea on board. He would still continually find her looking at him wistfully with her soulful, surgically debagged eyes, waiting for some sign of his relenting. She clearly believed it was only a matter of time before he saw the error of his ways and came back to the haven of her waiting arms.

Being out of a relationship with Cookie was, in its own way, as exhausting as being in one. Charles Paris couldn't wait for the tour to come to an end.

Cookie Stone wasn't the only reason he felt that during the Brighton and Newcastle weeks. There was also the unresolved problem of Tony Delaunay.

Charles had had to be careful how he handled Claudia Lear. The girl's antipathy to her mother was so strong that he had to try to keep Lavinia out of it. Eventually he decided his only possible approach was complete honesty. He shared his suspicions with Claudia, told her he thought that Mark Lear had been murdered by Tony Delaunay.

It was a risk, but it paid off. Though the girl had had no suspicions of foul play, once the idea was planted in her mind, it generated fury and a strong desire for revenge. She was determined to bring to book the man who had killed her neglectful but beloved 'Daddy'.

So, that very Sunday evening, while Charles was still there, and her mother still out of the room, Claudia Lear had rung the police in Bath.

And then . . . nothing happened. Or at least, so far as Charles Paris was concerned, nothing seemed to happen. Throughout the Brighton week, he kept catching Tony Delaunay's eye, only to be further goaded by the company manager's complacent smile of immunity.

One early evening, towards the end of the Brighton week, Charles tried to enlist Ransome George's help to nail the murderer. Ran had been involved in the original recordings, surely he'd be prepared to investigate further. Charles bought his fellow-actor a pre-show drink and tentatively raised the topic.

'Forget it,' Ran said with a complacent

smile. 'I'm doing very nicely as it is. No way I'm going to upset the apple-cart.'

'What do you mean — "doing very nicely as it is"?'

Ransome George gave the grin that, later in the evening, would bring the house down halfway through Act Two, and confirmed Charles's long-held suspicions. 'Look, I've known about Bernard Walton's involvement in those recordings for years, haven't I? And the more famous he's got, the more it's been in his interests for me to keep quiet about it. That's what I mean by "doing very nicely".'

'So you don't deny that you're blackmailing Bernard?'

'Ugly word — blackmail,' said Ran, in a way that would drag a laugh from the most recalcitrant audience in the country. 'Let's just say we have an agreement.'

'How many other people do you have "agreements" with? I suppose you've been blackmailing Tony Delaunay for years as well?'

'No. It wouldn't matter to Tony. He's gay, anyway. And, apart from that, he's not a star. Nobody's that interested in what a company manager gets up to.' Even when it's murder, thought Charles. 'But with Bernard,' Ran went on, 'it works just fine, has done for years. Mind you . . .' He looked with sudden suspicion at Charles. 'Now you know all the details, I wouldn't advise you to start trying to do the same thing.'

'What, blackmailing Bernard, you mean?'

'Mm.'

Charles was affronted by the suggestion. 'I can assure you, Ran, there is no danger that I would ever do that.'

'Good.' Ransome George sat back with another sleek, complacent smile. 'Because at the moment the deal I have with Bernard is perfect. I get regular money — never ask too much, you know, doesn't do to be greedy in this sort of business. And then he sees to it I get parts in a lot of his shows too. Same kind of deal as he does for you, eh, Charles?'

Charles Paris was so flabbergasted by the accusation that, before he realized what he was doing, he'd lent Ran a tenner.

It was in Newcastle that the situation changed. For the first few days, Charles's frustration at his own impotence was as great as it had been in Brighton. Then suddenly, on the Wednesday, Tony Delaunay wasn't there. He'd been around for the matinee, but by the time the evening performance started, he had gone. By the beginning of the following week, in Cardiff, a new company manager had been appointed by Parrott Fashion Productions.

Details of what had happened to Tony filtered slowly through the *Not On Your Wife!* company. Plain clothes policemen had apparently arrived at the theatre in Newcastle to interview him, and he had left in their company. Nobody knew why, and, preoccupied — like most actors — with themselves, nobody was that interested in the reasons for his departure.

By the time Tony Delaunay came to trial, charged with the murder of Mark Lear, the tour was over. Individual actors may have been shocked over their breakfast newspapers, but there was no company left to experience communal hysteria.

Not for the first time in his life, Charles Paris wondered how closely the police investigations had been shadowing his own. Even though their official enquiry didn't possess Lisa Wilson's information about the studio doors having been locked, some kind of researches must have been going on, to be presented at the adjourned inquest on Mark Lear. The police too must have been checking out the phone calls he made on the day of his death. And surely they too, in time, would have made contact with Claudia Lear.

Charles didn't talk to the girl again, though he often wondered about her, and how — if at all — her self-destructive relationship with her mother would be resolved. Lavinia Bradshaw had tried to reinvent herself, but Claudia's anorexia was part of the cost of that transformation, a constant reminder that the past can never be completely cut off.

Charles did speak to Lavinia once again. She was delighted by the news that her husband had been murdered. That meant there was no longer any threat to her insurance money.

Charles also heard from Lisa Wilson a few times over the next months. She had been given a fairly rough time by the Bath police for withholding information. At one stage there had been talk of charges against her, but in the event none materialized.

Once that threat had dissipated, her telephone conversations with Charles became less frequent, and finally ceased. Lisa Wilson seemed to be managing to make a new start. Business at the studios, she told him in one of her last calls, was really picking up. At the same time she mentioned casually that she was into a new relationship, which 'seems quite promising — at least he's a teetotaller for a change'.

So was Charles at that point, but he didn't think it worth mentioning the fact to Lisa Wilson. Whatever there might have been between them was now long gone. Besides, although she had been the motive force which made him give up drink, now he was doing it for himself. The abstinence made his evenings very long and slow, but he did feel healthier for it. Also, he needed some kind of self-punishment.

He found a letter at Hereford Road on the Sunday between the Bristol week and the Manchester week. He didn't recognize the name or address on the notepaper.

Dear Mr Paris,

I am writing to inform you of the death of my sister Ruth. As you probably know, she had been in and out of hospital for some months, and so in some ways her passing on must have been a relief to her. I have been through her address book, and am writing to all the people in it to inform them of the sad news, and also to say that a funeral service will be held . . .

But the date had passed. Charles felt bad.

He'd had no idea Ruth was so ill. It compounded his general sense of being an emotional cactus, someone whom no woman could approach without getting hurt.

He kept meaning to ring Frances. But he didn't.

The *Manchester Evening News* gave his performance as Aubrey one of those notices that Charles knew he would never be able to flush out of his mind. 'Charles Paris,' it ran, 'acts as if having a love affair is only marginally preferable to an attack of piles.'

Two months after the *Not On Your Wife!* tour ended, Maurice Skellern rang to say that Charles had been offered another three-month tour. Again of *Not On Your Wife!* Bill Blunden's slow process of perfecting the comic machinery of his play was set to continue for another crawl around the provinces.

Charles Paris's first reaction was to say 'No', and he knew his first reactions were always right. He was sick of the play, for one thing. And he couldn't face another three months of reproach from Cookie Stone.

On the other hand . . . he had no alternative prospects for the year ahead, the bank balance was dwindling, and three months' work remained three months' work. Then again, as Maurice Skellern said, 'There's always the chance it'll "come in", Charles. When you're on West End money, you won't regret all those endless months of touring, will you?'

So Charles Paris said 'Yes'.

In fact, sure enough, a year later *Not On Your Wife!*, finally rewritten to Bill Blunden's satisfaction, did 'come in' to the West End, for the start of what proved to be a very long and successful run.

There were a few cast changes, though. Pippa Trewin hadn't even done the second tour, because she was playing the lead in a movie. And for the West End run, Cookie Stone was replaced by an actress straight out of drama school. The girl was really not old enough for the part, but she was Pippa Trewin's younger sister. Mind you, she'd changed her name to Samantha Driver. Like Pippa before her, she didn't want anyone to think she was getting preferential treatment just because she was the daughter of Patti Urquhart and Julian Strange.

Oh, and in the West End, the part of Aubrey was played by an actor called George Birkett.

Charles Paris was philosophical about all this. Bloody annoyed, but philosophical. He'd long since given up the expectation that life would be fair.

Possibly to compound its unfairness, in the Queen's next Birthday Honours, Bernard Walton was knighted for 'charitable work and services to the theatre'.

The day Charles Paris agreed to do the second tour of *Not On Your Wife!*, he felt in need of a little celebration. It wasn't that he was celebrating the decision; more that he wanted to shut his mind to the fact that he'd made the decision.

And he had done nearly two months off the booze. That was almost unprecedented. He had proved he wasn't an alcoholic. He could take it or leave it, stop whenever he wanted to. He deserved a little treat.

So that evening Charles Paris went out and got drunk — two-second pause — merry — two-second pause — tiddly — two-second pause — tipsy — two-second pause — blotto — two-second pause — pissed — two-second pause — rat-arsed . . .